Darling Pericles

MADELON DIMONT

Darling Pericles

HEINEMANN : LONDON

William Heinemann Ltd
15 Queen Street, Mayfair, London, W1X 8BE

LONDON   MELBOURNE   TORONTO
JOHANNESBURG   AUCKLAND

Printed in Great Britain by
Willmer Brothers Limited, Birkenhead

For Penelope

Athens, 429 B.C.

1

I'T's ridiculous. Here I am, sitting shivering on this veranda on a cold winter's day, writing you a letter you will never read. I am supposed to be the most intelligent—some say the most beautiful—woman in Athens. At the moment I feel like a mindless, ugly old crone. Yet I am only thirty-six. I can't even be bothered to comb my hair, and I am huddled inside an old, threadbare cloak of yours.

Perhaps if I try to describe our life together—you, Pericles, the aristocratic statesman, and me, Aspasia, the talkative young rebel—I shall be able to forget you and start a new life on my own. Our sixteen years together were so wonderful, unbelievable almost, that it's impossible for me to accept the fact that you're no longer here. If I write it all down, at least it won't be lost.

A slave sweeping the courtyard is eyeing me warily, as if I were a dangerous animal. He has probably never seen a woman writing before. Few Athenian women can. And I suppose the only reason why I can read and write is because of my eccentric father, Axiochos, and his conviction that women ought to rule the world.

My father genuinely adored women, any women; and he was frightfully bored by men. There was no place for him in our men-dominated society where true love is homosexual and women just household commodities. So he ignored society. He shut himself up in a country villa, surrounded himself with women, and set out to prove his theory that we are the superior sex. He might not have got away with it in strait-laced Athens, but in decadent Miletos nobody cared. Provided you had the money—and he had—you could live as you liked without being bothered.

The only men I met in the first fifteen years of my life were my father, our tutor (who hardly counted) and our downtrodden slaves. The old man wasn't exactly against his own sex; he simply

3

pretended it didn't exist. He must have told us a hundred times that Woman is the Queen Bee, man is the drone. The worker bees were conveniently forgotten. I wonder if he ever realised how inconsistent his own position was: a sort of stud stallion with exclusive rights to a herd of brood mares. I've no idea how many women he had altogether, or which ones he was married to and which ones not. It made little difference since he'd invented his own marriage rite which mainly consisted of prostrating himself on the ground and promising to love, honour and obey the bewildered girl who from then on was to be his 'queen'. As a child I must have danced and sung at at least ten such ceremonies, so perhaps he needed a new wife every year.

Most of the girls, like my mother, were freedwomen or even slaves (he generously gave all his women slaves their freedom, though I doubt if he ever went through the legal technicalities. Females, he insisted, could never be slaves). The citizens of Miletos ignored him just as he ignored them and wouldn't have dreamed of condemning their daughters to life in our madhouse.

It really was a woman's world. His wives lived in comfort in the best rooms while he himself slept in poky 'men's quarters' at the back of the house (whence he emerged on the prowl at night to 'pay homage' to his queens in turn. So in fact he rarely slept in his own Spartan cell). At meals it was the women who lay on the couches while he made a pretence of serving them. On special occasions he even used to wash their feet.

I might have thought all Greece lived that way if it hadn't been for Chloe, the Spartan nurse who took me under her wing when my mother died. She was a fearsome old woman with a heavy moustache, huge sagging breasts and an exaggerated respect for omens. On the day I was born she saw a pair of ravens copulating; this upset her so much she went all the way to Delphi to ask the oracle what it meant. The oracle told her enigmatically: 'Put garlic in the sausage' (or it might have been 'put garlic in the cottage' — the last sacred word was a bit blurred). On the day she got back to Miletos a year later I was bawling my head off because I was hungry and in a sudden flash everything was clear: her mission in life was to look after me. It couldn't have been more convenient since my mother was very ill and died a few days later. I must have asked Chloe a hundred times how she elicited this god-sent message from the riddle of garlic, sausages or cottages, but she refused to be pinned down, just looking at me pityingly and muttering that

4

Apollo moves in mysterious ways. For once I have something to thank Apollo's oracle and the omens for.

Chloe was freeborn but poor, and had been with families all over Greece. Why she ever came to us I don't know since she couldn't stand my father whom she referred to scathingly as 'The Old Toad'. He in turn was convinced she was a man in disguise, and treated her accordingly. She launched a secret crusade to save us girls, and me in particular, from his evil, wicked influence by teaching us ladylike behaviour. We heard how proper, respectable households should be run, with men as the masters and women their servants. We had it drummed into us that women should be seen and not heard, that the greatest virtue is silent submission, that men are always right and women must have no opinions, and above all that they should never ever voice their feelings. It all sounded very peculiar. And since Chloe, like my father, practised the exact opposite of what she preached, I listened politely and thought the omens had turned her head. She instructed me in religion, which I found bewildering, for the gods all seemed such unpleasant characters (Father had no time for the deities, being too busy worshipping the goddess Woman). She even taught me 'domestic accomplishments' on the sly—weaving and spinning and cooking—so that one day I could make someone a dutiful wife. They were easy enough to learn, but I found them painfully boring.

I was wildly happy till I was about twelve, when I began to sense there was something wrong in the 'palace of queens'. Particularly among the newer recruits to my father's herd who just could not or would not adapt to their 'superior' status. He would buy a girl from a dealer, often a nice child from a good family, sold into slavery because of some idiot war. He would bring her home, free her, go through his personal marriage ceremony, force her to attend lessons, and expect her to be an instant genius. They were always very beautiful—he had good taste and picked his superwomen carefully. But the poor darlings were not, on the whole, very bright. They had been brought up to worship Man the Master and had no idea how to play father's game. They obviously longed to escape to the seclusion of Women's Quarters where they could spin and gossip and discuss their babies. Instead of which they were expected to loll about elegantly in the main hall, drinking wine and making intellectual conversation. Half of them couldn't even get the hang of the alphabet. And they were terrified of father who became more irritable as he got older and would forget his supposedly inferior status to yell: 'Talk, damn you, talk! You're wonderful people,

5

you've got wonderful brains. Don't keep your pearls of wisdom from me, let me hear you TALK.' Of course this made them even more tongue-tied.

The only person who wanted to talk was me. So as soon as I was old enough to eat grown-up dinner I devised a system for getting the wives out of their misery. At the beginning of the meal I would pipe up and say something like: 'Thalia (or Leto or Xanthia or Elpomene) and I were discussing the true meaning of knowledge today. She says it's a gift sent from the gods, but I disagree because . . .' I would prattle on and on, utter rubbish if necessary. For Father didn't really listen; he just liked to sit on the floor basking in the company of beautiful women exercising their beautiful minds. In fact he very often went to sleep. I must have been intolerably precocious, and the wives all regarded me as an awesome freak. But they were grateful to be able to lie there nodding sagely at what they thought were appropriate moments. Some of them even became brave enough to hazard 'indeed' and 'quite right' when I paused for breath.

Another cause of tension was the fact that none of the later wives seemed able to produce anything but boys. The birth rate in the household was on the wane anyway as my father got past his prime, and for the last five years of his career as a would-be begetter of superwomen not one girl was born. Every pregnancy was nine months of hope and solicitude, every birth a cause for recrimination and despair. It was the one occasion when the meek, obedient wives tried to stand up for their own rights. But they always failed. For the rule of the house was that boy babies must be exposed—packed in an earthenware pot and left in the open to die. My father personally made sure this was done and he was quite unmoved by the mothers' pleading. One wife managed to hide a boy baby in the stables for about two months before he found it. The child was exposed, even then. And the wife herself ran away a few days later. I secretly hoped she found her baby still alive and took it with her wherever she went.

My own mother died after giving birth to a boy. My father told me she died in childbirth, but from what I could gather from Chloe she caught a chill afterwards and simply hadn't the will to fight it. She might have lived if she could have kept the baby. Even in civilised Athens today new-born babies are exposed, especially girls. It isn't considered murder because there's just the *chance* they might be picked up, by someone prepared to go to the trouble of raising a future slave, or by a brothel-keeper specialising in children.

6

So our community conscience is not troubled. And nobody pays attention to the feelings of the mothers. Surely we go the wrong way about it—there should be some method of preventing conception, instead of forcing a woman to carry a child for nine months just so that it can be killed. Abstinence is no answer; nor is an exclusively homosexual society. At least we women have one thing that men find desirable and their boy-friends haven't got. And we can provide them with the sons they take such pride in.

My father would have hired a woman to teach us if he could have found one. But although he searched all twelve Ionian cities and even asked friends in Athens, it seemed there was no woman, free or slave, capable of teaching his wives and daughters to read and write. He himself educated us in his own, highly personal versions of the myths and legends, in which the goddesses were good and the male gods bad, the women all heroines and the men all scoundrels. He somehow managed to portray Clytemnestra as a paragon of virtue and Perseus as a cunning schemer, and had an extremely ingenious theory that the Trojan War was really fought by women. It was all such nonsense that not even children could take it seriously—not this child anyway. The stories were charming, but they simply didn't make sense.

Apart from imaginative history he taught us the poems of Sappho —'the greatest poet who ever lived.' The poetess of Lesbos was indeed a genius and I found her verses deeply moving. Yet, despite Father, I was sure she couldn't be the *only* poet who ever lived. Fortunately I had the chance to find out, when Father quickly tired of teaching a mob of little girls the simple arts of reading and writing (I've sometimes wondered if he was all that proficient himself). He was convinced we must be literate if we were going to become intellectual leaders of the world, so was unwillingly forced to employ a male tutor.

At least I suppose Menexenos was a male. He wore his tunic short and had a wispy beard, but apart from that was the most unmasculine representative of manhood my father could have hoped to find. He was scared stiff of the regiment of women he was required to teach, and suffered special agonies in the summer months when we used to slip off the tops of our tunics and sit there in class bare-breasted.

But although he quivered with terror for the first five minutes of every lesson, he had a good brain and was a painstaking teacher. It wasn't easy for him, limited by order to a curriculum of Sappho and texts extolling women, and he struggled for the first few months. Then he discovered that the unprepossessing little chatter-box in the front row was really anxious to learn. Little by little he began to devote more time to me alone, leaving the others to their own devices. They were relieved and grateful, I was ecstatically happy. Father would have been furious, but he never found out.

We studied forbidden texts, like Homer, Hesiod and Alcaeos. We studied mathematics, astronomy and geography. Menexenos loved his city and fired me with some of his enthusiasm for Milesian history, Milesian literature, and above all the great Milesian philosophers who set out to explain scientifically what the world was made of. They all reached different conclusions; I was more fascinated by the reasoned, logical methods with which they reached them than the ultimate answers themselves.

Menexenos also kept me informed about what was going on in the world. I heard that Athens and Sparta, the two great powers in Greece, were at war, then made an uneasy peace. I learned the history of the Persian war, then dragging to an end. Menexenos spoke with mixed approval of the famous Athenian general, Pericles. He was a great soldier, statesman and patron of the arts, yet seemed to be becoming almost a dictator, undermining the world's greatest democracy. According to Menexenos this superman was under the spell of Anaxagoras of Clazomenae, an upstart philosopher who challenged all the theories of our own Milesian thinkers. I thought he sounded interesting.

Father used to refer to me affectionately as his 'problem child' and was, I think, rather baffled by me. I was the only one of the whole bunch who actually became articulate, the only one who even half-proved his theory that women can use their brains (perhaps my sisters were too influenced by their mothers. They were certainly happier in the kitchen than the class-room). Yet I was an ugly, gawky girl with a quick temper. And, looking back, I realise how irritating I must have been. For I have never stopped talking. I started asking awkward questions when I was three years old and began answering back when I was four. My sisters called me 'know-all Asp' and avoided arguing with me if they could. They played interminable games while I tried to find someone to talk to. And they all had mothers while I only had Chloe—another fact which made me 'strange'. They thought I was even more weird when I adopted Menexenos.

Of course father just wasn't consistent. For all his theories about

8

the higher reaches of the female mind, he would have been miserable if his women had really turned into a gaggle of questioning philosophers. He was in love with all things feminine, from soft clinging fabrics to pots of rouge, from jewels to exotic perfumes. Every time a ship came in from the East the wives were showered with expensive presents. And he adored women so much he couldn't believe they didn't have perfect brains to match their bodies. When I turned into a brain without a body to match he was appalled. After particularly heated arguments, which I always won by elementary reasoning, he used to make me strip to make sure I wasn't a boy.

Since we never wore much anyway, and there were always women in various stages of undress sprawling about the house, this didn't worry me. I was sorry for his sake that I was skinny and flat-chested, but I couldn't help it. I used to fidget impatiently as he waxed lyrical to the assembled household on the glories of true womanhood. 'You are all my noble queens,' he would proclaim, 'and I am your humble servant. Remember, darlings, that you're all great people, that the world is yours for the asking. Remember that your brains are just as good as men's, if not better. And remember above all that you are women, beautiful, sensuous, desirable women. You are not equal to your unfortunate male admirers, you are far, far superior.'

He would get carried away by his own eloquence, usually to the bed of his newest wife. And when I tried to ask him why, if our sex was so supergifted, it was despicable men who ruled the world outside, he almost got to the point of ordering me to be seen and not heard.

Although Father would have been proud and pleased if he could have seen what I became, he never knew me as anything but an ungainly problem child. For just as I was in fact starting to look less like a blade of grass and more like a young female, he suddenly got very ill. He was in great pain for several days, but refused to let his queens' nurse him. And I think what finally killed him was Chloe's insistence on fetching a doctor from the town. When he opened his eyes to see a man standing over him, the old man-hater pulled himself up in bed, coughing and spluttering. With his last breath, he ordered the bewildered doctor out of the house. Then he groaned, fell back on the cushions and died. He left a household of about twenty females, enough money for them to live comfortably for the rest of their lives, and no arrangement about who was to become their legal guardian.

Thanks to Father, I could read and write. But although I had learned everything Menexenos could teach me, there was nothing I could do with my knowledge. I was fifteen years old—the age when well brought up Athenian girls are given in marriage. But I doubt if any man in his right senses would have taken me on then, even if I had had a dowry of ten thousand talents. I was tall, thin and gawky, all arms and long legs, clumsily conscious of my swelling breasts and growing hips. I was a child who developed late; and when womanhood did come it overtook me much too fast. It was some time before I got used to it. I had unmanageable brown hair, a nondescript sort of colour, dark brown eyes, an ordinary nose, high, wide cheek-bones, a determined chin, and a mouth which seemed to stretch from ear to ear. I was very self-conscious about it. The wives had tried to teach me ladylike behaviour: I could play the lyre, dance stiffly, and sing in a fluty treble. My speaking voice was clear and almost musical—at least it wasn't shrill. I wasn't interested in clothes or jewels and rather wished I'd been born a boy (in different surroundings, of course). I was certainly not attractive—interesting, perhaps. I had a pretty name: Aspasia means 'lovable'. And my greatest defect was my tongue: I never stopped talking.

Despite my lack of womanly charms, soon after Father's death Chloe started muttering about a local banker's son who was looking for a wife. She had even been ordered by Apollo to give me half her life's savings as a dowry. I wondered miserably whether she really could hand me over to the banker's son like a piece of unwanted property. It probably wasn't legal, without a man to sign the marriage contract. But there was no arguing with Apollo. And with His help, Chloe was capable of almost anything.

The trouble was that I had no idea what I did want to do— except that I didn't want to get married. And there wasn't really much alternative. There's very little a single girl *can* do except sit at home and wait for something to happen. I hadn't enough money to set up house on my own, and no relatives I could go to. I wished I were a man so I could travel and see the world.

Salvation arrived through Manto, my favourite among Father's wives. She was a kind, pretty girl who had always felt unhappy and out of place in our all-woman home, however hard she tried to get used to it. For her mother had been a notorious Miletos courtesan who died suddenly while simultaneously entertaining six clients; Manto had been brought up among men, she was hired out to men almost before she could walk, she enjoyed men and she liked men.

Father was fascinated by her sensuous curves and 'married' her after her mother died. Manto was then about twenty and had nowhere to go; by the time she realised what she had let herself in for, it was too late. The luxury and laziness of life at our villa were just to her taste, but she couldn't adjust to life without men. Father was past it, and in any case shared with the others. Menexenos fled when he saw her approaching. The slaves were locked in their own quarters, beaten and whipped and threatened with castration if they so much as looked at one of the wives. She couldn't bring herself to make love to women. Poor Manto was miserable.

One day about a month after Father died she got a letter. She came lolloping up to me in the courtyard, squeaking: 'Asp, Asp, come here, come here *quickly*. Look what I've got ... a MAN brought it!!!'

It was a battered roll of paper, addressed to Manto at her mother's house.

'He was a sailor from Athens, and when he asked for me at Mother's they told him to come here. Just think of it! Go on, Asp, open it, read it to me, go on, go on, I can't wait!'

I broke the seal and read out loud:

'Darling Manto—Do you remember your friend Chrysis? Well, you'd hardly know me now, I'm so grand. I've got my own house and six slaves and a chest full of lovely clothes and even a little dog! Yes, really, they all belong to *me*. All the most important men in Athens say Good Morning when they see me in the street with my slaves, and most of them come to my parties and bring me gorgeous presents. It's like being a real lady, only not half so boring!

'It's much much better than your Mother's and a very superior type of client. So why don't you come and get rich, too? We could set up together and enjoy ourselves, just like old times. Remember?'

It was signed 'Your dear friend Chrysis' and ended with a post-script: 'There's plenty of room in the house for you to stay as long as you like. They do things differently here, so there aren't people coming and going all the time.'

Manto and I looked at each other and gasped in one breath: 'Athens!' Then to my immense surprise she flung her arms round me and started to cry. 'Come with me, Asp,' she sobbed, 'don't stay here in horrid old Miletos. You've been so good to me, I couldn't have managed without you. I can't just ... just abandon you here.'

I was touched and confused, as well as being semi-suffocated. 'But what could I do in Athens?' I asked.

'I'd look after you,' she cried. 'I'd turn you into a really pretty girl and show you the ropes and make sure you weren't cheated. Besides, you're so clever you'd always get by somehow. Please come with me, Asp, please, PLEASE!'

I hesitated and made weak excuses. But deep down my mind was already made up. Athens. Where there were writers and poets and thinkers. Where people were questioning, debating, creating. Athens, mistress of the sea, head of a vast empire, leader of the civilised world. It seemed such an obvious place to go I wondered why I hadn't thought of it before. In Athens nobody would try to marry me off to the banker's son. In Athens I could listen instead of talking. In a month in Athens I could learn more than Menexenos had taught me in eight years. Athens, Athens, Athens—I wanted to leave at once.

Manto was obviously going to earn her living as a high-class prostitute and I worried that I might not be good at it. I told myself philosophically that the only way to find out was by trying— and went to break the news to Chloe.

I had anticipated a scene and the wrath of Apollo, but she was unexpectedly reasonable.

'You always were a restless child,' she said gloomily, 'so I'm not surprised. Mind you, I'd rather you settled down and married here, but if you've got to go charging across the world, Athens is the best place. The women there are modest and keep out of the way— you'll be able to follow their example. Thank the gods I taught you to spin and weave—it's perfectly respectable for free women to seek household employment these days, I'm told. I'll give you a letter to my former employer, the Lady Diotima. She'll see you come to no harm.'

She seemed oddly distracted, as though not really interested. And I almost felt she was glad to be getting rid of me. Had I offended Apollo? Apparently not, since she insisted on giving me more than half her life's savings.

She also decreed that we must take a slave with us. There weren't any females, so it had to be a male. Chloe marshalled them all in the courtyard and inspected them from top to toe, even opening their mouths to examine the state of their teeth. They looked even more terrified than they had been of father's whip. In the end she selected a tall young Thracian with a thatch of blond hair, called Micon. 'He's strong and healthy,' she declared, 'and speaks a bit of Greek. He should last you a long time. I'm not sure he's not a bit too good-looking'—she looked meaningfully at Manto—'but he's the only one of these decrepit weaklings capable of defending you.'

It was Manto who decided when we were going. 'There's a ship leaving for Athens in seven days' time,' she announced a few days after getting the letter.

'But how do you know, Manto? You haven't been out of the house.'

She studied her toes, which were rounded and pink.

'Well you see, Asp, that sailor who brought the letter just happened to be passing the house, so he came in to see if I'd written an answer. And he told me they're sailing for Athens then.'

I pretended to see nothing unusual in an Athenian sailor 'just passing by' a house out in the wilds of the country.

'And did you tell him we want a passage?'

'Oh yes. He said he'd ask the captain. He'll probably be passing by again tomorrow so he can let me know then.'

He must have passed by, for Manto came running up to me next day, flushed and dishevelled, crying: 'It's all fixed, Asp, we sail at dawn in five days.'

If I hadn't been so overwrought with excitement and busy weaving Athenian dreams I might have realised sooner what was the matter with Chloe. I didn't find out till the day before we sailed, when she beckoned me into her own bare little room, scene of countless childhood memories.

'I want to talk to you, Aspasia.'

I prepared myself for a harangue on the dangers of the big city, advice on how to be a lady and a flood of Apollo-sent warnings. But it wasn't that at all.

'Now you're going, I shan't be needed any more,' she began.

There was nothing to say. It was perfectly true.

'I ought to find a new family. But I don't think I can, not after being like a mother to you.'

She sniffed defiantly and I began to feel horribly guilty.

There was an embarrassed pause. Then she suddenly changed mood, and declared brightly: 'Yet it's just as well you're going— though mind you I don't approve of your going with that shameless whore. Because with you off my hands I'm nicely placed—I'm going to marry the banker's steward, Stephanos.'

I wanted to roar with laughter, from relief, delight, affection. Instead of which we sobbed happily in each other's arms. Apollo, it seemed, fully approved the match. One up to him. And she admitted coyly that Stephanos had first proposed five years before, but she had felt she couldn't leave me to the whims and mercies of the Old Toad. Darling Chloe. And perceptive Stephanos to see through the forbidding, shapeless exterior to the kindly soul which lay underneath.

I met him for the first and only time the next morning, when he arrived to drive us down to the town in his waggon. Chloe insisted on coming too, to read the omens. Whatever they were, they were favourable. We found the ship easily, bustling with activity and ready to sail. The captain himself, a weather-beaten, taciturn man, came on shore to welcome us and looked agreeably surprised by Manto's shapely charms. I huddled inside my cloak—it was late summer and the dawn was damp and cool. I had a moment of panic —perhaps it was all a mistake, perhaps I should stay behind in Miletos and marry the banker's son. But there was no time for reflection. I quickly hugged Chloe, who was fighting back her tears, shook hands with Stephanos and followed Manto up the narrow gangway. The slave Micon came behind us, carrying our few belongings.

Even Manto seemed unsure of herself. She took my hand as we stood uncertainly on the deck, out of the way of the hurrying sailors. In no time at all the anchor was up and the ship itself came alive as the banks of oars started to creak. We moved away from the rising sun; Chloe and Stephanos became puppets waving on the shore. I have never been back to Miletos again.

Looking back, I can't think how we dared do it. We must have been either very brave or very foolish; or perhaps we were just too ignorant to understand fully what we were doing. We were a strange trio: a 21-year-old prostitute with a lovely face and superb body whose experience of life was confined to her mother's Milesian brothel; a 15-year-old girl with a head full of book-learning, unacquainted with anything except her father's dream world; and a handsome young slave with frightened eyes about whom nothing was known. When I think what *could* have happened to us I'm almost inclined to thank Apollo for his protection. I'm sure Chloe was sacrificing daily to make sure it was given. Anyway, with or without Apollo's interest, without meeting pirates, Spartans or Persians, by luck, good fortune or the law of probability, ten days later we sighted Athens.

14

2

I HAD found out enough in those ten days to make me realise how inexperienced I was. And we certainly hadn't chosen the gentlest introduction to the world—straight from the rarefied atmosphere of our sheltered villa to the rough, tough discomfort of a trading ship. For me it was like being suddenly set down in a foreign country where I knew neither the language nor the customs. For two days I sat speechless in a corner of the deck, simply watching the men. Manto was so worried about my unusual silence she kept asking if I was ill. But I wasn't sea-sick. I was fascinated, over-awed and frightened.

They were so powerful. So confident. So beautiful. Not the soft, fragile beauty I had seen in women, but a beauty made of muscle and bone, strong brown hands and glistening bare backs, sturdy thighs and hairy chests. The sailors were all free-born Athenian citizens. They looked proud and arrogant, as if the world was theirs by right.

On the third day I began asking questions. Why did they do this and what was that for and where was the next port and when would we get to Athens? The sailors were amused and puzzled. They answered my questions with good grace and sometimes even let themselves be drawn into conversation. They couldn't make me out—a garrulous overgrown child, patently innocent. Yet I was travelling with the luscious Manto who had disappeared to the other end of the ship on private business, making up for the previous year.

The captain himself was intrigued. Two nights out of Athens he wandered casually up to where I was lying on the deck and sat down beside me.

'Everything all right?' he asked hesitantly.

'Yes thank you,' I answered primly. 'It's a beautiful night.'

'Indeed.'

He had nothing more to say, but apparently intended to stay, for he stretched himself out on the deck. After a few moments he leaned over and kissed me clumsily. I was surprised and interested.

'Have you ever been kissed before?'

'No, not by a man.'

'Did you like it?'

'Your beard tickled.'

'Oh. Well I can't help that.'

He tried again, more successfully. The beard still tickled but his mouth found mine. It was wet and sloppy and tasted faintly of salt. I didn't know what to do. If this was what sex was all about I wasn't sure I didn't prefer women.

When he finally stopped, I asked curiously:

'Why did you do that?'

'Because I wanted to, of course.'

'Yes, but why did you want to?'

'I don't know, I suppose because you're a pretty girl and it's a beautiful night as you said and, well, it seemed a good idea.'

This was the longest speech he had made so far, but I wasn't going to let him escape that easily.

'That's nonsense,' I persisted. 'In the first place I'm not a pretty girl. And secondly you don't care about the beautiful night. Every night is like this, and you're so used to it you don't notice. I think you were just curious to see how I would react. You probably had a bet with the First Officer about whether I would or wouldn't.'

He burst out laughing and suddenly became human.

'You win,' he chuckled. 'You may not be pretty but you've certainly got character. And you make me feel like an old fool.'

From then on we were firm friends. He sat beside me most of the night teaching me about the stars, and put his arm round me when it got cold. I felt safe and protected—perhaps men did have their uses.

The next day I stood proudly beside him on the bridge, asking incessant questions which he answered patiently. Manto was startled and delighted. 'I see I won't have to teach you much, Asp,' she remarked with a broad wink before vanishing again on her own affairs.

The captain asked where we were going, so I explained about Chrysis.

'Hmm,' he mused. 'I've heard of her, of course. Everyone must have done. They say she's beautiful, witty, and moves in the top circles—generals, nobility and so on. A very high-class companion.'

16

'How do you mean— a companion?' I queried.

'Well, since you'll probably end up as one if you stay with Chrysis, you'd better know. They're girls who keep men company, at banquets and parties—and afterwards. Personally I prefer just to go to a State brothel and pay my obol. I'm uneasy with the expensive women—full of modern ideas and clever conversation. Perhaps I'm old-fashioned. Some companions, like Chrysis, live on their own. Others can be hired by the month or bought outright. They put on a lot of airs, though half of them are no better than common prostitutes.'

He looked at me thoughtfully.

'I can't really see you as a companion, young lady. Though I don't know, in a few years time perhaps, when you've filled out a bit . . . You're certainly entertaining. And that's what they're for really—to keep their men friends amused.'

The captain had also heard of the Lady Diotima, Chloe's former employer.

'That'll be the wife of Aristippos. The most pious woman in Athens, they call her. Won't let her husband out of her sight in case he's corrupted by those wicked companions.'

He laughed. 'You might be a match for her. But for your own sake, I think you'd be better off with Chrysis. They say she's a kind girl, too, despite her profession.'

She was not only kind. She was exquisitely beautiful. Her long honey-coloured hair hung round her head in ringlets, encircled by a thin gold band. Her oval face was white and smooth except for her red cheeks and full crimson lips. She had big brown eyes made larger by her darkened eyelids. And she was bubbling over with happiness and excitement.

I hung back shyly as she and Manto rushed into each other's arms with squeals of joy. The captain himself had escorted us to the door of her house, uncertain, I thought, whether to be pleased or embarrassed at being seen in the streets of Athens with two such striking young women.

I sensed the feeling of luxury in Chrysis' house even as we walked in from the street. The slave at the door was a magnificent negro wearing a turban. There was a fountain playing in the courtyard. And everywhere a faint smell of perfume. I felt awkward and out of place in my rough woollen dress, embarrassed about my tangled hair, my freckled face, sunburned from ten days at sea. Chrysis was wearing a deep purple dress of some soft, diaphanous

material that clung to her tiny, well-formed body. She made Manto
—up to now the most elegant woman I'd seen—look like an over
dressed country servant.

For the first time in my life I minded about my appearance. And
there and then I decided that I, too, would be a beauty. I didn't
pretend to be Helen of Troy, and I could never be a china doll like
Chrysis. But I had two eyes, a nose and a mouth. I had a slim figure
and long, straight legs. Above all, I was young. And it was obviously
possible to improve on what nature had given me.

It was Chrysis who noticed me standing awkwardly in the
shadow, and looked inquiringly at Manto. She probably thought I
was a slave.

Aghast, Manto dragged me out into the open.

'Oh how awful, I'd quite forgotten you, I don't know how I *could*!
You shouldn't just have stood there, you silly girl, Chrys is dying
to meet you.'

I don't think Chrys (Manto couldn't resist abbreviating names)
was aware of my existence. And she could hardly hide her surprise
as Manto explained me:

'This is Asp. You'll love her and she's a genius. You mustn't be put
off by the way she talks because she's ever so nice really and she's
so clever she's bound to think of something to make us lots of
money.'

It was an odd sort of introduction. But I could see Chrysis was
fond enough of Manto to accept her friends without question. She
gave me a big smile and said: 'Welcome to Athens. I hope you'll
stay here a long time.'

I haven't left since.

I spent the next few months growing up—at least in appearance.
It was clear I would have to earn my living as a companion, and I
never really considered doing anything else. I certainly had no
intention of calling on the Lady Diotima. Chrysis was a companion,
and her way of life seemed near-perfect to me. Her house was her
own, bought out of her savings. But all household expenses were
paid by her current lover, Titormos, a wealthy land-owner who
showered her with presents and visited her every afternoon. He
was extremely fond of her and would probably have liked to live
with her. But he was also attached to his wife and devoted to his sons.
So he supported two households, and in return had the best of both
of them. It suited Chrysis admirably not to have him around all the
time. She was one of those people who love everyone—man or

woman—and was probably incapable of being in love with anyone. Which, of course, is why she was such a successful companion.

I kept out of the way during Titormos' afternoon visits, taking refuge in what would have been the women's quarters of a 'respectable' house. It was boring, with nothing to do and no-one to talk to, but I didn't feel ready to start my career. And I refused to admit to myself that life wasn't really all that different from home. After all, I was still surrounded by women. And I might as well have been in Corinth or Megara or even Sparta for all the culture and creativity I'd encountered. Yet at least I was there, in Athens. And somewhere outside in the teeming city were the people, the men, I was determined to meet.

First things first. I had to be fit to meet them. If I was going to be a companion I must do it properly—and that meant becoming a desirable woman. So I practised doing my hair and painting my face, I spent hours trying on Chrysis' clothes and jewels. I doubt if any girl can ever have made such a determined effort to become an accomplished prostitute. I expect I overdid it and looked ridiculous. Though I don't know—I have always had good taste, a sense of style. Manto was far, far prettier than me, but I soon realised I could be much more elegant.

Chrysis and Manto were eager to help with my 'transformation', and I couldn't have had two better teachers. They spent every morning playing with me as if I were a doll, trying this hair style and that hair style, this face and that face. I would never have guessed the same set of features could look so different depending on where you put the light and the shade, the black and the red. In the end we settled for a face which, with only minor variations, has been mine ever since. I am naturally pale, but still smooth white lead under my eyes and along my cheekbones. Rouge below them makes the lines even firmer. With colouring on my eyelids my eyes look enormous. And ever since someone described my big mouth as 'generous' I have happily painted it deep red. I can't hide it, so I might as well show it off.

Nearly all companions have fair hair. Men like it, just to be awkward (very few Greek women are natural blondes). So Chrysis summoned the best hairdresser in Athens to do something about my anonymous brown. He smeared on a sticky paste which tingled and told me to let it dry in the sun. When Manto brought me the mirror I could hardly believe it—my dull, dreary hair had turned a deep shade of gold. Either I was lucky or Amyris the hairdresser is a magician—too often dyed hair comes out a bright lemon colour.

But mine went a rich burnished gold, and when he'd rubbed oil on to make it soft, it shone and glistened in the sunlight. We left curls over my forehead, and pinned it up at the back of my head so it hung down in ringlets. Looking in the mirror, I could hardly believe it was me.

I spent most of Chloe's savings on clothes—how horrified she would have been. But after wearing rough white wool all my life I couldn't resist the colours and fabrics the dealers brought round. There were soft linens and featherweight fabrics I had never seen before; reds, blues, greens, purples, yellows; stripes, patterns, fringes, tassels. Chrysis' slaves made me a dozen cloaks and dresses, some with sleeves in the new fashion but mostly simple tunics, pinned at the shoulders, held in by a girdle at the waist, falling to the ground in soft pleats. They seemed less fussy and suited me better.

Then there were shoes, for the day when I finally went out. Here I kept up with fashion, for the new high-heeled sandals with cork soles were perfect for my arched insteps. Having hardly ever worn shoes at all, I practised walking in them for hours.

Chrysis examined me naked from head to toe before deciding I didn't need underclothes. She, poor love, was on the plump side and squeezed herself into an alarming array of breast bands, stomach bands, hip bands and the gods know what else, only to take them all off again before Titormos arrived in the afternoon.

Finally, I was ready. After a final pat to my hair one morning Chrysis sat back, looked at me, sighed with satisfaction at her own handiwork and said solemnly: 'Aspasia, you are beautiful. Now all we have to do is find you a lover. He must be young, handsome, and very very rich.'

Manto suggested a few names, but Chrysis wouldn't hear of them. She felt personally responsible for me now, and nothing but the best would do. Also, it wasn't as if Manto herself had found a lover. Titormos often brought friends on his afternoon visits and they slept with her for an hour or two. She had been given a few presents and been out to a few parties. But even though she was pretty and alluring, nobody seemed interested in a permanent arrangement. The ironic thing about Manto was that despite her passion for men, she was basically a women's woman. We all loved her dearly and would have done anything for her. Men found her a joke: they pinched her cheeks, slapped her bottom, cried 'Good old Manto,' and went to somebody else. It seemed unfair. Even if she was a bit vulgar, even if she did have appalling taste, at least she wasn't pretentious and affected like most of the other companions I met

20

later. She was naive, ignorant and willing, and would have made someone a perfect wife if only she hadn't been the daughter of a battered old prostitute and an unknown father.

We were sitting on the veranda discussing potential lovers when Titormos walked in, alone for once. I hadn't realised how late it was, and tried to escape through the back door. But he slipped round behind me and barred my way saying, 'Oh no you don't. We haven't been introduced and I don't know who you are, but I'm not going to let a vision like you slip away in a hurry.'

Chrysis remarked calmly: 'I told you about her, darling. This is Aspasia of Miletos, Manto's friend.'

'But I thought . . . I mean, you said . . .'

He was nonplussed, and I was delighted.

'You thought I was an ugly little girl from the country, a companion's poor companion,' I laughed. 'May I present myself, maidenly mathematician, chaste astronomer, virginal poet and pure philosopher.' I swept a deep curtsey and fell over the shoe I had been trying on.

It was a good start. He picked me up and carried me over to the couch where Chrysis was sitting, and even though he said nothing, did nothing, I knew he was attracted to me, I knew he wanted me. It was a heady, giddy feeling. I was only in his arms for a moment, yet in that moment I caught a glimpse of what attraction between men and women could be. I wanted to find out more.

But not with Titormos. He belonged to Chrysis. And although I liked him I was slightly repelled by this fleshy, thick-set man with a debauched face and a spreading stomach. Athens, I had been told, was full of men, at least half of them interested in women.

Titormos put me down beside Chrysis saying: 'You wicked woman, why have you been hiding her away? You made her out to be some sort of monster, yet she's a ravishing beauty!'

Chrysis and I exchanged meaningful glances. It was amazing what bleaches and paints could do.

He insisted on bringing out some of the best Chian wine to celebrate our meeting, and the four of us settled down to talk. Or rather, the two of us. I felt at ease with him, so started pestering him with questions about some of the famous names I had heard from Menexenos. Everyone in Athens knows everyone else, at least by sight, so he was able to give me superficial but witty sketches of most of them.

'Do you know Anaxagoras the philosopher?' I queried.

'Vaguely. A funny old chap who lives in the clouds. They call him The Mind. Pericles thinks highly of him, but I don't think much of these modern philosophers you know. I've other things to think about.'

'Like what?'

'Well, city business, and my farm, and my sons, and Chrysis here'—he patted her affectionately. 'This year I've been taxed with fitting out a warship and they may decide I'm rich enough to finance a theatre production as well. I've plenty to do.'

'But aren't you interested in what the world is made of, don't you wonder what we're here for, what we're trying to achieve in life?'

'Yes of course I do. I'm very interested.'

'Well then, surely it's worth listening to what the new thinkers say, if only to make certain you disagree. You can't reject something without knowing what it is.'

He shrugged in mock despair.

'All right. I'll go and listen to your precious Anaxagoras and bring you a full report.'

Chrysis laughed happily. 'You must have been bewitched by her to take that so meekly. If you're really so smitten you can do her another favour.'

'Anything,' he declared melodramatically.

'Find her a lover then. The most eligible man in Athens. It doesn't matter if he's married or not, but he's got to be rich, handsome, and prepared to put up with her talk. I know many people who wouldn't.'

Titormos was delighted. 'There'd already be lovesick suitors queuing up in the street if you hadn't kept her hidden away so long. What a pity I'm otherwise engaged—or perhaps I don't qualify as handsome?'

She kissed him reassuringly as he clapped his hands in inspiration.

'I've got it—we'll give a banquet. A banquet to launch Aspasia. The biggest, smartest banquet ever held. All Athens will come. And then the fussy young lady here can select her own paramour.'

Chrysis and Manto were enchanted with the idea. And the banquet was fixed to take place in three days' time.

I couldn't quite overcome the feeling of unreality, as though all this wasn't happening to me but to another shadowy person who had nothing to do with me at all. Despite the new hair and face, I still felt like 'know-all Asp'. I had never kissed a man, except the captain. I had never talked to a man on equal terms, except Titormos.

Yet I was about to be launched as a fully-fledged companion. I was just sixteen, and I had to earn my living—money was getting low. I tried to suppress my confusion, the feeling that this wasn't really what I had come to Athens *for*. It wasn't hard, as we were frantically busy with preparations for the banquet.

Chrysis decided I'd better have some lessons in the art of seduction. So we all three trooped off to the big bed she shared with Titormos.

'Now then,' she ordered, brisk and businesslike, 'lie down beside me and pretend I'm a man. Let down the top of your dress—that's right—and try to look all loving.'

I pulled such a face we burst out laughing.

'No, not like that. You've got to be soft and melting. Flutter your eye-lashes or something. That's better. Now put your arms round me—no, no, don't grab me, *stroke* me. That's it. Kiss me a bit, on the mouth and the body—keep your teeth *away* you beast—and put your hand here. Ouch, Aspasia, STOP IT—this is a lesson, not an orgy!'

We rolled on to the floor in fits of laughter.

'Oh dear,' Chrysis remarked, sitting up and drying her eyes, 'I'm not much of a teacher really. I suppose I'm out of practice. At Manto's mother's place we had to work really hard with some of the drunks and odd types who came in. These days I'm more used to being seduced myself. But you seem to have got the basic idea, and anyway you'll learn with practice. They all want something different.'

A thought suddenly struck her. 'I suppose you do at least know what a man looks like?'

'Well, I've seen statues.'

Manto, who had been raptly watching the performance, was all for bringing a slave in to show me. But I wouldn't hear of it—they do have their dignity. So the girls attempted to give me a description. According to Manto every male was equipped with a penis as big as a tree-trunk and testicles the size of an Olympic discus. Chrysis' average man, on the other hand, needed coaxing to make him function at all. It made me wonder about Titormos. They got into a heated argument about the best way to induce an erection and I was left none the wiser.

Then Manto took it upon herself to give a solo demonstration of the most usual positions. Chrysis couldn't bear it. 'No, no darling,' she protested, 'if you thrash about like that you'll put them off. Men do want to feel they're in charge, not that *you're* using *them*.'

She turned to me. 'Of course you've got to look as if you're enjoying it, but without going into a Bacchic frenzy—unless he happens to like that sort of thing. I'll show you.'

She pushed Manto off the bed, lay down herself, and went straight into the motions of an orgasm, accompanied by little whimpers and gasps. Then she sat up and said brightly: 'It's easy. With a bit of practice you can do it half-asleep. They never notice you're acting because they're too carried away themselves. And with them you can *tell* if it's real or not. Some of them like you to talk while you're doing it. Others may want to bite you, or hit you, or do it on the floor or standing up or back to front. You'll learn. Just pretend you like it, whatever it is, as long as it doesn't hurt too much or leave ugly marks.'

'But . . .' I was more confused than ever. 'But what if you actually do enjoy it?'

Chrysis shrugged. 'It depends. You're there to please the man, and it's not a good idea to get so worked up you forget all about him. Not that any man has ever really given me pleasure—they're too selfish and impatient. I always have to do it myself, afterwards. But some girls—like Manto here—enjoy it every time. I don't think it helps, for a companion. It's much better to pretend and stay in control.'

The day of the banquet I felt like a bride on the eve of her wedding. Or Iphigeneia being led to the sacrifice. Titormos had been wildly extravagant, determined to do things in style, and the house was full of people rushing about—merchants, decorators, hired cooks, musicians, tradesmen of every sort. The big room had been hung with new tapestries, bright new cushions had been made for the couches, flute players and dancing girls hired, and the most popular companions invited. There would be about fifty people altogether: magistrates, generals, orators, writers—all the top society of Athens.

I was tempted to wear white, just to stress the sacrificial virgin idea. But it would have been going a bit too far. Instead I chose an apple-green dress of a soft, clinging material, so light it was semi-transparent. It had gold stripes at the hem and sides, I wore a gold band in my hair, and a delicate gold necklace which Titormos brought me that afternoon 'to give you luck in your chosen profession'. Chrysis wore pale blue and Manto bright red. We must have made a striking trio.

I have never been good at connecting names and faces and there were too many that evening to register anything but vague impressions. Titormos, flanked by his women, greeted every guest at the door—presenting me heartily as 'our new little flower', or 'the philosopher princess'. Some men bowed, some nodded, some stared admiringly, others looked me up and down as if I were a slave in the market. A few—the ones who came in pairs—took no notice of me at all.

There seemed to be total confusion as people milled about uncertainly, slaves darted in and out washing feet, Titormos welcomed late arrivals and a group of chattering girls appeared from nowhere. Then at last everyone settled down, girl slaves started to bring in the food, and I could look round and see what was happening.

There were two double rows of couches back to back down the room with five or six couches crossways between them like rungs of a ladder. Titormos was lying on the middle rung, with Chrysis and me squeezed one on each side of him. So we were right in the middle, within shouting distance of practically everyone. The men all lay back in comfort, festooned with wreaths and garlands. One or two had already pulled a girl down beside them, while the rest of the girls perched where they could.

The food went on and on, course after course, brought to the diners by an army of slaves. I sat there listening to the talk, trying to make sense of it, suddenly shy. Most of the conversation seemed to be about the day's business in the Assembly, and again and again I heard the name Pericles.

'Didn't you invite Pericles?' I asked Titormos. 'You promised everyone would be here.'

A man next to us burst out laughing. 'You really are a child-in-arms, aren't you? I'll pay ten minas to anyone who entices the Olympian out—even to an all-male gathering. What I wouldn't give to see our Pericles let his hair down at a party like this.'

He saw I was baffled, so explained more kindly: 'We all gave up inviting him years ago. The man's a monster—he simply never goes out in the evening. He says it's because of weight of work, problems of State and all that. But if you ask me, it's because he's frightened of showing he's human. He's a strange man, brilliant in many ways and surprisingly likeable. He's been known as The Olympian since he was a young man because his eloquence and austerity are almost god-like. Perhaps because of this, he tries too hard to be perfect, to keep up the image. He never relaxes.'

He paused, and added perceptively: 'I wouldn't be surprised if he's lonely.'

Having found my tongue, I began asking questions. I discovered my neighbour's name (Meidias), age (48), income (average) and interests (heterosexual). I learned that he had been a general three years before, that he dabbled in poetry, attended the Assembly regularly and had a wife and three sons.

By this time the drinking had started, and I lost count of the times I drained my cup. I may have been drunk—I was certainly flushed from the heat and the noise. Whatever the reason, I ignored the insipid-looking girl draped across my new friend and asked him outright:

'Do you love your wife?'

He looked puzzled. 'Yes, of course.'

'Then why aren't you with her now? Or why isn't she here with you?'

'My dear child . . .' he began, but I cut him short.

'I know what you're going to say—that it just isn't done for respectable women to attend a banquet. But I want to know *why*. Why can't a citizen's wife enjoy herself in mixed company? What has your companion there got that your wife hasn't? Education, perhaps, but why is it forbidden to respectable women? Why, for that matter, can't your companion be received in a respectable home? Why are some women destined from birth to be inside, others eternal outcasts? Why should it depend entirely on where they were born? And why are all women, Athenian or not, denied any say in the way your city is run?'

Everyone round us had stopped talking, taken aback by my sudden outburst. As I stopped for breath they all began babbling at once and Titormos, amused, waved for silence. 'One at a time,' he ordered. 'Our infant prodigy wants to know why we live the way we do, so let's try to give her a satisfactory answer.'

They couldn't. It was the first—but by no means the last—debate I started on women's rights, or lack of them. And no man has ever been able to answer my questions—or had the courage and honesty to say 'we like things the way they are and don't care about your feelings'. There is no answer, except to admit that logically the system is ludicrous. And while Athenians are normally reasonable, tolerant men, they won't hear a word against 'their' civilisation. As long as women keep quiet and don't ask questions, the whole puzzling question can safely be ignored.

They tried very hard to find the answers. Women aren't educated for politics, they claimed. (Well, why not?) Citizens' wives prefer their own company. (Have they ever been given a choice?) Women don't want to go to school. (When were they ever invited?) Com-

26

panions would feel uncomfortable in a family atmosphere. (Why?) And so on and so forth. None of their arguments held any water, and they were unwillingly forced to admit it. The other companions were triumphant, drumming every point home and appealing to me if stuck for the next move. I reflected that I really was my father's daughter. He would have been proud of me.

Titormos was ecstatic. 'I've never given a banquet like this,' he whispered. 'Usually people just sit about gossiping or cuddling. But this is intellectual, everyone's talking, everyone's interested. You're a darling, darling girl and you'll be the toast of Athens.' He flung his arms round me and kissed me sloppily.

The men managed to find a culprit to blame for one of our complaints. It was Pericles' fault—that man again—that respectability meant 'born in Athens'. The year before he had sponsored a law limiting citizenship to men of Athenian descent on both sides. So citizens could no longer marry foreign girls, because their sons wouldn't be Athenians. I vowed to tell this Pericles what I thought of him if ever I met him. (And you can't accuse me of not keeping my promise.)

When the men finally realised they couldn't win the argument they set out to prove they were still the masters in any case. The girls were forcibly silenced as dresses slipped down and couples locked together.

Titormos had a problem, with two girls on his hands. There were plenty of unattached men in the room, but he seemed unwilling to let me go and couldn't decide who to surrender me to. He had had a lot to drink.

Then his Idea hit him. He tried to sit up straight, swayed, fell back on the cushions, then finally got unsteadily to his feet.

'Gentlemen,' he shouted, 'and ladies—if you must be called that —your attention please. We are here tonight to launch this timid young child (roars of laughter) in our civilised society. She is embarking on a career for which she shows natural talent and aptitude. But someone has yet to initiate her into its true, deeper mysteries.'

There was more laughter, and I wondered what he was leading up to.

'That someone will be getting a rare privilege, granted to most of us only once in a lifetime, on our wedding nights (loud sniggers). 'He must be prepared to pay for it. How much is it worth to shut her mouth and open her lips? You may never have the chance again. Gentlemen—not ladies, you're out of this—be generous. I am offering Aspasia of Miletos, to the highest bidder.'

I wanted to collapse with hysterical laughter. This was really the height of romance—to be auctioned off like a cow or a slave. And it certainly wasn't my superior mind they were going to pay for. Yet I had to start somehow, somewhere, with someone. This way at least I would be sure of making some money.

Titormos lifted me up onto the couch so that everyone could see me, inspect what they were bidding for. I wondered whether I should strip. In my transparent dress it was hardly necessary.

Someone at the back shouted, 'Ten drachmas,' and was instantly booed by the rest of the room.

'Come, come,' cried Titormos. 'It's an exceptional piece of merchandise we have here—turn round, dear, so the gentlemen can see you—worth much more than the price of a morning's shopping. I'd offer fifty myself if it weren't for my little lovebird beside me. There was a time when I would have taken on the pair of them. Now, alas . . .' He patted his paunch sorrowfully.

A voice shouted, 'Fifty, then,' and another cut in, 'I'll double it —one mina.'

'One mina, I am bid,' Titormos bawled, 'One mina ten, one mina twenty, one mina fifty. Are we going to value this precious jewel at the purchase price of an unskilled slave? Two minas—that's better —two minas fifty, three minas, four minas, five minas—now you're talking about money.'

Five minas, I thought in amazement. That was nearly as much as I had brought to Athens with me. I looked curiously at the men who were prepared to spend a small fortune on something they could get in a State brothel for less than a drachma.

It didn't stop there. My neighbour Meidias, who seemed to have mislaid his insipid companion, joined the bidding and pushed it up to six. A big red-nosed man with bushy eyebrows went to seven, and a languid-looking youth drawled 'Eight.'

Meidias shrugged. 'Sorry, my dear. I don't want to end in the bankruptcy court. It'll be for another time, when you've come down to second-hand prices. Pity, though.'

I thought so too. I liked him.

'What, Meidias,' boomed Titormos, 'worrying about your wife? Come now, I am bid eight minas, it can't end there. Was that eight fifty? Yes, Parmeniscos offers eight and a half minas.' The red-nosed man had nodded imperceptibly.

'Nine, then,' said the languid young man, airily, as if it were all rather a tiresome bore.

'Nine minas, nine minas I am bid by Deinon. And nine and a half by Parmeniscos.'

There was dead silence in the room as the two of them went up and up. Ten, ten and a half, eleven, eleven and a half. Then a collective gasp as the younger man drawled: 'Really, this is too sordid. Fifteen.'

'Fifteen, fifteen minas,' cried Titormos triumphantly. 'Deinon has offered fifteen minas for one night with Aspasia of Miletos! Sold? . . . Sold!'

He picked me up, carried me over to the couch where the youth was lying and deposited me beside him, saying with a deep bow: 'She's all yours, you lucky man. I hope you'll both be very happy.'

So there I was. Sold for the night to this extraordinary young man about whom I knew nothing at all except that he must be rich. At least he was presentable—slim, fair, blue-eyed, obviously a dandy. He probably had a weak chin under his beard.

'Hello,' he said, smiling. 'You were amusing, before, when you had them all confused for an answer. I think we shall amuse each other now, too. Come a bit closer.'

He put his arm round me and slipped his hand inside my dress. 'Mmm . . . you have delightful breasts.' He pulled me over to him and kissed me, hard.

From that moment I had no doubts, no fears, no confusion. Chrysis' lessons were all forgotten. I didn't need to know what to do. I just did it.

Deinon's mouth stayed locked to mine, pressing and insistent, as his hand gently explored my body. My head swam, but not from the wine. I was throbbing with excitement.

'Easy now, little one,' he whispered. 'You'll enjoy it more if we take it slowly. Let's go.'

He stood up, took me by the hand and led me through the half-naked couples to the door. I followed in a daze. A faint cheer went up as we went out—from those who were still capable of noticing.

Out in the cool night air of the courtyard he took me in his arms and kissed me again. 'You're quite lovely, you know,' he said. 'I couldn't have let you go to any of those coarse old men. Which way is your room?'

Inside the cold, dark bedroom he undid my girdle, unpinned the brooches on my shoulders. My dress fell round my feet and I stood shivering, from cold or excitement or both.

'You won't be cold for long,' he promised. 'Stand by the door where I can see you. Perfect. Beautiful.'

He came over to where I was standing and ran his hands over me like a sculptor moulding clay. I was weak at the knees and no longer cold. Then he carried me to the bed.

I didn't realise then how extraordinarily lucky I was to have been bought by Deinon. He was an expert lover, gentle yet passionate, tender yet forceful. His languid affectation completely disappeared, though he would undoubtedly have said, if asked, that it amused him frightfully to play with a precocious virgin.

He teased me, calmed me, set me on fire again and, just when I was sobbing with satisfaction and exhaustion, began all over again. I kissed him, worshipped him, opened my legs wide for him, then became a part of him once more.

At last, towards dawn, he kissed me lightly on the forehead and said: 'You're a woman now, my love. You're a complete woman, every beautiful part of you. I don't know why, but I hadn't expected you to be as capable as this. Perhaps it's because you like it—so many girls just pretend, and I can always tell. You're not worth fifteen minas, you're worth a hundred and fifty. Go to sleep now.'

He squeezed my hand, rolled over and went to sleep. I lay beside him, my legs trembling, stunned with exhilaration. I had hardly spoken a word all night.

An hour or two later he woke up with a rueful grin and a dry throat.

'Hello. How d'you feel?'

'Marvellous. Drunk—I don't know.'

'What it is to be young and tarnished. I'm thirsty. And I ought to be down in the market-place already. Who cares.'

I wrapped myself in a cloak and went to look for a cup. In the banqueting room there were still several couples sprawling on the couches. Meidias, my friend from the night before, was lying by himself, a crooked garland still on his head. He opened his eyes and asked: 'Did you like it?'

'Yes.'

'Good. I'm glad it was Deinon if it couldn't be me.'

He shut his eyes again as I tiptoed out with a cup.

Deinon drank the water thirstily. We made love gently, gracefully, in perfect time. Then he lay back and said:

'What a pity.'

'What do you mean? What's a pity?'

'That I can't marry a girl like you.'

'Well why can't you?'

He laughed. 'Don't start all that again. Nothing is worse than a woman who preaches in bed—even if she's as pretty as you.'

'Why marry at all then? Just keep a companion.'

'I wish I could. It's my wretched parents. They think that by inflicting some stupid little girl from a good family on me they might force me to mend my wicked ways. Also they consider it's time I provided an heir to carry on the family name and honour the ancestors' graves. Fortunately there's one saving grace—so far my mother hasn't been able to find any girl worthy of being her daughter-in-law.'

At that moment, Manto appeared in the doorway. 'Young love,' she said scathingly. 'You made such a din you woke my man up.' I stuck out my tongue as she smiled wistfully and wandered away.

At last, unwillingly, we staggered to our feet and out into the sunlight. The slaves had already cleared away most of the debris, and laid out bread and wine in a corner of the veranda. Chrysis found us there, in heated argument about women's education. She sighed. 'Good morning, children. Aspasia, you sound just the same. I hope you didn't keep it up all night.' She peered at me blearily. 'But you look different now—I can almost see you glowing. Your first night was obviously a success. I'm pleased.'

One hour after Deinon left, a slave arrived with a money-bag. Fifteen whole minas. I was rich.

3

WHAT amazes me, looking back to the first night and the five years of nights that followed, is how thick-skinned I was, how little I felt. It could have been a traumatic experience losing my virginity to the highest bidder at the age of 16. Yet the only real shock was the discovery that I enjoyed it so much and could be so well paid for it. I suppose I was callous, insensitive, heartless; I was certainly happy. And it was probably this convenient inability to feel very deeply that made me such a success as a companion. It simply wouldn't have done to fall in love with every other man I met, or swamp them all with emotion—they would have fled in terror. But as it was, I was incapable of loving, and therefore of suffering. Although I think I was a reasonably kind girl, soft-hearted even, I had no idea what passion or anguish were all about, and no desire to know. My own life was one long frivolous party with little time for emotional drama. I must have been both conceited and opinionated, but at least I was contented.

I could argue that I was infected by the mood of Athens at the time, or rather the mood of the Athenians. It was a period of buoyant optimism when it looked as if nothing could go wrong, and it seemed that Athens was politically, socially, intellectually, in every way, the perfect city. Her citizens were bubbling over with pride and confidence and grand ideas. There was no time for sentiment—not that the Athenians have ever been sentimental people. They don't feel—they think. Today the city's mood is more like mine, bewildered and confused. But twenty years ago we were both too confident in our new-found glories to indulge in more than superficial heart-searching. We have made up for it since.

After the banquet, my life changed. Thanks to the fifteen minas I had become a celebrity overnight, and half Athens wanted to look at me. Every man Chrysis had ever known—and several she couldn't remember having met at all—came to 'renew their acquaintance', so that on some days the house became more like the colonnade in the market-place than a private home. Titormos complained that he and Chrysis couldn't get a moment alone to themselves and that he was being drunk out of house and home—but he was obviously pleased and flattered that 'his' girls were getting so much attention.

I was expected to repeat my party piece on women's rights, and I couldn't have been more delighted. I was exhilarated and intoxicated by having so many men to talk to; it wouldn't particularly have mattered if we'd been discussing the price of cabbages (being men, and Athenians, that would soon have led to debate on the need to standardise the Greek currency, the suitability of the cabbage as an offering to Athena, or the horrors of Spartan cooking). What was so heady, after being cooped up with acquiescent women all my life—essentially feeling rather than thinking beings—was the way the men questioned, probed, reasoned, used their minds before opening their mouths. It didn't matter if they were intelligent or stupid as individuals—they all had the same method of attacking a problem intellectually, and most of them were able to concede defeat gracefully if outwitted. They loved talking, about anything and everything, and I loved them for it.

Conversation is as essential to Athenians as food, drink or sleep. And although they would have been chattering away to each other anyway, in the street, at the baths, or in the gymnasium, I suppose it had added spice in the exotic atmosphere of Chrysis' home with a few pretty girls who not only looked on wide-eyed but answered back. Chrysis herself became more talkative: she turned out to have a considerable knowledge of poetry which Titormos had done nothing to cultivate. And two or three others girls began dropping in—there was Melissa, a dark-haired, vivacious girl from Corinth, and Callisto, pale and dreamy, who was interested in Ionian philosophy. At first they came with their lovers, then started coming on their own.

The afternoons were spent talking. And in the evenings we went to a banquet, or someone would provide dinner for the whole group. It was an easy, lazy life—everyone had enough money, nobody had any serious worries. The men must have worked some time, on their own and the city's business, they may have had problems with their wives and families and slaves. But that spring and summer nothing appeared to matter—except glorious Athens and glorious sex.

Athenian citizens are legally entitled to kill their wives for adultery. But they have no such rights over their companions. With the exception of Chrysis, watched over by her Titormos, we exchanged partners or acquired new ones from month to month, even from day to day. I spent the night or an afternoon 'rest' with any friend who asked; I usually enjoyed it, though soon realised that Deinon had been an exceptional lover. Like Chrysis, I learned to pretend. After all, I was doing a job and getting paid for it—not at a flat rate of so many drachmas an hour, but with presents of money, perfume, jewels, even food. It never ceased to amaze me that men should be so lavish, so extravagant with me when they could perform exactly the same act for one obol—a sixth of a drachma—in a State brothel, or do it free at home with their wives. When I asked them why, they usually said it was because wives and prostitutes (for once classified together) were boring company. I fail to see what difference this makes in bed—but didn't refuse the gifts.

I came to the conclusion that it wasn't a good idea to get tied to one man. Melissa had just freed herself from a possessive type who locked her in the house all day. And even Chrysis sometimes gave the impression that she was tiring of Titormos but too kind to tell him so. It gave her security to have someone paying the enormous household bills. But with her looks and talents she could probably have made even more money on her own. We were lucky, of course, to be able to choose. Many girls were hired out by the month to a man or even bought outright, and they had no say in the matter at all. Thanks to Titormos' wealth and generosity I found myself among the Athens elite instead of starting my career from a brothel in the Piraeus. I was and am grateful. But it doesn't alter the fact that Titormos is, for an Athenian, a vulgar boor.

Meidias, my friend from the banquet, dropped in every few days 'to see how I was getting on', and we soon became good friends. He took himself much more seriously than Deinon and his friends, perhaps because he was older: he spoke regularly in the Assembly, took his civic duties very seriously and was a member of what was loosely known as the 'Pericles set'—a group of eminent politicians, speakers and artists, mostly from aristocratic families. When Meidias came we abandoned the others and sat talking in a corner —or rather he talked and I listened. He taught me what was happening in the city and the world. He explained the Athenian system of government, whereby all forty thousand citizens were their own rulers, meeting five times a month in the Assembly to debate and legislate. The presiding committee was chosen by lot, as was the five hundred-man Executive Council, responsible for city administration. The only officials, in fact, who were elected for their merit, were the ten generals. Meidias was both interested and well informed, and I couldn't have had a better teacher. I think he was flattered to have such an eager and decorative pupil.

One day after a pleasant afternoon with Deinon, Meidias came bursting in with the news that peace had at long last been signed with Persia. It was thirty years since Athens had crushed the Persian fleet at the battle of Salamis—Meidias had fought there—and there had been no serious threat to mainland Greece since then. But the war had been dragging on, in Asia Minor, Egypt and Cyprus, costing the city a fortune in ships and manpower. Now at long last it was over, and the Persians had given up all claims in the Aegean.

Meidias didn't seem as pleased as I would have expected. 'It makes it very awkward for Athens,' he mused. 'For years we've been collecting tribute from our allies as payment for protecting them against the Persians. Now they don't need protection. But I hardly imagine we're going to stop collecting tribute. We've already transferred the allied funds from Delos to Athens, supposedly because they're safer here—that caused an outcry all over Greece. We're going to be even more unpopular now.'

'What does Pericles think?' I asked curiously. Democratic though Athens was, the people would undoubtedly vote for whatever he suggested.

'He's realistic. He says that even though it may seem wicked to have taken the tribute, it would be madness to let it go. Admittedly for the first time in nearly a hundred years we have no war on our hands. We're at peace with Persia, and a five year truce was signed with Sparta two years ago. But it's a very shaky truce. Look at Greece – divided into two big leagues, more or less evenly matched. On the one hand there's our own alliance of about one hundred and fifty cities and islands, originally formed for defence against Persia. The allies have all been paying tribute to us to help us support our navy, which in turn protects them. Most of the Athenian allies have democratic governments and believe the people as a whole have the right to run their cities. They try to follow our example by helping the underprivileged and preventing the abuse of power by conservative minorities. The Athenian navy is the biggest in the world and more or less controls the sea.

'On the other hand there's the Spartan league, headed by Corinth and Sparta herself. It is supreme on land: Spartans are raised to be soldiers and nothing else, with the result that their army is invincible. Sparta stands for oppression and intolerance; she puts power in the hands of a privileged few and encourages them to rule by fear. She is supported by many cities which are jealous of Athenian power and influence. We simply can't afford to upset the balance of power by disbanding our own alliance, even though we no longer need to defend ourselves against the Persians. The Spartans would overrun the whole of Greece and there would be no more freedom.'

'But the Athenian allies haven't much freedom either,' I objected. 'They're forced to be members and pay tribute whether they like it or not. It's not an alliance, it's an empire.'

He sighed, exasperated. 'Don't be so maddening. Of course you're right. Ideally every city should be free to govern itself its own way, ideally there should be no barbarians, no Persia, no Sparta, no wars. But they exist, and we can't leave free Greece to the mercies of those bigoted, backward Spartans. Put yourself in Pericles' shoes— what would you do?'

I had to admit, while disapproving on principle, that I saw his problem. 'Not that I'd ever have the chance to be in the Olympian's shoes, for the simple reason that I was born without a masculine appendage,' I added crudely. 'And you can't tell me he's virtual dictator of Athens thanks to his superiority in that department. From all accounts he hasn't got one.'

Meidias laughed. 'Aspasia, you are incorrigible. I can see the jealousy bursting out of you. As for Pericles, he has produced two sons, and I can assure you that when I saw him in the baths before coming here he appeared to be better endowed than most of us. You're just jealous because he's not crawling at your feet like every other man in the city.'

He sipped his wine, then said in a different tone of voice: 'Incidentally—I don't quite know how to put this, and I don't want you to get the wrong idea. You know perfectly well that I'd like to make love to you, but I haven't asked you and I'm not asking you now. That's not the point. I'm old enough to be your father, your grandfather even, so perhaps I take a paternal interest. What I wondered is . . . if you get fed up with this sort of life . . . I could give you a loan or something, a monthly allowance perhaps, so you'd be free to please yourself, not dependent on your lovers . . .'

He mopped his face with the edge of his cloak, ill at ease.

'The thing is, my dear, you seem so different from the general run of companions. It seems a pity that you have to sell your body when you have such a fine brain. I'm an old fool and perhaps I've become too fond of you. That's all I can offer you without any obligation on your part.'

I was deeply touched. And rather flattered. It must have been the first time anyone had offered to pay a companion *not* to have sex. But I would have been accepting his money under false pretences. The fact was that I *liked* sex and had no intention of giving it up.

Also, I found Meidias himself attractive. Although he was three times my age he was fitter than many of the younger men who lay about drinking all day. He had very broad shoulders and strong, muscular arms and legs. His face was ugly yet dignified, and his grey eyes under heavy black brows were lively and penetrating.

I pulled him to his feet and put my arms round his neck. 'You're the best grandfather a girl could wish for. But I'm afraid I'm past redemption. I'll prove it to you if you like.'

He burst into delighted laughter. 'You deceptive witch. There was I, trying to save you from the perils of the flesh and all you want to do is seduce me. Lead on.'

It was the most overwhelming sex I had ever had. Meidias was all man—in comparison even Deinon seemed effeminate, light weight. Even though I couldn't love him, I became deeply fond of him. We were lovers for about four years.

Although I couldn't actually take part in city life—the meetings of the Assembly, the endless debate in the market place, the baths and the sports grounds—thanks to Meidias I was always up to date with what was happening, what people were saying and thinking. I soon discovered that men like nothing better, under the guise of conversation, than to deliver a lecture on their own particular subject. If they find you know a little about it, better still. If you know enough to contradict and cross-question them, some get angry and flustered—it hurts their pride to be made to look foolish by a young girl. Those men don't come back. But others are provoked, challenged, pleased. These were the ones who became my friends, irrespective of whether I slept with them or not. For even with my enthusiasm for the pleasures of the flesh, I could hardly sleep with them all. Many, in fact, weren't interested. They came, diffidently at first, to laugh or sneer and stayed on to talk when they discovered they weren't actually being lured into a high-class brothel. Some returned, bringing their lovers. But nobody ever brought his wife.

I got to know the city. With one or two of the other girls and a couple of slaves I often went out to the shops and stalls, to the perfume sellers, the jewellery dealers or textile merchants. Heads turned as we passed—we were the only women out in the streets, except for slaves, and everyone knew who and what we were. I didn't care. Visually, Athens was disappointing—noisy, dirty and dusty with the temples on the Acropolis still in ruins from the Persian invasion thirty years before. Everything happened in and around the market place, but not even I could spend half the day joining in the talk and argument there. Besides, it was much more comfortable at home.

Sometimes I went out on my own, accompanied by Micon, the Thracian slave I had brought with me. Life in Chrysis' household obviously suited him. He no longer looked frightened, and had developed into a big, boisterous, incredibly handsome young man bursting with life. He was a favourite among the women stall-keepers in the market, old and young, and turned out to have a shrewd head for figures. He could have done all my shopping for me, except that I didn't really trust his taste when it came to perfumes or fabrics. I hadn't bought a female slave of my own because Chrysis had plenty and it would just have been another mouth to feed.

As the months went by and the novelty of me wore off, my regular visitors and/or lovers were a group of about fifty or sixty people known as the 'Aspasia set'. In fact there were two sets. The first was composed of wealthy young men of about Deinon's age and social position. They were mostly dashing, flamboyant types, many of them not yet married, who drank too much, wore the latest extravagant fashions and had an obsessive passion for thoroughbred horses. Yet, being Athenians, they could switch at a moment's notice from discussion of a fetlock to an appreciation of Sophocles' latest play or a heated debate on Pericles' foreign policy (which most of them considered too cautious). They would never have admitted that they came to our house for anything except the drink and the girls; though again, being Athenians, they often became so engrossed in an academic argument that they quite forgot their drinking and loving. They were great fun, if exhausting. Parties went on till dawn and sometimes ended with a mass expedition to the port of Piraeos or up on to the Acropolis to make love (profanely) among the ruins. They pretended to be wildly progressive and weren't at all. They were just bored young men with too much money to spend and nothing to do. They needed a war. My favourites, apart from Deinon, were Theocles, a witty story teller and hilarious mimic, and Tolmides, slightly older than the rest, a hot-headed soldier who did everything with reckless bravado. He had been elected general before he was thirty, had already led several successful minor campaigns, and did his utmost to live up to his name, which meant 'daring'. In peacetime all he could do was fight duels over girls or organise raids on other people's banquets. Even though he was nearing forty and beginning to go bald he clung desperately to his image as a firebrand; in this capacity he led the growing opposition to Pericles, and it made quite a change to hear the Great Man referred to as anything but perfect.

The other group, which wasn't a group at all but a collection of individuals, was made up of older men who presumably enjoyed my company. Many of them were also members of the 'Pericles set'. They didn't come for the wine or the girls, they came to talk. This doesn't mean they'd lost interest in sex or were teetotallers or faithful to their wives. Many of them had mistresses, whom they sometimes brought with them. Others had lovers. They drank, certainly, but seldom got drunk. It didn't occur to me at the time how exceptional it was for the top men in Athenian art and politics to spend hours talking to a teenage girl. I suppose they were intrigued and attracted by the contrast between my blonde curls and my relative articulacy. Whatever the reason, they came. And 'going to see Aspasia' became part of Athenian life.

Many of them were brought by Meidias; he knew the men I would like and which men would like me. I think secretly it pleased him to show me off. Particularly when the man concerned was sceptical, despised companions, didn't like girls or was convinced that nobody under the age of forty had a brain in his or her head. It was a triumph for Meidias if such characters came back again — and they usually did.

It was through Meidias that I got to know Anaxagoras, the revolutionary philosopher whom my tutor Menexenos had disapproved of so strongly. He was a vague, unworldly man, so obsessed with theories about what the universe is made of that he was quite oblivious to the everyday world as it is. He had no conception of time, place or money and hardly noticed whether he was in a temple or a fishmarket. He lived on a monthly allowance from Pericles. And he found nothing strange about our unorthodox household — in fact he'd probably never noticed there weren't any women round his normal teaching haunts.

He had an ingenious theory that everything in the world is made up of tiny particles called atoms — far-fetched perhaps, yet plausible. He believed the sun and stars are enormous balls of fire. And the creator and controller of the cosmic system was Reason, which had created order out of chaos. I found the last bit rather hard to accept, as if he'd thrown it in in desperation to account for phenomena even he couldn't explain scientifically. At least he didn't attribute the creation or government of the world to Zeus or Apollo; there was no place at all for the gods in his scheme of things.

I became very fond of the untidy, courteous old man with the flowing beard, known to everyone simply as The Mind. I tried to make sure he always had something to eat in case he forgot later. And when, as sometimes happened, he went on talking far into the night, we would bring him a couch and let him talk himself to sleep.

He seemed to like me, too. One day when I had been trying, half successfully, to find flaws in his Reason theory he patted me affectionately on the head and said: 'You're a bright girl, you know. Ought to go in for philosophy. I'd like to match you against my other star pupil, whatsisname, Xanthippos' boy. He wastes too much time with trifles instead of sticking to fundamentals.'

I would very much have liked to match my wits against those of Xanthippos' son Pericles. But although not a day passed without your name being mentioned, although you were a household word, although half my friends were your friends, you seemed totally inaccessible. And by all accounts not so much superhuman as in-human. I was curious, but I could do without you.

One very cold day during my second winter in Athens, Chrysis' steward came shuffling up to where Manto and I were huddling over a brazier debating what to do if she was pregnant (there was the same worry every month, probably because Manto couldn't count up to twenty-eight. I'd tried making a calendar for her, with a leaf to tear off every day. She forgot, tore off two or even three on the same day, and ended up with the usual panic—'Asp, it's late, what shall I *do*?')

'There's a young person to see you,' said the steward disapprovingly.

'Well, why don't you show him in?' I asked.

The steward sniffed. 'When I asked his name, he asked straight back what mine is. I hardly liked to ask his business but took the liberty, judging by his appearance, of telling him he'd come to the wrong place and directing him to the State establishment in the next street.'

'And then?' I was intrigued.

'He asked me why I didn't go there if it was so excellent.'

'And?'

'I was taken by surprise, so admitted I do go there. At which the young person clapped me on the back, said we should go there together some time, but for the moment he wished to speak to you.'

'Show him in, by all means,' I ordered.

The porter went away and came back leading one of the most extraordinary looking young men I had ever seen.

His face, or rather his features, were bulbous: he had protruding eyes, a round nose and an absurdly curving mouth. His beard and hair stuck out at all angles—it was more like looking at a comic actor's mask than a real face. He appeared to be quite young, probably a few years older than me.

This bizarre individual was wearing nothing, on that freezing cold day, except a cloak. No tunic underneath as far as I could see, and no shoes or sandals. His feet and legs were blue with cold.

He swept a low bow, rolling his eyes, and declared dramatically: 'The great Aspasia, I presume.'

'It depends what you mean by great.'

'Quite. Since I don't know what greatness is, you can take it in any sense you please. Perhaps I should have said "notorious". Wherever I go, I hear your name. Tolmides talks about you, Theocles imitates you, Deinon is obviously in love with you, Titormos boasts about you, Meidias praises you. When yesterday old Anaxagoras not only spoke highly of you but actually remembered your name, I decided I must come and see for myself. Otherwise I should either have been excluded from the conversation of half Athens or forced into the untenable position of discussing someone I don't know. So here I am.'

'Here you are indeed,' I agreed. 'But who and what are you?'

'My name is Socrates, stone mason by trade, nuisance by profession. I am twenty-one years old and have just come back from military service—otherwise we should undoubtedly have met before. When I left Athens the only talked-about woman was the goddess Athena herself. Now you seem to have deposed her.'

'How do you do?' I said gravely. 'For Athena's sake come and get warm.'

The more we talked—and he stayed for about three hours that day—the more we approved of each other. He had a crystal-sharp mind that probed and dissected every word it encountered, rejecting half of them as unnecessary, illogical or contradictory. With Socrates it was impossible to get away with a meaningless generalisation, a half-truth. With a sweet air of innocence he would ask: 'You're too clever for me. What exactly do you mean by that?' I

41

soon learned the game and played it back at him, to his immense delight.

At last, reeling slightly but none the worse for wear, he staggered off into the night saying: 'Farewell. Now I know what they are talking about. And I know why. They told me you were beautiful, seductive, charming, perceptive, intelligent. So are many women. They didn't tell me you have a logical mind, exceptional in a woman. And above all, they didn't tell me you have a sense of humour.'

He kissed me on the cheek, grinned mischievously, and was gone.

Socrates became a regular visitor to the house, often accompanied by a boy-friend or a group of hangers-on. I was devoted to him myself, but soon noticed he was getting on a lot of people's nerves. Tolmides, for one, couldn't stand him. After a few angry discussions which just made the would-be warrior look silly, the 'daring' one gave up in disgust and would walk out if Socrates shambled in (Socrates himself, needless to say, had no such delicacy and thought the whole thing a big joke). Meidias found him irritating and was, I think, secretly jealous. For the brash young man from a working class background had somehow made a name for himself in the city and was said to be respected by Pericles himself. This put the Olympian higher in my estimation, but Meidias simply couldn't understand it. 'What on earth is that young oaf's attraction?' he asked me angrily. 'He's ugly, shabby, dirty and ill-mannered. He has no respect for anyone or anything and appears to have had no education worth speaking of. All he ever does is talk in riddles. Yet he gets invited to Pericles' house, and whenever I come here, here he is again. Are you in love with him or something?'

I couldn't help laughing. 'Don't be such an idiot. You've told me often enough that I'm too self-centred to fall in love. And if I did—which the gods forbid—I certainly wouldn't choose a destitute stone mason with no interest in girls. Socrates amuses me, that's all.'

He complained grumpily that I sounded like Deinon, which was perfectly true. And Meidias wouldn't have appreciated one of the many reasons for my liking Socrates: he was extraordinarily nice to Manto. He never teased her, he never ignored her, he paid her compliments and listened to what she had to say; Manto blossomed whenever he was around, and I was grateful to him for his thoughtfulness.

If Tolmides couldn't stand Socrates and Meidias disliked him, Titormos positively loathed him. The people Socrates brought to the house were the sort he most despised—'useless young idlers'— and he felt it was somehow degrading to associate with them. Things came to a head one afternoon when Titormos discovered Socrates fast asleep on Chrysis' bed.

'What do you think you're doing here?' he spluttered indignantly.

'What are *you* doing here?' Socrates replied sleepily, opening one eye.

'What d'you mean, what I am doing here?'

'I mean what are you doing here?'

'How dare you?' raged Titormos. 'Get up, get up at once.'

Socrates raised himself on one elbow, rolled his eyes and said sweetly: 'Of course I'll get up, sometime. I can't stay in bed all day, even this delightful bed. But for the moment I'm weary, I've nothing else to do and I'm going back to sleep.'

He lay down again, pulled the cover over his head and began snoring, very loud. Titormos stormed out into the courtyard, marched through the front door and wasn't seen again that day.

A few days later Chrysis poured her heart out to me. 'I'm sorry, Aspasia, but you know what he's like. Once he's got an idea fixed in his head, it's absolutely hopeless trying to reason with him. And he says that either Socrates must stop coming here or he himself goes. He hates being made to look a fool.'

I had seen it coming. The only thing I wasn't sure about was Chrysis' real feelings.

'It's your house,' I reminded her, 'even if he does pay the bills. Is it really worth it, to have him dictating who can and who can't come here?'

'I don't know,' she said miserably. 'I really don't. You know I adore Socrates, particularly since he's so nice to Manto. And Titormos is getting more and more bad tempered these days. I think he feels inferior, he secretly worries that we might despise him in comparison to all your friends. Yet I really am fond of him. He's been very good to me. And I just can't face the idea of being independent again, or getting used to someone else. Remember I'm older than you, and I haven't got your brain. Also, I'm getting so fat I soon won't be much use as a companion.'

Poor Chrysis. It was true, she *was* getting rather plump. She was as beautiful as ever, but she might well have had difficulty finding another lover as generous as Titormos. She was too good-natured to suggest it, but the obvious solution was for me to get out, taking my entourage—and Socrates in particular—with me.

I found a house just below the Acropolis that had everything I wanted. It was a perfectly ordinary, rather large house with two inner courtyards—one for the men and one for the women—and several rooms big enough to hold a crowd of people. Its owner had died three years before and his heir was now selling off the house to raise funds for a niece's dowry. It was dilapidated and uncared for, but I loved it.

I had to buy slaves of my own. Micon, obviously, would become my steward, and it seemed logical to let him choose the men and women who would be working under him. We went down to the market together and chose four men. They all turned out to be hard workers and honest people, thanks to Micon's good judgment. But when it came to choosing women—I needed at least three—he hung back bashfully.

'What's the matter, Micon?' I asked. 'From what I've heard, you're the last person to be shy with girls. I thought you'd enjoy the women's market.'

'Well it's like this,' he said awkwardly. 'I don't quite know how to put it. But there's a young female belonging to your friend Chrysis with whom I have what you might call an arrangement. And I thought if your friend was willing to sell, well, then we might get married.'

'Why on earth didn't you say so before?' I laughed. 'Which girl is it?'

'Lamia. The one who does your hair.'

I knew her well, a pretty cheerful girl with a pleasant voice. 'I'm sure that can be arranged,' I promised him. 'I'll ask Chrysis as soon as we get back.'

'There's just one more thing,' he added apologetically.

'Yes?' I queried.

'I think if you were to buy the young female you might find you were getting an extra slave for nothing, as it were.'

'You mean she's pregnant?'

He nodded.

'Well in that case we shall need a female who knows something about babies. Lamia's too useful to waste time looking after her own.'

Micon's eyes lit up. 'You mean you'll let us keep the baby?'

44

'Of course,' I reassured him. 'No baby born in my house will ever be exposed, regardless of whether it's male or female, free or slave. But that doesn't mean I authorise you to go round serving children on every woman in sight.'

'Oh no,' he agreed happily. 'I wouldn't dream of such a thing.'

Chrysis was quite happy to let Lamia go once she heard about the baby. And I bought two more females—Andromeda, an untrained young girl, and Ismenia, a competent Phrygian woman who was a capable nurse and housekeeper.

The seven slaves were sent to put the house in order. And a few days later I moved in. It was a sunny spring morning with Athens looking at its best. As I proudly walked into my very own house I heard a strange tapping coming from the second courtyard.

'What's that?' I asked Micon.

'Visitors for you,' he replied mysteriously.

I went through the dividing door into the half of the house intended as women's quarters and there to my amazement was Socrates. With him was a bald, melancholy looking man I didn't know. They were tapping one of the walls.

'What on earth . . . ?' I began, but Socrates interrupted with a whoop of joy.

'Welcome, welcome,' he shouted. 'I had to be the first to greet you in your new house. I brought you a present.'

He stepped back and I saw a stone bust on a low pillar. It was a Hermes to stand outside the front door—something no Athens house, respectable or otherwise, could be without. But this was a Hermes with a difference. Instead of the noble godlike features generally seen on the household deity, this one had a wicked, mischievous grin and a jolly, almost tipsy expression. It didn't look unlike Socrates himself.

'Do you like it?' he demanded. 'I made it especially for you.'

I flung my arms round him and kissed him. Despite his preference for boys he didn't seem to mind. Then we both remembered the stranger, standing embarrassed on the veranda.

'I'm so sorry,' fussed Socrates. 'I quite forgot to introduce you. This is Pheidias, a sculptor. We thought perhaps he might carve a frieze to brighten the place up a bit.'

The melancholy man greeted me gravely. 'I would suggest a scene with the poets, or the muses, or both . . .'

I was enchanted with the idea. And mine became the only house in Athens with a frieze by Pheidias and a Hermes by Socrates the stone mason.

45

The gloomy sculptor dropped in to see me occasionally even after he had finished the frieze. I was never quite sure why—he talked very little and generally looked as if he were about to burst into tears. He was Athens' greatest craftsman, yet convinced he had no talent at all. He would glare moodily at his carving on my walls and mutter 'hideous, hideous', as if defying anyone present to contradict him. When someone invariably did, he would snort angrily and shake his head. Nobody, he implied, knew what he was talking about. He once confessed to me after a few cups of wine that his life's ambition was to create the biggest statue ever seen, of gold and ivory; but he was terrified that once he started he would be paralysed by the enormity of the job. 'I couldn't do it, my dear, it would be presuming too much. Just imagine, a towering, glittering Zeus or Athena, two or three times life size. I would stand there in front of the block of stone and my hands wouldn't move. I know they wouldn't.' There was no way of convincing him he was a great artist. I gave him another drink and changed the subject.

After a few days in my own house I wondered why I hadn't moved months before. Not that life was very different, it was just that I felt different, no longer dependent on Titormos' moods, no longer worried if Tolmides pinched the female slaves or Socrates collapsed in the best bedroom. More people, if possible, came than ever before and the Aspasia set seemed to include everyone who was anyone in Athens. With, of course, one notable exception. Pericles was as remote as ever.

I was as unpopular with Athenian wives as I was popular with their husbands. 'They think you're some sort of sorceress,' Meidias chuckled one day. 'Somehow the word has got round that you've bewitched every man in the city, and they're convinced that at the very least you must have three heads. I tried to tell my wife that you're just an exceptionally pretty, intelligent seventeen-year-old girl, and for some reason she burst into tears.'

There was no point in saying I didn't blame her. There were probably many wives with brains as good as or better than mine. They just hadn't been taught to use them. And Meidias, for example, would never dream of spending two hours explaining to his wife, as he just had to me, why Pericles' efforts to organise a conference of all the Greek city-states had failed. It seemed a good idea on the face of it: every city in Greece and the Aegean was invited to send a delegate to Athens for talks about restoring the temples destroyed by the Persians and setting up an effective system of naval defence. The trouble was that this really meant nothing more than restoring

Athens' temples and building up the Athenian navy. The Spartans realised this at once and refused to have anything to do with the 'all-Greek conference'. Without them, it would have made no sense, so was never held. The Greek cities never have been able to agree with each other, except when threatened by a barbarian power like Persia. They probably never will.

It seemed to me that the five year truce with Sparta was hardly worth the paper it was signed on. The year I moved into my house the Spartans sent an expedition to 'liberate' Delphi and the Delphic oracle from the control of Athenian allies. Pericles simply waited till the Spartans had gone home, marched on Delphi himself and gave it back to the allies. The Spartans had been granted precedence in consulting the oracle instead of waiting the usual ten or twenty days—an inscription to this effect was carved on the head of the bronze wolf in front of the temple. Pericles got a similar decree passed in favour of Athens, and inscribed on the right flank of the same wolf. I thought it was one of the silliest stories I'd ever heard; it simply went to prove how ridiculous war is. Why should hundreds of grown men march about the country in full armour just to ensure they wouldn't have to queue up when consulting the idiot oracle? Meidias was shocked at my irreverent attitude and I was equally shocked that an intelligent man like him could take the oracle seriously.

The months passed quickly, happily. I began to love Athens and feel like a true Athenian. It was an odd life, being the friend and confidant of nearly every man in the city but knowing none of the women. I still had friends among the companions, of course— Manto in particular often stayed with me for days at a time—but it seemed unnatural that shut away in hundreds of segregated apartments there should be a class of people I couldn't know at all. The only 'respectable' woman I ever met was Elpinice, the wife of Callias, a wealthy diplomat. She was a formidable old matron who didn't give a damn about tradition or convention. When her husband refused to bring her to see me she did the obvious, sensible thing and came on her own. In the past this remarkable woman had acted as go-between in a power battle between her brother and Pericles; she was generally supposed to have slept with her brother because she lived with him and kept house for him before her marriage; Callias was so much in love with her he married her without a dowry. I could never understand why she alone of Athenian wives defied the taboos and broke through into an all-male society. It must just have been her immense strength of character.

There was furious debate in the Assembly that year about Pericles' plan to use the allied funds for building new temples on the Acropolis in Athens. He claimed the money was for Athens to do as she liked with and that a public building programme would relieve the growing unemployment problem (hundreds of ex-soldiers were out of a job). The opposition maintained that the allied funds had been subscribed for defence against the Persians and should not be used for beautifying the city of Athens. Pericles won, as usual, and Pheidias was put in charge of the entire building scheme. He was delighted, and terrified by the responsibility — he told me he had begged Pericles to find someone else, but the Olympian had been adamant. Pheidias, he said, was the best sculptor in Athens, therefore he and no-one else must design the city temples.

Eighteen months after I moved into my house there was a disastrous, tragic, military campaign. A band of anti-Athenian exiles had seized two remote cities North West of Thebes and were not, as far as I could see, doing anyone any harm. But Tolmides, The Daring, saw this as a chance to assert Athens' and his own glory; he wanted to march against the cities straight away. Pericles was against the idea but for once was outvoted in the Assembly, so Tolmides set bravely off with a thousand men, including Deinon. The whole idea was mad: it was late autumn, the weather in the North was terrible, and a thousand men were no sort of army at all. They did manage to take one of the cities, couldn't make any headway with the other, and were ambushed on their way home. Half the Athenians were hemmed in and forced to surrender; the others died fighting. Both Tolmides and Deinon were killed.

It was Socrates who brought me the news, and I was grateful to him for saying as little as possible. He just put his arm round me and let me sob. It seemed so tragic, so utterly senseless for young men like Tolmides and Deinon to go merrily marching off to kill themselves for no reason at all except to show off Athens' power. And they didn't even manage to do that. I was heartbroken, and blindly angry. It shouldn't have been allowed to happen.

My life changed, after the deaths of Tolmides and Deinon. Sex no longer seemed fun, so at the tender age of nineteen I more or less gave it up. I missed Deinon horribly, more than I would have thought it possible to miss anyone, and when the next summer Socrates, too, went off on a military expedition I felt lonely for the first time in my life.

The younger group of the Aspasia set had more or less disbanded:

parties didn't seem the same without its two leaders. And most of the young men who came to see me seemed overawed, as though I were a formidable matron instead of a girl their own age. Ridiculous really, but I was glad they weren't queuing up to leap into bed with me. I didn't need the money: Meidias had invested my savings and assured me I could live comfortably on the income provided I wasn't too extravagant.

There were always girls around the house if anyone wanted sex. I generally had two or three young companions staying with me, girls who had just arrived in Athens to start their careers. And Manto seemed to spend more time at my house than she did at Chrysis'. I was glad to have them there, and left it to them to make their own financial agreements. I didn't take a share, but if, as sometimes happened, their lovers offered me a gift, I didn't refuse it.

One bright spot in that gloomy year was a new friend: Sophocles, the playwright, then aged about fifty and at the height of his fame. Our relationship was based on puzzled respect. For I couldn't understand how such a devout, conservative, in some ways narrow-minded traditionalist could write such moving, awe-inspiring poetry. And he could not understand how such an irreverent, cheeky child could hold her own in an adult argument. We argued for hours about the role of women: he thought they should be, ideally, like his own tragic heroines, sadly resigned to the will of the gods. I thought his heroines were mostly rather foolish girls who let themselves be used by gods and men without putting up a fight. Sophocles ought to have known about women—despite his piety, he was a rakish old man with an eye for a pretty face and pair of legs. But the girls he courted so assiduously were very different from the woe-begone, dismal creatures who suffered their way through his plays. I couldn't see why he didn't portray women as they are instead of as he thought they ought to be. Or why, if his ideal women were so strait-laced, he spent all his time in the company of women who were the complete opposite.

Socrates came back safely from an unsuccessful military campaign, and then it was the Spartans' turn to take the offensive. They marched on Athens itself, but when they were only a few hours away from the city inexplicably turned round and went home again. In fact it wasn't so inexplicable: it was more or less common knowledge that Pericles had bribed their commander, King Pleistoanax, to go away. The king was brought to trial when he got back to Sparta and sentenced to a heavy fine. He could afford it with the 600 minas he had received from Pericles. It seemed yet another example of the stupidity of war.

Pericles too, it seemed, believed that lives should not be sacrificed in the cause of meaningless words. That winter he sent envoys, including Elpinice's husband Callias, to Sparta to negotiate a lasting peace. Despite an outcry from the warmongers they agreed to give up all claims in the South in return for Spartan friendship. A thirty years' peace was signed.

Three months after the peace was signed I met you, Pericles. The thirty years peace lasted less than fifteen. Our love lasted sixteen years and seven months. My love, I thought, was everlasting. It was and is. But would you ever understand, I wonder, why I am now going to marry again, to become the wife of a man you wouldn't even have employed as a servant? You might forgive me, but I doubt if you would really understand. Lysicles, my future husband, may be only a sheep-dealer, but he is kind, he asks nothing of me and gives me dog-like devotion in return. Please, please try at least to see my point of view, to see why I am doing this.

4

IT is now several days later and I have just re-read everything
written so far. I didn't intend to write most of it—it just came
out as a sort of introduction, to what was, I suppose, the turn-
ing-point in my life. I seem to have been very confused, referring to
you sometimes as Pericles, sometimes as The Olympian, sometimes simply as you. From now on you are you. From now on, in
fact, you could take over: there's very little about my life in the
past sixteen years that you don't know. Yet I wonder if our
separate accounts of the same events, dramas, emotions would
bear the slightest resemblance, whether they would be recognisable
as dealing with the same subject. Perhaps not. This is one of the
things I miss most about you—your *different* way of seeing things
to counter-balance my own. It was like looking at the world
through another pair of eyes, and often discovering that my own
were blurred or distorting. I don't have much confidence in them
any more.

I had seen you once or twice in the street, so knew what you
looked like. And although you had never even looked at me I was
fairly sure you must know who I was, too (you told me later that
you did). We were, after all, the two most celebrated people in
Athens in our different ways. I had resigned myself to the idea that
I was never going to meet you, though I was curious to know why.
Were you frightened? And if so, of what? Were you a woman-
hater? And if so, why did you have a wife? Were you so completely bound up in affairs of state that you had no time or interest
for anything else? If so, you must have been a very remarkable
phenomenon, as worthy of my passing attention as a rare species of
wild beast. Whereas I don't have any particular affection for exotic
animals, I would always go out of my way to look at one, just once.

Three months after the signing of the thirty years' peace, you
suddenly woke up to the fact that I existed. You were never able to

give me a satisfactory explanation as to why; in my own opinion, having dealt with Persia, Sparta, the Acropolis and every other problem under the sun, you were bored with nothing to do. Whatever the reason, you reportedly started asking questions about me. You asked Meidias, you asked Sophocles, you asked Socrates — 'Who is this woman Aspasia?' They told you, in their different ways, then reported this extraordinary fact to me. You must have had a very confusing picture of me.

'Why doesn't he come and see me, then, if he's so curious?' I asked Meidias. 'There's nothing compromising about it — practically everyone else in Athens has been here.'

Meidias sighed. 'You know perfectly well he never goes anywhere. Every morning he walks from his house to his office. In the afternoon he goes to the baths. Early every evening he walks home again. It's a routine he's kept up for years, you could almost tell the time by his movements.'

'Perhaps I should simply turn up at his house, then. Elpinice does.'

He looked alarmed. 'Dearest, not even you could do that. In the first place you couldn't get past the door porter. In the second place Pericles' steward Evangelos has strict instructions not to let strangers into The Presence. The slaves would gossip, the word would get round that you'd been turned back at the door and you'd become the laughing stock of the city. Please don't try it, for my sake.'

'Well for my sake couldn't you try and persuade him to come here. You're a friend of his.'

'It's no use, Aspasia,' he replied, exasperated. 'He has literally never been seen in any street except the ones between his house, his office and the baths, and your house certainly isn't on his route. Do you realise that the last time he went out to pay a social call was about fifteen years ago, when he put in a brief appearance at his cousin's wedding. Even then he only stayed till the first toasts. You'll simply have to resign yourself to the fact that Pericles is not for you.'

I was annoyed. In those days I was used to getting my own way. It seemed absurd that someone should be going round asking questions about me, yet unwilling to come and find out for himself. But there seemed to be nothing I could do about it. 'He sounds like a pompous bore and I haven't the slightest wish to meet him,' I said crossly and untruthfully.

Socrates, however, didn't give in so easily (in fact I have never known him give in at all). I don't know how many months he must have spent nagging and pestering before he finally wore you down. I only know that for some time he was looking very mysterious, secretive and full of suppressed excitement. When I asked him what he was plotting he just grinned and said enigmatically: 'A little surprise. Wait and see. It's developing nicely.'

I can imagine the sort of tactics he must have used, referring incessantly to me, quoting me whenever possible, till you were tricked into asking yet again, 'What's so special about this woman Aspasia?' And Socrates, inexorably, must have replied: 'Come and see for yourself.' At that point you were more or less trapped, for Socrates demonstrated the illogicality of every objection you raised. And, as I later discovered, you prided yourself on your logical mind. He bullied and pleaded until you were finally forced to admit that none of your arguments were valid; the only reason, therefore, for staying away must be that you were frightened. But Pericles the Olympian could not possibly be frightened of a twenty-year-old companion. You had no choice but to prove it.

Had I known what he was up to, I should have enjoyed a day by day progress report. But Socrates loved springing surprises, and the first I knew about it was when he asked if he could bring a friend to see me in secret that evening.

'Yes, of course. But why in secret?'

'The man's a political exile. Nobody must know he is here.'

'Why bring him here, then? You know how many people there always are around the house.'

He totally ignored my question. 'He mustn't be seen by anyone at all, particularly not by any of Pericles' friends. It is extremely important that Pericles shouldn't know he's in Athens. Knowing your feelings about the Olympian, I thought you'd be willing to help.'

I was too pleased with the idea of outwitting Pericles to notice that his sudden coughing fit sounded suspiciously like laughter.

'Oh well, that's different, you should have said so before. I don't think I can get everyone out of the house because Manto and the girls will probably be entertaining. But you could come in through the back door, if I leave it open, and go straight to the little sitting-room on the left. I'll make sure the others are all in the other half of the house.'

'Wonderful! We'll be here two hours after dark.'

He kissed me on the cheek, rushed to the door and vanished, as if he were afraid I might change my mind. And it was only when he had gone that I realised I had quite forgotten to ask who the mystery man was, what his offence had been, or why he was in Athens. I was intrigued.

It was a chilly spring evening. I lit the oil lamps in the little sitting room and settled down to wait, after giving instructions to Micon that on no account was I to be disturbed. I was reading the first draft of Sophocles' new play *Antigone*, carried away by the beauty of the language but still irritated by the woodenness of the characters. Why *couldn't* poetry be written about people who were real? The only person who ever managed it was Homer.

Socrates hadn't bothered to explain why he wanted this political exile to meet me. As far as I had gathered he wasn't actually asking me to hide him in the house. If not, why was he coming to see me, risking being identified in the street? There was something that didn't quite tally about the whole story, but I couldn't work out what it was. I went on reading, finding it difficult to concentrate.

At last there were steps outside. Socrates pulled back the doorway curtain, looked round the room and whispered conspiratorially: 'Is it safe?' I nodded. He disappeared for a moment then sidled into the room, followed by a man dressed in a long dark cloak. I couldn't see his features in the dim light, and waited in silence as he unwrapped the cloak, handed it to Socrates, then stepped forward hesitantly to the couch where I was lying. It was you.

I was completely astounded. I stared, gasped, and stuttered: 'P . . . P . . . Pericles!'

You bowed gravely.

My astonishment turned to fury as I realised how Socrates had tricked me. I felt an utter fool and wanted to burst into tears. Trembling with rage I dashed over to him, leaving you standing in the middle of the room. 'How dare you do this?' I screamed. 'How *could* you invent all that nonsense about political exiles and secrecy? I hate you, I loathe you, I never want to see you again. Get out of here and take your friend with you!'

He was at his most maddening. 'Now, now, calm down, darling,' he purred. 'You're always complaining you've never met Pericles so I brought him to see you. I thought you'd be grateful.' Turning to you, he went on: 'Pericles, meet Aspasia whom you've heard so much about. She's hardly at her charming best at this moment but I assure you she really can be quite entertaining.'

I wanted to hit him. But it was your turn to be angry. 'Socrates, what's all this?' you exploded. 'You told me Aspasia had invited me here. Yet it seems she wasn't expecting me. What have you been up to? Explain at once.'

54

Socrates shrugged and studied his grubby toes. The wretched man was choking with laughter.

I took a deep breath. 'He told me he was bringing a political exile, someone who had to be hidden from Pericles, that is to say ... from you.'

'Oh. Well, I'm sorry. I'd better go,' you said stiffly.

We stood there awkwardly, at a loss. Then suddenly, mercifully, my sense of humour came back. It really *was* a comic situation — Pericles and Aspasia brought together in strictest secrecy in the middle of the night, and unable to do anything but lose their tempers. The comedy playwrights would have made a meal of it. I started to laugh myself, then glanced at you, still standing self-consciously in the middle of the room, uncertain what to do. You looked bewildered, hurt, vulnerable. Pericles the Olympian was embarrassed. He was shy and confused. He was human.

I stopped laughing, walked over to you and said gently: 'Please don't go. I'm sorry about all this, but you know what Socrates is. It's true, I *have* been longing to meet you and I'm very glad you're here. Lie down and have some wine.'

You glanced round the room in panic as if searching for an escape route, then lay down gingerly on a couch. 'Well ... if you're quite sure. You see, I have heard so much about you, and Socrates said ...'

'I think we should stop taking any notice of what Socrates says,' I said, turning to the young man in question. 'I suppose this was the surprise you've been plotting for so long?'

He nodded gleefully as you broke in: 'Surprise? But he told me you'd been begging him to bring me here for months. I don't understand ...'

'So she has, so she has,' said Socrates. 'But I had to tell her it was impossible until I knew it was a certainty — I wouldn't have liked to raise the poor girl's hopes and then disappoint her. And then when you insisted on all this secrecy I couldn't resist my little joke.'

He bounced over to where I was standing, fell on one knee and declared dramatically: 'Aspasia, my dearest, my sweetest, my fairest, forgive me! I kiss your feet, I prostrate myself before you. Forgive your unworthy and humble servant!'

He looked so ludicrous we both burst out laughing. The ice was broken.

I ladled out the wine as Socrates threw himself unceremoniously on to my couch. 'I suppose I do owe you both an apology. But the chance was too good to miss. I knew that if I told Aspasia who the visitor was she would have acted like an intellectual, heartless show-off, launching off about women's rights from the moment she met you. She was far too antagonistic. You would have found her insufferable. In fact she's quite a nice girl at heart even if she does fly into tempers.'

The awful thing was—he was right.

Socrates did most of the talking that first evening, playing the fool, making us laugh. You were silent, nervous, quite unlike I had imagined you. You only relaxed when he said something particularly idiotic; then you broke into a deep throaty chuckle. I was anything but my normal scintillating self. After getting off to such a humiliating start I found myself tongue-tied, unable to deliver all the lectures I had always promised to give Pericles if I ever met him. We lost some of our shyness after a few cups of wine, but even so our conversation was tentative, hesitant. I think we talked about Sophocles' plays, and you told us about some of Aeschylos' tragedies which Socrates and I were too young to have seen.

After a couple of hours Socrates rolled to his feet. 'Well, children, that's enough for tonight. We mustn't keep Pericles out too late on his first social call in years.'

We stood up, facing each other. Again, I noticed that uncertain, lost look on your face. I wanted to comfort you, reassure you.

'I'm glad you came,' I smiled. 'You were quite different from what I expected, very much nicer.'

'You too,' you replied, looking gravely into my eyes.

There was a moment's silence before you added awkwardly: 'I should like . . . I mean, could I . . . would it be possible to see you again?'

'I should love it.'

'Well, what shall we do . . . how can we arrange it?'

Socrates interrupted. 'It seems ridiculous, but Athens' leading general is afraid to let people know he is visiting a young lady. Don't ask me why; it's just the way he is. I would suggest that if you two wish to make assignations you can send a slave with a note to me and I'll make sure that it's safely delivered. You see, I'm a true friend after all.'

'Yes, yes, that's a good idea,' you said gratefully. Then you put your cloak on, clumsily kissed my hand and more or less bolted out.

Socrates paused in the doorway to look back at me with a broad wink and triumphant smirk.

The next day I asked Meidias: 'Tell me about Pericles.'

'What about Pericles?'

'Well, about him as a person, his family and so on.'

Meidias looked suspicious. 'Why the sudden interest? You seem to be obsessed with the Olympian these days. Don't tell me you've actually managed to meet him?'

The trouble with Meidias was that he was too shrewd. 'No, of course not. I was just curious,' I lied.

Fortunately he loved imparting information of any kind. 'Well, let me think. Pericles was born four years before the Battle of Marathon, which makes him forty-nine now. His father Xanthippos was a prominent politician and general. But it is through his mother, Agariste, that he belongs to the brilliant Alcmaeonid family, one of the oldest in Athens—they trace their descent back to King Nestor of the Trojan War. He has an elder brother, Ariphron, and a sister whose name I forget. There's a story that while his mother was pregnant with her second child she dreamed she was going to give birth to a lion. A few days later she produced Pericles.'

'Ridiculous,' I said, thinking how Chloe would have loved such a tale.

'As you like. Anyway, almost from the day he was born, he was treated like a young prince. Nothing was too good for him. He was given the best possible education—not only did he go to school like the rest of us, but he had Anaxagoras as a private tutor and his own music-teacher, Damon. We were all a bit jealous. But even as a boy he wasn't conceited. He had a sort of aloof charm that made him irresistible. And he worked, by the gods how he worked! When we were all enjoying ourselves with wine, women and song he was studying. When we were fooling about at the sports ground he was already speaking in the Assembly. He took himself very seriously indeed. Between you and me I think he was a bit shy of the rest of us and needed to prove himself in public before he dared try to make friends in private.'

This picture fitted in with the surprising Pericles I had met. 'Go on,' I urged.

'Well, he's been a general on and off for most of the past twenty years. As you know, they have to be re-elected every year, but I think Pericles has only missed two or three times. He is undoubtedly one of the most brilliant generals we have ever had, perhaps because he stops to think before he acts, unlike poor Tolmides.'

'Is he married?' I asked casually, although I knew the answer.

Meidias looked at me sharply, started to say something then thought better of it. 'Yes and no. It's an odd situation. I think he is still technically married to a distant cousin. She was the wife of Callias' son Hipponicos, but when she inherited a fortune she was obliged by law to marry her nearest male relative to keep the money in the family. The nearest suitable relative was Pericles; they married and had two sons, now aged about fifteen and thirteen. It was anything but a love match—I doubt if the Olympian had any time for her at all. Anyway, having done their duty by providing male heirs to the fortune, they parted amicably and she went back to her former husband, Hipponicos.'

As I digested this information, Meidias went on: 'It's a strange household, with no mother for the boys. And I heard the other day that Pericles has also become guardian to two younger children— Cleinias and Alcibiades—whose father was killed in Tolmides' campaign. They are cousins on his mother's side.'

I wanted to ask if you had a mistress, but it seemed a leading question. I compromised. 'Does he like boys or girls—or both?'

He shrugged. 'Neither, as far as I know. I've told you dozens of times—Pericles never goes anywhere, never sees anyone outside his own home except on business. I can't remember him showing interest in any sort of sex.'

'Extraordinary,' I mused.

'Well, he's certainly not for you, with your well-known appetite. Speaking of which—what about it?'

But I wasn't feeling like it and invented a headache. Meidias went away puzzled and disgruntled, leaving me to pace restlessly about the house, irrationally confused. I wanted to talk to Socrates, to ask him about you, about your reactions to the night before. But there was no sign of him that day and I knew if I went out to find him I'd have no chance of speaking to him alone.

He didn't turn up the next day, or the day after. Finally I sent a slave out to look for him and tell him I wanted to see him.

A few hours later he shuffled in, looking evil.

'At your service, my love. What's your problem?'

'No problem. I just wanted to see you.'

He sighed. 'What's the matter with you, Aspasia? Never in your life have you just "wanted to see me". Apart from anything else I'm the ugliest man in Athens, not remotely pleasing to the eye. You may want to talk to me, perhaps. That's different. In which case there must be something you want to talk to me about. Come on, what is it?'

I swallowed my pride. 'Pericles.'

'Of course. What about him?'

'I don't know really. I just wanted to talk about him.'

'Well go on, then. Talk.'

'Don't be so exasperating,' I pleaded. 'You know what I mean.'

He relented. 'All right then, you want to know what the Olympian said about the other night, what he thought of you. Correct?'

I nodded.

'Well, oddly enough, Pericles has done nothing but pester me to find out what *you* said about the other night, what you thought about him. I'm damned if I'm going to act as mediator between two supposedly adult people who should be able to communicate with each other. That's why I've kept away from here. I did my bit when I introduced you and now I'm not so sure it was a good idea. If you want to know what he thinks, ask him yourself.'

'How can I? I've heard nothing from him.'

'Look, Aspasia, what did you do when you wanted to talk to me?'

'I sent you a note.'

'Then for the gods' sake use your failing wits and send one to Pericles. It's very simple you know. Give it to me and I'll deliver it straight into his aristocratic hands.'

'But I can't! I mean, it isn't done for a woman to start sending notes . . .'

Socrates shrugged in despair. 'Have you taken leave of your senses? Since when has Aspasia of Miletos worried about whether or not something is "done" by a woman? Pull yourself together, darling.'

I must have looked miserable, for he suddenly laughed and said, much more kindly: 'Poor love. I can see I'd better reveal everything: our worthy and esteemed general is himself going through agonies of indecision about whether or not he should invite himself to come and see you again. You know he's really not used to this sort of thing, so I suggest you put him out of his misery by inviting him yourself.'

'Really? This isn't just another trick?'

'Truly. By Zeus, Apollo, and all the rest of them. Come on, write him a note and I'll take it to him straight away before he leaves the baths. Though why it should need me to instruct two of the finest brains in Athens on how to run their love affair I don't know.'

'What on earth do you mean, love affair? We've only met once.'

Socrates smiled enigmatically. 'You silly girl. When I see my two best and most talented friends behaving like perfect idiots I can only come to one conclusion.'

He had the irritating habit of always being right. And I knew it. I wrote, very correctly: 'It would be a pleasure to see you again. The back door will be open this evening and I shall be in the same room — Aspasia.'

Socrates tucked the note somewhere inside his filthy cloak and strode off, barefoot as usual, to deliver it. He looked extremely pleased with himself.

(I have never, in all the years I have known him, seen Socrates wear shoes or sandals, even though he spends most of the day outdoors, summer and winter. And I have never seen him in anything but the tattered cloak which I am sure is the same one he had on the day I met him. He wears no tunic underneath, his right shoulder is always bare, and I know for a fact the cloak is all he has on because when he falls asleep it rides up, leaving him naked from the waist down. I was often tempted to pinch him but thought he might be disappointed to wake up and find it was only a girl. He rarely goes to the baths, is always dirty, shabby and unkempt. Yet his friends — and he has hundreds — won't hear a word against him.)

The rest of the afternoon dragged by. I couldn't settle down to anything, didn't want to talk to anyone, and paced restlessly about the house, fussing at the slaves. I even snapped at Manto for asking what was the matter with me. Obviously hurt, she announced she was going to stay with Chrysis for a few days. I didn't care.

I didn't know what to wear. If I dressed up too much it would look as though I had done so on purpose, for a special occasion — and I didn't want you to think that. On the other hand, I did want to look my best. The more I worried the more I was angry with myself for worrying. I kept telling myself you were just another man, that it didn't matter what you thought. I had never felt like this before, not even before the first banquet, and it was infuriating to find I couldn't reason myself out of senseless, illogical panic. Were you going to come, or was it all another of Socrates' elaborate jokes? What sort of mood would you be in? Would you be disappointed in me? How could I impress you, after the abysmal exhibition I made of myself the time before? I knew so much about you, but didn't know you at all.

In the end I put on my most expensive dress, pale yellow and so light it almost floated. It made me feel good, and I told myself firmly that you would probably think I wore such fabrics all the time. I put silver bracelets on my arms and ankles then took them off again — they seemed vulgar. I made Lamia the slavegirl do my hair three times and even then it wasn't right. She asked curiously if I was going to a banquet and I told her crossly to mind her own business. When I looked in the mirror I thought I looked ghastly. And the worst thing of all was that I couldn't laugh at myself about the fact that I cared so much. I cared, and that was that.

Long before dusk I was in the little sitting room. Micon had produced a jar of the very best wine from Chios (bought the year before for special celebrations and people) and I mixed it strong—at least two parts wine to one of water. I drank about four cups, rather fast, and began to feel more confident.

For some reason I was convinced it would be a good idea if you came in to find me doing something domestic, just to prove I wasn't all that different from the women you must know. It seems stupid in retrospect—after all, surely my attraction was that I *was* different. Anyway, I had a loom moved into the sitting room (to Lamia's great surprise) and sat there trying to weave. Setting it up, the threads got tangled, I became hopelessly confused between the woof and the weft and warp—or whatever the wretched things are called—and discovered my hand was shaking. I reflected glumly that I was no Penelope. And banished the loom into the courtyard.

I hadn't specified a time in my note, so had no idea when to expect you. I didn't have a water clock with me, but remember giving up hope when it was at least three hours after dark and you still hadn't appeared. I had checked five times that the back door was still open, and was lying there miserably wondering if there could possibly have been a misunderstanding—Socrates might have forgotten, not found you, been knocked down by a horse—when I heard the back door click shut. My heart started thudding so unbearably fast I thought it would kill me. I think my face froze into an idiot grin. And then there you were, tall and terrifying in the doorway.

It seems so ridiculous now. That we were both completely inarticulate—from nervousness. You came in, fumbling with your cloak, babbling about children, Spartans, Anaxagoras. You made no sense at all, though I gathered later you had been held up because your precocious new wards had insisted on asking Anaxagoras questions about the Spartan way of life. And you couldn't leave the house till everyone had gone. Pericles, as we all knew, never went out in the evenings.

You were so obviously paralysed by fright that I felt momentarily a bit bolder. And once more had this entirely new feeling of tenderness, a wrench in the pit of my stomach. But I couldn't express it—it just made me more tongue-tied.

61

'Come in,' I fussed, grabbing your cloak. 'Did you have any trouble finding the house?'

'No, not at all.'

I made a bee-line for the wine jar and was already ladling out a cup for you, slopping it over the edge, when I realised I hadn't asked you to lie down. You were standing in the middle of the room nervously fingering your beard, at a loss.

'I'm so sorry, please take a couch,' I said as graciously as possible. 'I think that one over there is the most comfortable.'

You lay down gingerly as I carried over the cup of wine, spilling a quarter of it on the way, and lay down myself on the other side of the low table. There was a dog barking in the distance and I couldn't think of a thing to say.

My head was reeling from the amount I'd already drunk and I remember thinking that on no account must I show it. All my perceptions seemed sharpened and I was intensely conscious of every object in the room, the couches, the table, the cups, the flickering lamp, above all the two people lying there, their thoughts silently careering along separate courses, total strangers. I knew how you must feel, because I felt the same. But the knowledge didn't help, it just made me suffer twice over, for you and for me. Panic-stricken, I tried to reason with myself that this was ridiculous. But even if I had felt like laughing—which I didn't—I would have been afraid of offending you and making you feel foolish. I sensed, even then, that you couldn't bear to be laughed at.

The silence seemed interminable, though it probably only lasted a few moments. You broke it with a banal remark about the weather. We had an earnest conversation about how cool it was for the time of year, as a mocking voice in the back of my mind jeered at the picture of Pericles and Aspasia, alone together, solemnly discussing the climate.

You gulped down your wine and I gave you some more. You said how good it was so I launched into an account of who supplied it, where it came from, how much it cost. I was wondering what you were thinking, whether you might not be so bored you would get up and leave at any moment.

Having exhausted the subject of the wine, I cast about desperately for something else.

'Tell me about the new buildings on the Acropolis,' I hazarded. 'Pheidias is so secretive, so convinced he'll make a bad job of them, that I've no idea what they're going to look like.'

You smiled for the first time. 'Pheidias is maddening, but it's probably better than being too sure of himself.'

Then you began to talk, hesitantly at first, then with more and more confidence, until you seemed completely to have forgotten that you were alone with a young woman of doubtful morals in the middle of the night. Your eyes lit up, your voice took on a different, softer note as you described your vision of a new Athens gleaming with marble and gold, visibly the foremost city of the civilised world. I caught a glimpse of the calm, confident Pericles I had heard so much about. And for the first—but not by any means the last—time I sensed that your one and only true, overriding love was for your city, Athens. Anyone or anything else would always take second place.

Although not a great patriot myself, you were obviously so sincere, so glowing with pride in Athens and her achievements, that I felt rather humble. You described the Parthenon, the imposing new walls leading to the Acropolis and the great gold statue of Athena that Pheidias was frightened to sculpt. You had plans for new temples outside Athens, too, as well as a new Hall of the Mysteries at Eleusis and a covered concert hall next to the open-air theatre in Athens. I could see the new buildings already standing there, towering over the city and the sea. And when at last you stopped, saying apologetically: 'That's the general idea. I hope I've not been boring you,' it seemed small-minded to voice my doubts about where the money had come from.

But I was no longer tongue-tied. So I objected gently that perhaps your critics had a valid case in claiming that money raised for defence should not be used to beautify peace-time Athens. And you explained, equally gently, your point of view: the money was earned; it was paid by the allies for protection and so long as Athens protected them it was no one else's business what she did with the surplus.

I wasn't entirely convinced and never have been. Yet I could see how your unruffled sincerity swayed the Assembly, why you were called the Olympian. Your reasoning was faultless, your faith tremendous. The financial ethics were totally irrelevant, minor inconveniences to be ignored.

I laughed. 'They've been telling me for years you're the one man in Athens who could beat me in an argument by sheer force of conviction. I hate to admit it, but they're right. Don't imagine I agree with you—but at least I'll give in gracefully.'

You looked pleased. 'Thank you. I'd hate to be disapproved of by anyone as beautiful as you.'

There was an awkward pause. Never before had I been at a loss about how to acknowledge a compliment. Never before had I been so ridiculously thrilled by a few trite words—which coming from you didn't sound trite. I think I must have blushed. At any rate I couldn't look you in the eyes.

'You must have known a lot of beautiful women,' I faltered, half hoping to hear more. But the ploy didn't work—it just embarrassed you.

'No, not at all,' you said. 'In fact'—and you were stumbling over your words—'I don't think . . . I'm not sure . . . I don't remember ever having talked to a woman before. Alone, that is.'

I was shocked into spontaneity. 'What on earth do you mean? You are, or were married weren't you? How can you possibly never have talked to a woman?'

'Well, I mean . . . I put it badly . . . yes of course I talked to my wife, and my mother and the nurse and the slaves. But they were never interested in anything that interested me, they just sat there nodding politely, neither listening to nor understanding a word I said. In the end I gave up trying. I felt like an outsider in my own house. You are the first woman, except Elpinice perhaps, who has ever argued with me about politics, the first woman I have heard discussing theatre, the first woman with a mind of her own.'

I had a vision of my father's long-suffering wives obediently trying to use their bird-brains, and wanted to launch into my celebrated lecture on women's rights. How could you *expect* your women relatives to be intelligent when they had never been given a chance? But I glanced at you and saw you looking confused and miserable.

You said: 'I'm so sorry, please forgive me. I didn't mean to talk about myself. How stupid. I don't know what came over me . . .'

I could almost see you writhing with embarrassment, and heard myself saying gently: 'Don't be sorry. Please. Come and talk to me as often as you like. You're not an outsider here.'

I shall never forget the look in your eyes. Amazement, incredulity, hope flashed through them as you stammered: 'But surely you haven't time. I mean, you have so many friends, you're such a lovely girl . . . how can you spare time for me?'

I didn't answer, unsure of what to say, so you went on: 'I'm just a middle-aged soldier with no social graces. I don't sing or dance or know how to flirt. I'm hopeless at witty conversation. How can I possibly impose myself on the most brilliant girl in Athens?'

I leaned across and took your hand.

'Please, Pericles. I mean it. Come whenever you want to, as often as you like. I'll make sure nobody knows. I want you to come.'

You stood up, pulled me to my feet and stood looking down at me, your hands on my shoulders. I felt very small.

'Thank you, my dear,' you said gravely. 'I should like that very much. This has been a memorable evening.'

You kissed my hand, picked up your cloak and strode out almost jauntily. I went to bed feeling exhausted, bewildered and extraordinarily happy.

5

I⊤ seems amazing, now, that it was at least two months before you even kissed me. Although we saw each other frequently, although we spent hours alone together in the privacy of that dark little room, although the underlying tension was almost unbearable at times, we did nothing about it. I remembered what Meidias had told me: that you simply weren't interested in sex. And even if he was wrong, you probably weren't interested in women. Also, I was frightened to try to find out in case you thought I was just another companion chasing an important man.

You, I learned later, were terrified to make advances to me in case I thought you thought I was just another companion. . . . You were so sure I had dozens of other men, so anxious to prove that what you valued in me was something different. How wrong, how stupid, how shy we both were. So we talked and talked and talked, longing to kiss and caress each other but both holding back out of mistaken 'consideration'. Sometimes I was happy, sometimes I was miserable, sometimes I was plain frustrated.

Those two lost months seem such a waste, now that we can never make them up. I would give anything to have them all over again— and this time they would not be wasted. We would be in each other's arms from the very first moment and never let go. There were times during our sixteen years together when words were hopelessly inadequate, when the only way to express a hundredth part of my love for you was to grip your narrow, bony hand and hope some of my pent-up feeling would somehow flow through into you. There were times when I felt literally sick with love, times when we would lie locked together for hours, just kissing. And each long, lingering kiss conveyed all the tenderness and yearning we could never express in words. Sometimes we fell asleep with our mouths sealed together. And one of us always had an extra arm which got in the way wherever we put it.

66

Oh, darling. I shouldn't let myself remember. It makes it so much harder to face the stark, final fact of never again. Never. I still don't believe it. I can't, won't believe it. I won't believe that we shall never again wake up side by side, touching each other for reassurance. Or that we won't lie through the dawn in a cocoon of intimacy, unwilling to get up and let the outside world in to break the spell. Or that never again shall I kiss your absurd protruding forehead that you were so selfconscious about, pretending to lick it away. Or complain that your beard tickles. Or laugh to myself as you stand there naked and shivering, angrily denying that you're cold. Athens was, to you, such a perfect city that the climate had to be perfect too. You were convinced it was never too hot, never too cold. Every winter you announced firmly that the freezing cold was just a chill in the air, went out without your cloak to prove your point, and came home coughing and sneezing. Because of the dust, you said. After the first two or three winters I learned not to nag you, but simply to keep a brazier burning in the bedroom all day and whisk it out before you got home.

You were forty-nine when I met you, and looked in some ways older. Your thinning hair, once black, was beginning to go grey. So was your thick beard. Yet you were anything but a doddering old man. And, to me, you were far more attractive than handsome youths of half your age.

This is how I should describe you to someone who had never met you: Pericles, son of Xanthippos, was a tall man with a tough body. You could tell from his physique that he was an aristocrat: everything about him fitted, was in proportion. He had long legs and long hands. He was neither stocky like a peasant nor slim and graceful like Socrates' boys; although he didn't have bulging muscles he was immensely strong and, even in his fifties, extremely fit.

His head was like an upside-down pear—his mother swore it was bulging with too much brain. He was very self-conscious about it and wore his helmet most of the time to hide his forehead. His greying hair was slightly wavy and never allowed to straggle down to his shoulders. He had it trimmed frequently, together with his bristly beard which was full and strong, carefully cut to follow the line of his jaw and chin and elongate his face. When he had his helmet on, most of his face seemed covered with hair, as if the beard and moustache were a half-mask over his mouth and ears. In it there was a generous hole for his full-lipped, sensuous mouth.

67

His teeth were regular, well-formed and rather yellow—with a visible gap when he smiled.

He had a long straight nose, prominent cheek bones and melancholy blue-grey eyes. Heavily lidded, they often seemed to droop at the outer corners—until he opened them wide and they sprang to life.

He dressed neatly but traditionally in white, brown or grey tunics of the very best wool. He wasn't interested in fashion, so never tried out new styles or colours. In fact he was happiest in full armour.

Although an aristocrat himself, he was a champion of the people: he believed there should be equal opportunity for everyone, rich or poor, noble or tradesman. Throughout his career he had supported the cause of the people against reactionaries of his own class who longed nostalgically for rule by a privileged minority instead of by the whole citizen body; by introducing payment for public service, he ensured that every citizen could *afford* to take part in the government of the city.

He was a great orator who didn't waste words. His voice was deep and well-measured, and he always thought before he spoke. I never heard him gabble. His movements, too, were slow and deliberate. When nervous or unsure of himself he fiddled with his beard.

And you almost tied your beard in knots during those two months. Your barber must have wondered whatever you'd been up to. You were attracted to me like a moth to a lamp, but once in my presence you were baffled and confused. You hated yourself for acting illogically, tried to keep away, and came back for more.

The day after our first evening alone together, a slave arrived with a package. Inside was a pear-shaped gold pendant on a delicate chain. A note said: 'Thank you for a wonderful evening. I shall come again tomorrow, a little earlier I hope, unless you send word through Socrates that this is not convenient. Pericles.'

I wanted to hug the slave but sent him away, grinning broadly, with a lavish half-drachma tip. I put the pendant round my neck and have worn it ever since—except for a few days when it was being repaired after we broke the chain during a quarrel. It is round my neck now as I write, and I am fingering the smooth gold as though it were a lucky charm. I love it because it is the first thing you ever gave me. And also because, although you certainly didn't realise it, the pendant is the same shape as your head. I wish Pheidias could have done a gold bust of you, just for me. It would have become my household god, my inspiration. As it is, I have to rely on memory.

That evening with you and the ones that followed were much like the first one. Although some of your shyness wore off you were still very unsure of yourself. You came every three or four days—it was the first summer in years you didn't have a military campaign on your hands so you had plenty of time to spare. But you were terrified of anyone finding out that we were seeing each other. And I didn't know you well enough to complain that I was nothing to be ashamed of.

In fact, I guessed—correctly—why you wanted our meetings kept secret. It was simply that you were frightened people would laugh at you. For the austere, inhuman Pericles, the relentless worker, the man who refused all invitations, the noble Olympian, was making a fool of himself over Athens' most notorious companion. I knew that I was generally thought to have slept with every man who came to the house, as well as many who hadn't. It would hardly have enhanced your dignity to become the latest addition to the long list.

It's easy to see, looking back, that we were falling in love. But at the time we fought it, resisted it, denied it vehemently to Socrates and ourselves. Athenians just don't fall in love with women—apart from the few who have passionate and short-lived infatuations for companions. Love marriages like Elpinice's are the exceptions that prove the rule. It's inevitable really: love, as opposed to lust, requires some sort of mental togetherness to keep it alive. Many Athenians feel deep affection and a sense of protectiveness towards their meek and dutiful wives, as well as fierce sexual jealousy. But they fall in love with young men who combine beauty and brains, who stimulate them, tantalise them, sometimes torture them, and never ever bore them.

I wonder what happened in the past three hundred years to reduce 'respectable' women to the status of uncomplaining sheep. In Homer's time it was different: Helen of Troy must have had something besides beauty if the Greeks actually united to go and get her back. The Trojan women—Hecuba, Cassandra, Andromache—were all educated and articulate, far more interesting characters than their husbands. Odysseus' wife Penelope was anything but a nonentity. In those days men had to pay for a bride; nowadays fathers pay out vast dowries just to get rid of their daughters. Only one hundred and fifty years ago, Sappho was running a prestigious school for young ladies. Now an Athenian girl could no more go to school than run in the Olympic Games. In Sparta, admittedly, it's different—the girls learn athletics and gymnastics and all-round toughness, with the impossible aim of making them as much like boys as possible. I am baffled by Sparta, by its ugliness, its bigotry, its single-minded dedication to turning out citizens who are anonymous, efficient instruments of war. They are hemmed in by prejudice, allowed no contact with the outside world, have no choice but to believe what they are told. Having won their wars, what are they going to do?

It was unthinkable, therefore, that Pericles of all people should fall in love with a woman. It was equally unthinkable that Aspasia should fall in love. Among people who didn't know me I had the reputation for being cold and calculating. My friends saw me as an entertaining mind graced with a pretty face and attractive body — or perhaps it was the other way round. Nobody thought I had a heart. And I don't blame them: until I met you I was a talking doll who mouthed, spoke, thought even — but rarely experienced any deep feeling.

I was infuriated by the effect you had on me. For years I had been vowing to lecture you, to humiliate you, and now I couldn't bring myself to do it. I would spend all day before you came rehearsing long harangues on women's rights, social equality, religious hypocrisy or whatever I happened to disagree about most at that moment. But when you arrived, timid and uncertain, all I wanted to do was take you in my arms and reassure you that you were loved, that you were not alone.

When you were actually there, my prepared speeches always seemed childish, prompted by envy or pique or the urge to be argumentative. And although we did argue at length, our discussions were generally friendly and reasonable, with both of us conceding almost as much as we gained. My personality, when with you, seemed to change. I thought before I spoke, I stopped trying to be clever for the sake of it, I wasn't cruel at other people's expense. I had seen you wince when I made a supposedly witty but cutting (and highly exaggerated) remark about Meidias, and immediately felt bad about it. He was, after all, my friend.

I may have been a dignified, adult character with you, but I was impossible with everyone else, myself included. I was sweet as honey one day, unreasonably irritable the next. Nobody could predict my reactions. I refused to go out or accept any social engagements in case Socrates came with a note from you. I slept with Meidias a couple of times and hated myself for it, bursting into angry tears after making love. He was worried and concerned and begged me to tell him what was wrong. I just cried all the more. I suppose I only did it to spite you, to prove to myself that I didn't love you. It had the opposite effect.

You too were anything but your usual dispassionate self. Socrates reported that you were distracted and bad-tempered, that you were snapping at your friends, that when a group of colleagues called to see you one evening you even appeared to be drunk. Athens was already buzzing with rumours and far-fetched suggestions but so far nobody had hit on the truth. Those who knew you well imagined you were just frustrated, with no war to fight. They were right about your being frustrated.

Things came to boiling point one hot summer evening. It had been one of those days when a heat haze hung over the city, the scorching sun blazed relentlessly and hardly a thing moved. The evening wasn't much cooler—it was hot and airless inside the little room I had come to think of as ours, but we didn't dare sit in the courtyard in case someone saw us. We had drunk more wine than usual, hoping it would cool us down. It just made us flushed.

We had been arguing about the position of women in Athenian society; I had said they were only there to provide male children, and for their husbands' convenience when wanting a woman. The wine must have made me bold, for I went on to ask whether you thought your wife had actually enjoyed making love. You said you thought not, and countered by asking whether companions really enjoy it either.

It was difficult to be truthful. We had never discussed sex before, and every word seemed intensely personal, dangerous. I did my best, explaining that some girls pretend, some girls enjoyed it, but that it was a profession like any other and one did one's best to please. I suddenly hated myself.

'What about you?' you asked casually.

'It depends on the man.' I felt flustered, trapped. 'I don't know really—it's a long time since I worked properly as a companion. I think I enjoyed it most of the time. But nowadays I don't really need to work.'

It sounded wrong. I added quickly: 'But let's talk about you.'

You looked alarmed and stood up. 'Another time. I must be going now.'

I walked over to the door and looked out to make sure there was nobody in the courtyard. It was cooler out there and I stood for a moment breathing in the night air. When I turned round you were standing right behind me, a towering dark shadow. As I looked up at you half questioningly you took my head between your hands,

71

held it for a moment, then leaned forward and kissed me. Gently at first, then harder and harder as though all the pent-up frustration of the past two months could be released in that one kiss. You closed your arms round me and pushed me back towards the couch.

We lay there devouring each other, touching, kissing, clinging in a frenzy of expectation. But just as I thought you were going to take me you gasped, gave a stifled cry and went limp in my arms.

You got up and sat on the other couch, your head in your hands. 'I'm sorry. I don't know what came over me.'

'Don't be sorry. I'm glad—I've been wanting you to kiss me for months.'

'But . . .' You decided against whatever you were going to say and stood up. 'Oh well. I'd better be going.'

I walked over to you, took your hand and kissed it gently. I didn't want you to go. You caressed the top of my head, almost absentmindedly.

'May I come again tomorrow?'

'Of course.'

The briefest of hugs and you were gone. But we both knew for a certainty that the next day we would make love.

It was the longest day I have ever known, hot and sultry and suffocating and never-ending. I couldn't stop thinking about you, was obsessed with erotic fantasies about you, with visions of you and me in every known position, inextricably entwined. I hardly noticed the people round me, only half-listened to what they said and replied distractedly when spoken to. They probably thought I'd got sunstroke. In the afternoon I retreated to my bedroom and tried to fill in time reading Sappho. But for once she failed to calm me: her love poems were very beautiful, very moving and far too pure. I wasn't in the mood for chaste love between girls.

You were going through the same agonies. Socrates dropped in during the early evening to report that you were jittery and tense.

'What on earth have you done to him?'

I don't believe in discussing my sex life with friends, not even with Socrates, so answered truthfully: 'Nothing.'

'Well in that case you'd better do something, quickly. The man's a bundle of nerves and infecting everyone round him.'

My hand was trembling as I put on my most revealing dress and drenched myself in perfume. The prospect of sex had never affected me like this before. But then I'd never had to wait two months before for a man I wanted. And I'd never wanted a man so much.

72

It was hotter, if possible, than the night before. You were glistening with sweat as you pushed aside the curtain and stood for a moment in the doorway, looking at me or through me. You flung yourself down on the couch and gave disjointed answers to my questions about the day's business in the Assembly (I couldn't have been less interested, but one had to say something). The previous day's intimacy seemed like a dream.

You were unusually brusque and off-hand; I guessed you had drunk quite a lot—you were certainly gulping down my wine as if it were water. The atmosphere was strained and tense as we discussed the weather at length, listening neither to ourselves nor each other. We were both asking the silent question—when?

I ladled out your fifth, or perhaps your sixth cup of wine, carried it over to you and put it down on the table.

'I'm glad you like the wine.'

You looked up at me. I looked down into your eyes. We were mesmerised for a long moment until you said, sounding half-choked: 'Damn the wine'—the first time I had ever heard you swear. You pulled me down on top of you and I was in your arms.

We kissed at first, locked together like limpets. We were drenched in sweat and I could hear your heart pounding. Then your hand slid hesitantly down my body. I wanted to grab it, you, anything, but sensed that I mustn't be too eager or give the impression that it was all part of a day's work. I could hardly pretend to be virginal, but there was no need to demonstrate how very non-virginal I was.

You stood up and took off your tunic. Your body was strong and supple.

'Take your dress off. You'll ruin it.'

'You do it,' I said, untying the girdle.

You gingerly pulled it over my head, then stood there looking at me.

'You're quite perfect.'

I stood up, too, and locked my arms round your neck. For a few moments we were locked together, then you pushed me backwards on to the couch and were on top of me.

I don't think you ever forgot what happened next, although I did everything I could to convince you it was unimportant. To you it was the most shameful and humiliating thing in the world. The simple fact was that your body wouldn't cooperate. And the more you tried, the limper you became.

You were getting angrier and angrier, cursing under your breath like a foot-soldier. There were several things I could have suggested,

73

but didn't dare for fear my expertise would inhibit you even more. You were near to tears as you got up dejectedly and slumped down on the other couch. There was a long silence before you said:

'I'm desperately sorry. I don't know what's wrong with me. This has never happened before. Really. I just can't explain it . . .'

It had happened to me before, several times. Generally when a man was making love to me for the first time, had been looking forward to it too much, was nervous and keyed up and had been drinking. I was disappointed, but it served me right for dreaming all day instead of realising that this was likely to occur. I laughed glumly to myself and resisted the temptation to tell you that you were not by any means the first man to suffer this overwhelming tragedy. I knew that next time it would probably be all right. But you were convinced it was the beginning of the end.

You went on: 'I don't know what you must think of me. I'm no use to you at all. Perhaps you think I like boys, that I was only trying to make love to you out of curiosity. I swear it isn't true. I desperately wanted you—I've thought about nothing else all day. And now this. Pericles the Great Lover who can't do anything about it when the most beautiful woman in Athens is lying naked beside him. You'd better send me away and stick to younger men who can do something for you.'

'Don't be a fool.' I gave you another cup of wine. 'It's not the end of the world. I expect you wanted it too much, that's all.'

'I still do,' you said despondently. 'I've wanted you since the first day I met you. I never stop wanting you. This should have been the happiest day of my life. Instead, I feel an utter idiot.'

I sat down beside you and kissed you. 'Stop torturing yourself. Everything will be all right. I know.'

'You're a marvellous person,' you said, stroking my head. 'I didn't know anyone like you existed.'

We stayed like that for a while, close and crestfallen. Then it was time for you to go. Reluctantly, you stood up and put on your tunic.

'Don't think too badly of me, my dear,' you pleaded. 'I was ashamed. But you've made me feel a lot better.'

I smiled. 'I'm glad. Will you come tomorrow?'

'May I?'

'I'd like you to.'

'Even after . . . this?'

'Especially after this. You're not to sit at home and brood.'

You kissed the top of my head. 'I doubt if you could keep me away. I'll try to be early.'

There was a thunderstorm next day which cleared the air. And since you were obviously terrified of repeating the non-performance of the night before, we just lay together on a couch and talked about ourselves and kissed and felt very loving. All the tension had somehow vanished, and I felt peaceful and protected in your arms.

We kept off the subject of sex. I told you about my father and you told me about your first love, for a curly-headed boy called Leogoras. You worshipped him for two years but were always too timid to do anything about it. We talked about your sons, then aged 15 and 13; you were bitterly disappointed in the elder boy.

'He seems to have a grudge against everyone and everything,' you said sadly. 'Nothing's ever right for him, though the gods know I've tried to give him the best of everything. His brother is quite different, a charming, intelligent, modest boy. But the elder one appears to have gone wrong somewhere.'

You sighed. 'It's been hard for them, I know, growing up without their mother. But what could I do? We only got married in the first place because she is a distant cousin and the law said we had to. Once she had given me sons to carry on the family name she wanted to go back to her former husband. I had no reason to keep her, so I divorced her. But obviously my sons had to stay with me and be brought up in the Alcmaeonid family.'

I felt very sorry for your unfortunate wife.

'What about the two other boys I hear you've taken in?' I asked.

You smiled. 'You know a lot about my household. They're the sons of a first cousin whose husband was killed in Tolmides' campaign. My brother and I are their joint guardians, but we agreed the children should live with me so they can have the company of the other two boys. My brother is a widower and lives with my sister Anactoria, who is anything but a motherly type. I think the family expected me to marry this cousin, too, just to make things tidy, but although she seems a pleasant enough woman I really didn't see why I should. As it is she and the children live in the house and I see them about once a month—they're no problem at all. The eldest son seems rather a backward boy. But Alcibiades, the younger boy, is the most precocious five-year-old I've ever known. He's always in some sort of trouble but invariably manages to charm his way out of it. And he seems exceptionally quick-witted for his age, not to say intelligent. He's a true member of our family.'

I was envious of you for being part of a family, with brothers and sisters and cousins and children and customs and traditions. I belonged nowhere, and, not being an Athenian, never could. Suddenly lonely, I buried my head in your chest. You held me tight, as if you understood.

It was a good evening, and so were the ones that followed. There was a new, relaxed intimacy to our conversation that hadn't been there before. We knew we should make love again. And we also knew there was plenty of time, there was no need to hurry. By now you were coming every evening as a matter of course and I had given you the key to the back door. As far as everyone else was concerned, I was simply going to bed early every night. They must have thought it extraordinary, but I didn't really care. With any luck they might suppose I was pregnant. I couldn't be bothered to think up an elaborate lie.

It was on the seventh day that it happened—naturally, spontaneously and successfully. You simply rolled over on top of me and went ahead. It wasn't actually the greatest thrill of all time—the first time seldom is. We were both trying too hard to be considerate, to please the other, while not knowing what gave the other pleasure. But we made up in love what we lacked in technique. The greatest pleasure of all was hearing you whisper: 'I love you, I love you; Aspasia, darling, I love you.' I knew you might not mean it, that you might not know what you were saying—but I hoped you did.

Afterwards, when you were lying exhausted with your head in my lap, I bent down and kissed your forehead.

'I love you, too.'

You looked up at me. 'Darling. Darling Aspasia.' And I could tell from your eyes that you did mean it.

6

'IT's delightful to see young love blossoming,' said Socrates, wolfing a bunch of grapes. 'Quite touching in fact. But what are you going to do about it?'

It was a month later, one of the happiest months of my life, a month in which I had thought and dreamed of nothing but you. I had been putting off asking myself this question. But trust Socrates to bring it up.

'I don't know. Nothing. What *can* we do?'

'Don't be silly,' he said paternally. 'You really are an exasperating girl at times. Of course you two can't go on like this for ever. Apart from anything else, the Olympian's not getting enough sleep—he looks positively haggard. And sooner or later, you know, people are bound to find out. I rather think Manto has guessed already, and I doubt if she's capable of keeping a secret.'

He was probably right. In any case, I found it almost impossible to keep it to myself. I wanted to tell everyone, to go round shouting about it. And I must have dropped enough broad hints for anyone with a grain of intelligence to guess what was going on. Chrysis had said to me a few days before:

'You're in love, aren't you?'

I couldn't bring myself to lie about something I was proud of.

'Yes. Is it that obvious?'

'About as obvious as the sun in the sky. Presumably one can't know who the lucky man is, or you would have told us. I'm not going to nag you even though I'm dying of curiosity. He must be very special.'

I longed to tell her, to talk non-stop about you all afternoon. I didn't because I couldn't trust her not to pass it on to Titormos who would then have told all Athens 'in confidence'.

We did talk about you most of the afternoon in fact. It was

77

she who brought your name up, I don't know whether intentionally or not, and I did my best to chatter about you impersonally while longing to confide 'he thinks . . .' and 'in his opinion . . .' At the end Chrysis commented drily:

'You certainly seem to have changed your ideas about Pericles. There was a time when he couldn't do a thing right. Now anyone would think you worshipped him.'

I wasn't certain, but I thought she was laughing.

Socrates had in fact asked the one question I preferred to forget. It was true we couldn't go on like this for ever. But I didn't want to break the spell by forcing you to discuss the future and make decisions. You might well have said it had got to be like this or not at all.

Yet even though I refused to admit it, I knew something had to happen. I was falling more in love with you every day: I wanted to be with you all the time, not just for a few stolen hours in the evening; I wanted to do things for you, to look after you and belong to you, to share all your life instead of just a part of it. I wanted to marry you, but obviously couldn't. For the first time I really minded being a foreigner and social outcast.

I knew that thinking about it wouldn't help, that however much we talked about it we should still find no way out. We couldn't marry. You couldn't or wouldn't wreck your career by living with me—that would be asking too much of you. So the only thing was to go on as we were.

I think you were so obsessed with me that it couldn't have stayed secret for ever, however careful we were. And you hated the furtiveness as much as I did. You explained apologetically one evening:

'I don't want you to think I'm ashamed of you, darling. I'm the proudest man alive. Some day, I know, we can be open about our love. But now I'm thinking of my sons . . . they might have a very bad time of it if people knew.'

I understood. You didn't want them teased about their father's affair with Athens' most notorious companion. There was also the precious family name to be considered. Not that understanding made it any easier to accept the situation. And I don't know what would have happened if the decision had not been taken out of our hands.

You were becoming more and more reluctant to go home at night —you would stay 'just a little longer' and 'just another moment', till very often it was nearly dawn before you finally left. We had started going to my bedroom once everyone else was asleep, since the bed was larger and more comfortable than the sitting-room couches and it was a rule of the house that nobody ever walked uninvited into anyone else's bedroom. It seemed perfectly safe.

But, as Socrates said, you never got enough sleep. You were awake most of the night with me, and arrived in your office soon after dawn. Two or three times you fell fast asleep beside me and I had to shake you to wake you up and smuggle you out of the back door before the slaves started moving around and you could be recognised on the streets.

One night you were even more weary than usual. After a heated finance debate in the Assembly you had ridden out to your country estate to inspect the wine harvest. When you got home you had a furious row about money with your eldest son Xanthippos who had lost all his month's allowance gambling. Then people had come to talk business and stayed on and on till you finally had to send them away, pleading tiredness. You told me Meidias was among them, and we laughed to think how shocked he would have been if he'd known where the poor tired general went next.

I had had a hard day too, with swarms of people expecting to be entertained. My slavegirl Lamia's baby was ill, and we had to get a doctor. Manto dragged me out to the slave market. One of the other girls announced she was pregnant. And finally I had to endure interminable cross-questioning from Meidias about why I wouldn't sleep with him any more, why I was always too busy or tired to see him, what was the matter with me, and if I wouldn't tell him how on earth could he do anything to help? In the end I told him crossly to mind his own business and he went out in a temper, presumably straight to your house. I felt guilty because he had been so very good to me. He obviously didn't believe my weak excuses, yet I couldn't tell him the truth.

We went almost straight to bed that night and made love with a last burst of energy conjured up from the gods know where. I remember you kissing me tenderly then rolling over with your back to me. The next thing I knew it was broad daylight.

It wasn't too much of a disaster as long as I could get you out of the house without being seen and nobody recognised you in the streets nearby. Unfortunately my bedroom opened right on to the main courtyard and veranda. I picked up your cloak, which was the nearest thing to hand, threw it round my shoulders and without waking you tiptoed out to see if the coast was clear.

Meidias was sitting there on the veranda right outside the door. As I pushed my way through the curtains he jumped up and stretched out his arms.

'Dearest, at last! I've been waiting for hours. I just had to come and say I'm sorry for being such a beast last night.'

I panicked. He mustn't see through the now half-open curtains. He must be got rid of somehow, quickly. I had to warn you in case you woke up and came out to see what was happening.

It must have shown in my face, for his expression changed from apology to consternation.

'What's the matter, my love? You look as if you've seen a ghost. Here, sit down, drink this.'

He pushed me on to a chair and gave me a cup of wine as I mumbled something about a nightmare. My mind was racing in circles—what could I *do?* Obviously the first thing was to warn you.

'I . . . I must go and put a dress on,' I stuttered. 'I can't sit about like this.'

'Why ever not?' he asked, reasonably. 'I've seen you with much less on. Besides, you look perfectly charming in that.' He looked closely at your cloak. 'I don't think I've seen it before, and yet it looks familiar . . .'

'Well anyway I must do my hair,' I gabbled, and without waiting for his answer bolted back into the bedroom.

You were still asleep, snoring gently. You looked relaxed and peaceful, and when I touched you your hand groped for mine.

'Pericles, wake up,' I whispered, shaking you.

Unlike me, you were always able to snap straight out of sleep into wide-awake awareness (it was probably because of your army training). You opened your eyes, took one look at my worried face, and asked:

'What's happened?'

'Sssh . . . It couldn't be worse. Meidias is sitting just outside the door. I don't know what to do.'

You sat up and frowned. You were thinking very hard.

'If it's not Meidias it will be someone else,' you said in a half-whisper, talking to yourself. 'They'll already have missed me at home and in the office. There's no reasonable explanation . . .'

I could almost see you shouldering the responsibility. You were mentally preparing to face the enemy as you sighed, stood up and said:

'This is it, my love. Lend me a comb.'

You combed your hair and beard, grimaced at yourself in the mirror, stood for a moment bracing yourself. Then you put your arm round me and we walked out together into the sunshine.

It was almost worth it, just to see the expression on Meidias' face. His jaw literally dropped and he simply sat there staring as you walked over, sat down and said casually:

'Good morning, Meidias. You're here very early. Do you mind if we join you?'

The poor man was genuinely shocked. After all it was he who had told me countless times, in complete good faith, that you weren't interested in women. He thought he knew everything about both of us and was in my confidence if not yours. I sensed the amazement giving way to anger as it began to dawn on him how he must have been tricked. You felt it, too.

'I think we owe you an apology,' you said chattily, toying with a piece of bread. 'We've been behaving like a pair of underhand conspirators—at my insistence. Aspasia hated fooling you, but she did it for me.'

You leaned across and kissed my cheek. I had never seen you so self-possessed, so much in command of a situation. For the first time, I caught a glimpse of Pericles the public figure, statesman and diplomat.

Meidias was still speechless, so you went on:

'I know we could have trusted you. Yet things somehow leak out in this city, and it seemed best to tell nobody at all. To be quite honest I'm glad you've caught us out. And I shall be proud and pleased if the whole of Athens knows that Aspasia and I are lovers.'

It took great courage for you to say that. I squeezed your hand and you smiled. It was good to be out in the daylight.

'But . . . but how did you meet?' Meidias was bewildered. 'I thought . . . I mean . . .'

I prayed you wouldn't mention Socrates, knowing how much Meidias disliked him. But you dodged the question cleverly, saying:

'The whole city was praising Aspasia and I felt left out. So I came to see her.'

Meidias was struggling with conflicting emotions. He worshipped you, yet you had deceived him and stolen his girl.

'Well, it does explain a lot,' he said hesitantly. 'You've both been behaving rather oddly, you know. But I would never have guessed that Pericles . . . that is to say . . .'

You helped him out: '. . . that Pericles would ever meet a companion, let alone fall in love with one. Having met her, do you blame him?'

Poor Meidias. He had no right to be jealous, and knew it.

81

'No, of course not,' he said bravely. 'I suppose it was inevitable really.'

After a moment's thought he went on:

'I'm very fond of both of you, so naturally I'm pleased. It was just such an unexpected shock. You needn't worry—of course I'll keep your secret.'

I think he meant it, but at that moment Manto and Melissa came into the courtyard and it would have been useless even to try. You lost some of your self-assurance in the presence of two strange girls, until Manto made us all laugh by saying:

'Pericles? Pericles? Aren't you the one who always wears a helmet? Where is it then?'

It had been on the floor by my bed, but before I could answer a slave appeared carrying the helmet as if it were a precious urn.

'That proves you're not an impostor,' I joked. 'Put it on, then Manto might recognise you.'

You clamped it firmly on your head—it looked rather out of place at breakfast time—and Manto clapped her hands in delight.

'That's better—now you look like Pericles the Olympian. I'd have known you anywhere. Just wait till I tell Chrysis I've met you.'

You and Meidias and I exchanged glances—by now we were allies. You shrugged: it was obviously hopeless to try and keep anything secret.

'I'd better be going,' you said. 'People will be wondering where I am. Thank the gods that at least it's not an Assembly Day—I wouldn't like to be covered in red paint.'

'Why would that happen?' Manto was wide-eyed. 'Just for sleeping with Asp?'

You laughed and explained that on days when the people's Assembly met—five times a month—the streets were patrolled by Scythian guards carrying ropes soaked in red paint to 'pull in' anyone who arrived late. She was rather disappointed.

'Are you coming down to the market-place, Meidias?' you asked. He nodded, still a bit bewildered. 'Good, then we'll go together.'

You put your arms round me in front of everyone and kissed me hard on the mouth.

'Goodbye, my darling, have a good day. I'll see you later.'

I was slightly dazed myself. I sat there blinking as the two of you walked out of the front door—it had all happened so quickly, so unexpectedly. And what happened next? I had no time to think it out, however, for Manto and Melissa launched into a barrage of eager questions—how? why? when? where? what?—and I was completely worn out by the time they finally went rushing off to spread the good news.

They did an excellent job. Socrates told me that afternoon—only a few hours later—that no fewer than nine people had already asked him conspiratorially: 'Have you heard . . .?' In a city of 40,000 citizens news spreads like wildfire. By that evening there can have been hardly anyone who didn't know that Pericles and Aspasia were having an affair.

I told Socrates what had happened, and for once he was rather serious. 'Of course it had to come out sooner or later,' he mused. 'But I wonder if Pericles can take it.'

'How do you mean—take what?'

'You should have seen his noble fellow-citizens down in the market place this morning. Those who weren't sniggering were whispering in corners; there were even some who laughed openly as he walked through, and made obscene gestures behind his back. His friends were embarrassed to talk to him, not knowing what to say. It must have been an enormous strain for him—you know how sensitive he is behind that mask of aristocratic indifference.'

I did. And I also realised how little I really knew you. The Pericles I had had to myself for months, the shy, considerate lover I met in stolen time, must be very different from the revered statesman the rest of Athens knew. I hoped my own, private Pericles would not be eclipsed by the city's Olympian.

'It's the biggest, juiciest piece of gossip Athens has heard for years,' Socrates went on. 'Everyone knows Pericles, and nearly everyone has heard of you. I imagine anyone who has actually met you can understand why the Olympian has fallen from his lofty pedestal of celibacy. But those who haven't are treating it as the bawdiest joke of all time. I wish people would think before they open their mouths.'

So did I. It might all have passed unnoticed had you been anyone but Pericles. But you had been a paragon of high-minded virtue for so long that your passion for a twenty-one-year-old companion caused a real sensation. Needless to say, nobody thought it was anything but a sexual infatuation. Generals and companions simply don't fall in love, still less when they are Pericles and Aspasia.

Dozens of people turned up at the house that afternoon, most of them presumably hoping you would be there. Nobody actually said anything, but I too sensed whispering behind my back, and the unspoken question: 'Is it true?' Some of our friends must have

83

found the whole thing so incredible they refused to believe it till they had actual proof. If they had asked me I would have told them—but that would have been too simple and spoiled the intrigue. Others merely came to gloat. I noticed Manto holding court in a corner of the veranda, far more popular than usual. She was presumably describing the morning's encounter, with embellishments.

Chrysis, at least, was straightforward. A slave arrived with a note from her saying:

'I might have guessed! We always said you must have the best man in Athens! T. is charging round in a daze muttering "Fantastic . . . Incredible . . ." and can't understand why I think it's perfectly natural. Would love to meet your Olympian sometime —if you still deign to talk to ordinary girls like me. At least I won't interrupt your breakfast.'

Dear Chrysis. She was much too good for Titormos.

The only visitor that afternoon who was quite unaware of what was going on was the philosopher Anaxagoras. The Mind ambled in, peered in amazement at the crowd of people in the courtyard, patted me on the head and settled down in the shade to hold forth about the nature of the universe to anyone who would listen. Socrates joined him, and very soon they were engaged in one of those verbal duels that sometimes went on for days and nights. They were both geniuses, but their brilliance flowed in two completely opposite directions so that the more abstract and grandiose Anaxagoras became, the more Socrates confused him with apparently ingenuous but subtly provocative questions. At least Anaxagoras never lost his temper; he always gave in cheerfully when he was logically proved to have been talking nonsense. I have seen lesser philosophers storm out in a rage when made to look foolish by Socrates' implacable logic.

Sophocles the playwright couldn't resist asking the question on everyone's mind. He came straight up to me, kissed me on the cheek and said:

'Forgive my asking a personal question, my dear, but what's all this I hear about a romance between you and my old friend Pericles?'

The buzz of conversation suddenly stopped as at least twenty pairs of ears strained to hear my answer.

'It depends what you've heard,' I said drily. 'Pericles is my lover, if that's what you mean.'

'Congratulations,' said Sophocles. 'We all thought he was impervious to female charms. Now perhaps he'll stop lecturing me for my little flirtations.'

84

There was general laughter as he went on:

'But I do think one of you might have told me—after all Pericles and I grew up together, we're almost like brothers. Why all the secrecy? I never try to conceal these things.'

He couldn't have done if he'd tried—at that very moment his eyes were straying towards a pretty companion sitting on the other side of the courtyard. He would probably have gone over to her there and then if a voice behind me hadn't made all heads turn.

'Good day, Sophocles,' you said. 'What a pleasure to find so many friends here.'

Sophocles embraced you. 'Good day, General. What a pleasure to find *you* here. You seem to be invading my territory: we have always agreed that while you command on the battle-field, I am general-in-chief where affairs of the heart are concerned. Are you trying to depose me?'

You laughed. 'Stick to poetry, where you have no rivals. You can't excel at everything, you know.'

Then you walked over to me and kissed me. This was the proof Athens had been waiting for—there could now be no doubt whatsoever that Pericles and Aspasia were lovers.

We stood together rather awkwardly on the edge of the courtyard as everyone else seemed either suddenly tongue-tied or engrossed in their own conversations. I wasn't used to being with you in public and wasn't sure what to do. Sophocles, satisfied with what he'd heard and seen, had made a bee-line for the pretty companion.

Fortunately Anaxagoras spotted you. He broke off what he was saying to exclaim:

'Pericles, my dear boy! What a pleasant surprise! I have always said you must come to Aspasia's and I see you've finally taken my advice. Have you been introduced?'

At this Socrates leaped up, dragged us both over to where Anaxagoras was lying and said solemnly:

'Pericles, may I have the pleasure of presenting Aspasia of Miletos? Aspasia, this is Pericles, one of Anaxagoras' pupils.'

It was difficult to keep a straight face as he hissed in my ear:

'Don't just stand there. Hold out your hand to be kissed.'

I bowed my head as graciously as I could, stifling a giggle. There was no point in confusing the old man, who was obviously delighted to have brought us together. He made us sit down with him and lectured us for hours on his atom theory. Your old tutor treated you exactly as if you were a ten year old schoolboy. Socrates kept unusually quiet and just sat there grinning.

It was hours before we could be alone together. Anaxagoras had no sense of time and stayed till long after dark, rambling gently on as people came and went, we moved inside, ate dinner and lay back contentedly to enjoy our wine. Socrates was there, and Manto and Melissa and one or two other close friends. Meidias came in after dinner and stayed for a while. I sat on your couch, leaning lazily back against you. It all seemed unreal, like an idyllic dream, as The Mind droned on, lost in the higher reaches of his own private universe.

He did come down to earth once, smacking his lips as he finished eating and half-heartedly brushed the crumbs from his flowing beard.

'Excellent my dear, excellent,' he said, peering round the room for me. When he saw me lying practically in your arms he beamed all over his face.

'I'm glad to see you two children have made friends. Pericles, you should take note of how Aspasia runs her house. It's comfortable, hospitable, not like that barn of yours.'

Anaxagoras always believed he had been responsible for introducing us. And nobody ever saw any need to disillusion him.

At long last Socrates took pity on us and led the old man away, still talking. Socrates was such an unpredictable friend: at times his practical jokes made me long to wring his neck. At others he showed such tact and diplomacy I wanted to fling my arms round him and kiss him.

That particular evening, however, it was you I kissed, as soon as the others had wandered off into the night. You looked tired but happy.

'How did the day go?'

'I don't know . . . not too badly, I suppose.' You frowned. 'It all seems a very long time ago. And I still can't believe I've been sitting here openly with you, all these hours. This time yesterday it wouldn't have seemed possible.'

'I know. It's the same for me.'

You looked round the room and sighed. 'Anaxagoras is right— it's so friendly and relaxing here. There's a welcoming atmosphere. And it doesn't seem at all strange to have men and women mixing together, talking together. I never knew there could be anything like this.'

You lay back, pulled me close and kissed me.

'To be perfectly truthful, my love, the day was torture. I have never felt so self-conscious, so estranged, such a curiosity. As I walked here this afternoon everyone was staring and whispering and giggling. I didn't mean to upset you by telling you. But now it doesn't seem to matter very much. I was tense and nervous when I arrived. Now thanks to you—and dear old Anaxagoras—there seem to be no problems at all.'

I was very very happy. 'I love you,' I whispered. 'Let's go to bed.'

7

U NFORTUNATELY the problems didn't vanish for ever. In fact
they got bigger. Your many enemies had been waiting for
years to find a chink in your armour of selfless devotion to
the city, and the 'Aspasia affair' was a gift sent directly from the
gods. They never let you forget it.

It was to go on all your life, and you never really got used to it.
Later you did at least manage to stay outwardly calm, but at the
beginning you would come home trembling with humiliation and
fury. There was very little I could do to help.

What you minded most was the gossip about me.

'They're calling you a whore' (or a harlot or a slut), you would
rage. 'How dare they? How can they? I'd like to kill whoever set
that rhyme going around.'

(The rhymes were mostly offensive but good-natured. I remember
two of the milder ones:

'Our general has lost one war
He's captivated by a whore.' and:
'Olympian he may be, but—
He's fallen to a foreign slut.')

I tried to calm you down. But of course I *was* or had been a
whore, even if the word 'companion' sounded less vulgar. And
apart from the fact that it was impossible to find out who started a
particular rhyme or lampoon or rumour, or who had been daubing
walls with crude jokes and drawings, there really was no law against
it. Athens was a democracy which respected the right of free speech,
at least when it concerned mortals. The gods, as I was to discover
later, were quite another matter.

Personally I was used to being a curiosity, so wasn't too bothered
by the attacks. People in the street shouting 'Where's your helmet,

then?' or 'Make way for the Olympian's mistress!' just made me laugh. In those days I didn't mind what most people thought, as long as those I liked and trusted were on my side. I had yet to learn the frightening power of public opinion.

For you it was different. You had always been a near-idol, a shining example of respectability. And now you were suddenly the butt of every crude wag and wit in the city. Wherever you went there were whispered references and not-so-cryptic half-asides about Miletos, blonde curls, middle-aged infatuations, nights of love, companions' pets and so on and so forth. It was almost too much for you when in the Assembly itself an insolent young man criticising your appeasement policy towards Sparta sneered:

'If it were Miletos, of course we should understand.'

Meidias told me you flushed, appeared to be on the point of walking out, thought better of it, then stood there impassively till the wave of laughter had died down and you went on with what you had been saying.

I seethed with fury when I heard about this, but there was nothing I could do. You were desperately hurt, and far too sensitive about what the people thought. What you never realised is that half the time they don't think, they just repeat what they've been told with a few embellishments. Athenians adore gossip and intrigue. And there were many, of course, who jumped at the chance to get their own back for real or imagined wrongs you'd done them in the past. You *can't* be the leading public figure in a city like this and not have enemies. I told you so again and again, but you would insist on trying to be perfect, on doing the right thing by everyone—which inevitably became the wrong thing for someone else. You were an infuriating idealist and I loved you.

Things weren't always easy at home, either. After that first day you more or less lived at my house, coming straight there from the baths or your office and staying till the next morning. You said it made you feel safe—at least once inside my front door there were no more sneers and giggles. And on the few occasions when you decided you must go to your house to talk to your steward or settle some domestic crisis you were always back again within an hour or two. I think quite honestly you were so much in love you simply couldn't keep away; at the age of 49 you had suddenly discovered a whole new dimension to life and for a while it became your life. You were a person who took everything you did extremely seriously, including falling in love. You would never have been capable of a half-hearted flirtation—for you it was either total commitment or nothing at all.

But you didn't really fit in with the easy-going atmosphere in my house. In the first place you were used to being master in your own home and felt ill at ease living in mine. Even though you insisted on giving me money, you were still a guest just like the others who drifted in and out at all hours of the day and night. Then you were stiff and awkward with the others girls—there were about six living there at the time. And they in turn were intimidated by you. I had never interfered in the slightest way with what they did or whom they entertained, as long as they didn't interfere with me. It seemed there was plenty of room for everyone. But I sensed that you were embarrassed in the presence of their lovers, most of whom you knew. And although I'm sure nobody was actually spying on you, it was inevitable that they should be curious to see how Pericles was settling in at Aspasia's.

You had always known that I was a companion, that I had other companions living with me, but while we were meeting alone in private it had been easy to 'forget'. Now that you were sharing my everyday life you were faced with constant reminders that my home was basically a high-class brothel and its mistress therefore a prostitute. You made superhuman efforts to be reasonable, but you couldn't help being jealous. You said miserably one evening:

'I'm obsessed with the idea that every man I meet here has been your lover. Yes, I *know* it's not true—half of them aren't interested in women any way. But there's this nagging voice at the back of my mind insisting that they must have been. Then it reasons that if they've slept with you once they feel they've the right to sleep with you again. And they're hanging round here all day while I'm working ... Oh, I'm sorry, dearest. I can't help it. Please understand.'

I did. And although I told you time and again that there was you and only you, I knew it made no difference. For the first time in your life reasoning didn't help you at all. You were a slave to your emotions, and the more you fought them the more baffled and angry with yourself you became.

I had to be very careful about sex. You weren't exactly a clumsy lover, but you were inhibited and inexperienced. I could have suggested a hundred ways to make it work better, dozens of variations we could have tried. I knew what excited me and was slowly learning by trial and error, what did most for you. Yet I couldn't actually say 'Let's do it this way,' or 'It's better like this,' because you would immediately have wondered who I learned it from or did it with, and the ghosts of all those former lovers would come between us again. You were so *considerate*—constantly worrying about whether or not you were giving me pleasure, when the greatest pleasure you could have given me would have been to enjoy yourself. However, we were in love, and that made up for nearly everything.

We lived on love that autumn, and most of the winter too. You were so very patient, so anxious to be forgiven for your occasional outbursts of rage or fits of gloom. I was trying hard to reassure you that you weren't just the latest in a long line of lovers. Love was something entirely new for both of us and we had a lot to learn.

We were living together yet not living together, since you felt like a stranger in my house even after months of staying there every night. We obviously couldn't go on like that for ever, but it was hard to see any alternative. I was frightened it might become too much of a strain for you, that you might begin to regret you'd ever met me and simply take the easy way out by going back to your old empty life without emotional problems.

I didn't realise quite how committed to me you were; you didn't talk much about love, and in any case words wouldn't have convinced me. I did know you were fond of me and attracted to me, but in those days I hadn't yet learned that Pericles did nothing by half measures, least of all loving. So I began to panic when for a few days you were unusually silent and distant, evidently worried about something you couldn't or wouldn't tell me.

'What's the matter, darling?' I begged. 'I know there's something wrong. Please tell me.'

'No, it's nothing,' you murmured evasively, and changed the subject. Yet I sensed there was some sort of battle going on inside you and if, as was likely, it concerned me, I wanted to be able to fight.

Then one afternoon you beckoned me away from a group of people sitting round a brazier in the main room.

'Can we go somewhere and talk? It's important.'

Judging by the look on your face it was deadly serious. I took your hand and we walked through the two courtyards to the little sitting-room where we had first met. I thought I knew what was coming and was frantically trying to think of any logical, conclusive reason why you shouldn't leave me. As a result, I was completely unprepared when you said calmly:

'I'm going to marry you.'

'*What?* But . . . but, darling, you can't!'

D

'Not only can I, but I'm going to,' you said firmly. 'Unless, of course, you have any objections.'

'But I don't see how ... What about the law ... ? What will people think ... ?'

You suddenly looked weary. 'I've been into it all, over and over again. The law says I can't pass you off as an Athenian wife, but it doesn't say I can't marry you. I wouldn't be pretending you were Athenian or claiming citizenship for you. In fact you would be little better than a concubine. But we can go through some sort of ceremony and you can come to live with me—if you want to.'

I was still taking all this in as you went on:

'I suppose I'm taking a lot for granted—after all why should you leave this house and all your friends to move into a strange family? But the fact is, darling, I can't bear it any more. I'm neglecting my sons, I'm cut off from half my friends who won't come here, I'm living in a place where I don't belong and never shall. Yet I can't live without you And to be honest, it's killing me to see you surrounded by all these men, day and night. I want you all to myself. Please believe me, I've thought and thought about it—this is the only solution.'

You buried your face in your hands and all I could see was the top of your helmet. I was still bewildered—this was one thing I had never even dreamed of, that you would actually take me, a Milesian companion, to live in your own house.

'But I still don't see ... I mean it just isn't done. How can I possibly live in your home, *as* your wife, when I'm not an Athenian?'

'Look, darling,' you said patiently. 'Until a few years ago dozens of citizens had non-Athenian wives—Elpinice's brother did, for example. Now that I've fallen in love with one myself I understand why and I wish by the gods I'd never had the citizenship law changed. Before then foreign wives became Athenian by marriage and their children were born citizens. Now, as you know, children of a mixed marriage can't be citizens.

'The thing is'—you were almost talking to yourself now—'there is still no law forbidding me to marry a foreigner. The marriage just won't have the same effects as if you were an Athenian. But surely it's better than nothing?'

You were pleading with me, begging me to agree that it was a good idea. But I had never heard of such an arrangement, or considered getting even half-married—for this was what it would be. I hadn't thought it possible.

'Even if it *is* legal,' I objected, 'it's going to cause a terrific scandal. It was bad enough when people found out about us—but at least there's nothing unusual in having a mistress. It's unheard of to take her to live with you in the family home. You might even be prosecuted for impiety.'

'No I won't. I've gone into that. And there's so much malicious gossip about you and me already, it could hardly be worse. We might just as well give them something to gossip about.'

I tried to think straight. 'I'm . . . I'm overwhelmed,' I said. 'And I'm not sure you realise what you're suggesting. You're risking your reputation, your career, your family name, your everything. I don't think I should let you. It's too much to give up, just for my sake.'

'Aspasia,' you said quietly, 'do you love me?'

'You know I do.'

'Will you marry me?'

What could I say? I could see from your eyes that you were never going to change your mind. Once it was made up, you were the most stubborn man on earth.

'Yes, darling,' I whispered. Then I flung my arms round your neck, and burst into tears.

You held me tight till I had finished sobbing, and then you began to talk. You talked and talked and talked, pouring out all the tension and worry of the past few days and months. You had considered setting me up in a house of my own, you said. But what was the point when I already had a house? You would still be just visiting me instead of living with me.

'And you would still be my mistress. I don't want you to be my mistress. I want you to be my wife. I want you close to me for ever.'

You had worried about what your sons and brother would think but decided they would obey as they always had. None of them had the courage to oppose you openly. And above all you had worried that I would be unhappy in a strange house among hostile people.

'Please believe me, darling,' you insisted, 'when I say I want you to be my wife, not my slave. I admit I'm jealous, but I'll try to control it. You can live exactly as you do here; I don't care how many people come to see you or how late they stay. They will liven the place up a bit. The difference will be that I shall feel I'm supporting you, protecting you, caring for you under my roof— all the time. I shall be sure at last that you are really mine. People won't come to Aspasia's house where Pericles is one of the guests. They will come to see Pericles and Aspasia.'

I knew what you meant. And little by little most of my misgivings faded as I began to look forward to belonging somewhere, to being almost part of a family. I would never be fully accepted, I knew. But I would be halfway towards becoming a 'respectable' woman.

Once we were unofficially 'betrothed' you were impatient to get on with it and would have moved me to your house that same evening if you could. But there were dozens of little practical details to be settled and organised, not least the wedding ceremony itself. It was quite obvious that it couldn't be a traditional affair with torchlit processions through the streets, 'introduction' of the bride and groom, and serenades outside the marriage chamber. I wasn't a 14-year-old virgin being handed over from father to husband. And our betrothal hadn't exactly been arranged by our families. I would have liked to do without the sacrifice and prayers as well—they meant nothing and seemed out of place. But you were obstinate; they were a family tradition and The Family, I was beginning to discover, meant a great deal to you. Rather than forsake The Family for Aspasia, you were going to make her almost a part of it.

'Look at it this way,' you insisted. 'I want my sons and my wards to respect you, to treat you as my lawful wife. So we must go through the proper rites—otherwise they'll always think you're just a mistress I'm keeping in the house.'

I agreed, doubtfully. It really was inconceivable that a companion from Miletos would ever be accepted by one of Athens' oldest and most aristocratic families. Weddings were private, domestic affairs, however, arranged to fit the traditions of the families concerned. I remembered my father's annual marriage rites—if he could invent his own wedding ceremonies so could we.

I was adamant about one thing: 'I am positively not going to be waited on by a group of handmaidens, or whatever it is you do. The idea of Chrysis and Manto giggling and simpering at your relatives is simply ludicrous. And all my girl friends are companions.'

You agreed hastily. In the end we asked Elpinice, the only Athenian woman I knew, to act as bridal chaperone. She was highly amused, particularly since her step-son was married to your ex-wife.

'I never thought Pericles had it in him,' she chuckled. 'For years he's been preaching about upholding family tradition, honour and all that nonsense—and now he himself is marrying a foreigner. I couldn't be more delighted. I promise you I'll play my part just as if you were my own niece!'

Then there were finances to be sorted out. Meidias had always been my legal 'guardian' since no woman, Athenian or foreign, was allowed to handle her own business affairs. We transferred the guardianship to you, but when Meidias had explained my financial situation—and I was surprised to discover how wealthy I was—you asked him if he'd mind looking after my money as he had before.

'If I took over it would look as if Aspasia was bringing me a dowry. And I am most certainly *not* marrying her for her money.' You grinned. 'In any case she's probably richer than I am, and we all know how these wealthy women feel they've a right to boss their husbands about once they've contributed a few minas to the family funds. They did things better in Homer's time when a man had to pay to get a bride instead of being paid to take her.

'Seriously, however, I want her to be able to keep her own money for herself rather than its being lumped together with mine. I can't be bothered to supervise the household expenses—I sell the produce from my farms in bulk once a year, give some of the proceeds to my steward Evangelos and let him buy all we need. It's worked perfectly well so far, but I don't want Aspasia to have to come running to me every time she wants a few drachmas for herself. I imagine the house-keeping will go on as before—if Aspasia wants to change things she can sort it out with Evangelos.'

It amused me that the man who jealously guarded and budgeted every talent in the city treasury should be so casual about finance in his own home. Fortunately Meidias loved dabbling in any kind of business, and was very good at it, so you formally authorised him to act for you in respect of my monies and properties. It was an excellent arrangement which we never changed.

I didn't want to sell my house, as it had become a sort of refuge for girls who arrived in Athens with nowhere to go. But someone had got to be in charge of the slaves and house-keeping and see the place didn't degenerate into a real brothel. Manto was out of the question: she was hopeless at figures, knew nothing about anything domestic and would cheerfully have offered hospitality to anyone, man or woman, who asked for it simply because she 'felt sorry' for them. Melissa, the dark-haired girl from Corinth, was more practical and had some experience of running a house (a wealthy lover had set her up in a home of her own for a couple of years). She was thrilled with the idea of being in charge of a house again while staying independent. So we agreed that she would collect rent from the girls who could afford it (or from their lovers), pay the household expenses from it, then share any profits with me. They turned out to be considerable, but since you never interfered in any way in my private business affairs you had no idea where my income came from. I felt it was better to keep quiet about this particular source once I was a semi-respectable 'wife'. In any case I gave a lot of it away to girls who were penniless.

Very unwillingly, I decided to leave Micon and Lamia at my house. Micon was used to being master among the household slaves, and since your steward Evangelos sounded like a domineering character himself I thought they would probably clash. Also, Micon and his wife would be a great help to Melissa: they had practically run the house for me and would continue to do so for her. They didn't want to leave me, but after rather a tearful scene they agreed to stay 'just for my sake'.

I didn't want to start life in a strange house without anyone I knew at all, and anyway you told me you only had one or two female slaves (you were remarkably vague about how many people actually lived in your home, who they were or what they did). So I took Andromeda, one of the slaves who had been with me right from the beginning and had grown from a scared, pale, jittery girl into a beautiful self-possessed young woman. I was very fond of her and hoped she would settle in well in her new home—but not half as much as I hoped I would settle in myself.

I suppressed my panic with frantic last-minute preparations. There were dozens of instructions to give to Melissa and Micon, a hundred little things to fuss about. The actual move was no problem—I would take a few clothes with me, then see what else I wanted. You told me that traditionally brides wore white, so I had a new dress made for the wedding, out of the finest wool, since it was winter. It wasn't exactly virginal, but rather less revealing than anything I had worn for years. I worried about my hair, my complexion, my make-up. To my own half-amusement I actually began to *feel* like a bride.

The evening before the Great Event my house was crowded with friends. We had only told a few people our plans but, as always, everyone seemed to know. It developed into a noisy, rowdy, impromptu banquet at which everything anyone said seemed hilariously funny and we all had far too much to drink. Even you seemed relaxed and expansive, perhaps because it was the last evening you would be spending there. When somebody proposed a toast

'To Pericles and Aspasia' you picked me up in your arms and smothered me in a bear-like hug. There was a roar of applause which died down as you made the shortest speech of your career:

'Thank you. We expect to see you all again soon—in my house.'

Soon after that we staggered to bed, laughing that we were doing such a shocking thing as sleeping together the night before our wedding. I couldn't sleep in fact, and lay there with a growing headache, more and more terrified by the prospect of the next day. You were snoring with your back to me; I felt completely alone and increasingly panic-stricken. I was going to be a stranger in your house, a total outsider imprisoned with a tribe of enemies. I wished you would wake up but didn't want to depress you, too. So I just lay there, trying not to cry.

At dawn you got up and left while I pretended to be asleep. There was nothing left to do and I lay in bed all morning trying to sleep and, when that failed, trying to reason with myself. It didn't work. At midday you came to fetch me. We slipped out of the back door without seeing anyone. And defying all tradition, custom, convention and religious law we walked hand-in-hand towards your house and our wedding.

8

L ETTER from Ariphron, son of Xanthippos, to Callias, ambassador:

'Excellency,

I entreat you to use your influence and powers of diplomacy in the matter of my brother Pericles, who has taken leave of his senses. For unless someone of your eminence can persuade him to abandon his mad course of folly, the General will bring ruin to our ancient and noble family and discredit to the city of Athens itself.

There is no need for me to explain my meaning: it is common knowledge that the unfortunate Pericles has fallen under the spell of a certain Aspasia, a notorious prostitute from the island of Miletos. This woman has reduced the once noble General, my brother, to a pitiful condition in which he is no longer responsible for his own words or actions. He fawns on her, he dotes on her, he spends his days dallying in her house of ill fame, neglecting his sons, his wards, his home and his city.

Ever since he met this siren he has been helpless in her power. When he should have been attending to city business he has been lounging in her brothel, when he should have been educating his sons he has been fornicating in her bed. He has not even tried to conceal his shameful infatuation, and has been impervious to all pleas from those who truly love him and have his interests at heart. He even accused us of interfering in his private affairs—hardly private when they were known to every beggar in the city.

Now the scandal has gone too far. Pericles has the audacity, the effrontery to propose bringing this woman to his own house—home of the Alcmaeonids for countless years. What is more, he insists on going through a travesty of the marriage rite with this harlot, this foreign whore, so that she shall "command respect" from his own sons, future Athenian citizens, born to him by your dear daughter-in-law, Hipponicos' wife. And he has even dared order his relatives to witness this shameful ceremony.

Callias, I beseech you, this madness must be stopped. The Milesian female will corrupt the innocent young boys in my brother's home, she will turn the Alcmaeonid family seat into a den of shame and vice, she will bring disgrace and disaster to the most noble name of the Athenian aristocracy. It must not happen. As you value our friendship, as you value loyalty to our kinship and devotion to our city, I implore you to speak with him, to dissuade him from this ignoble folly.

Yours in dismay, Ariphron.'

Elpinice showed me this letter to her husband long after the wedding was over. Callias, she said, had simply roared with laughter and wondered how Pericles could have a brother as pompous and pig-headed as Ariphron. He was one of those people who could never do anything right—he obviously had no idea that Callias was a friend of mine or that his wife was going to be my bridal chaperone.

Their own marriage, she told me, had caused a terrific scandal at the time, and the Ariphrons of the day undoubtedly condemned Callias for marrying a woman who was 'known' to have slept not only with her brother but with half the men in Athens. Conduct which was simply unthinkable for a purebred Athenian girl. But all that seemed to be forgotten now—as Elpinice pointed out, scandals only last until they become stale.

Not that this thought was much consolation on that grim winter afternoon. I sensed the hostility the moment we walked through the front door into your house. The place was bristling with antagonism and resentment—even the door porter looked surly and disapproving, barely nodding as you said 'Good afternoon, Conon.'

The house itself was bleak and cold with a feeling of being unlived-in. I realised later that of course nobody *had* been living in the rooms round the front courtyard. The children, their nurses, the slaves, all the day-to-day household living went on behind the closed door leading to the women's quarters. No wonder you had found it cheerless.

We stood there hand-in-hand in the dark empty courtyard, unsure of what to do next. If it had been your first wedding and I had been an Athenian virgin you would have gone to fetch me from my home in a horse-drawn carriage and half Athens would have turned out to cheer us on our way back to your house. As it was, I don't think any couple had ever walked together to their wedding through the muddy streets.

A lugubrious middle-aged man appeared silently from nowhere, looked hard at me, and stood to attention, as if expecting orders.

'Good morning, Evangelos,' you said, then turned to me.

'Aspasia, this is my steward Evangelos. I trust him more than most free-born Athenians and leave everything entirely in his hands. You can do the same or take over from him, as you like. Evangelos, Aspasia is your new mistress. Please do everything you can to help her.'

I had been more frightened by the prospect of this 'perfect' steward than by anyone else in the house. Knowing how powerful they could be in their own little kingdom, I was certain he would resent any intruder, let alone a foreign prostitute, being in authority over him. But I was agreeably surprised. Evangelos had a mournful, dejected face which seemed to announce that everything is wrong with the world. Yet he didn't look unkind. He didn't appear to be the sort of man who would believe gossip heard in the streets and market place. And he was obviously imperturbable. If his master had announced he was going to marry a Spartan slave-girl he would probably just have sighed and got on with the arrangements.

I greeted him politely and asked: 'Has my girl Andromeda arrived?'

'Yes. She was shivering with cold so I gave her some hot soup. She's waiting for you now inside.'

He looked questioningly in the direction of the door leading to the women's quarters (in my house it had always been open. Here it was firmly closed).

'I'd better go, then,' I said uncertainly.

'Yes. We might as well get it over with.' You laughed nervously. 'Evangelos will show you the way.'

I followed the steward across the bare courtyard and through the double doors that would have shut behind me for ever if I had been an ordinary Athenian bride. I felt very small and alone.

The second courtyard was a complete contrast. There were noise and bustle and confusion and the sound of children's voices. Elpinice was giving instructions to a group of slaves; she broke away as soon as she saw me, kissed me effusively and led me into a small, warm bedroom.

'Here you are at last—I thought you were never coming. Don't look so miserable; you're not going to your funeral, you know. Here, have some wine; it will make you feel better.'

She handed me a cup of the strongest wine I had ever drunk—it was hardly watered at all. I gulped it down and she refilled it at once. By the time I had drunk four cups the whole performance began to look much more like a big joke. (Evangelos, I learned later, was performing the same necessary service for you—undoubtedly on Elpinice's orders.)

'Now then,' she fussed, 'first things first. I know you're clean, but tradition says you must have a bath in this "pure" water.' She pointed to a bowl in the corner.

'What's so pure about it?'

'Nothing. If anything, it's dirtier than the normal water from the well. But the rule is that both bride and groom must bathe in the water of the nine fountains. The boys went half way across the city this morning to get it. They're still grumbling.'

So did I, because the water was freezing cold and I was indeed perfectly clean. I stood there shivering as Elpinice and Andromeda splashed it over me, and was standing naked beside the brazier when a voice from the doorway said:

'Hello. You're pretty.'

I looked round, and there was the most beautiful child I had ever seen. He had everything—golden curls, big brown eyes, a tilted nose, a bow-shaped mouth and pearl-white teeth. He was five or six years old.

'Hello,' I said, thinking rapidly. 'You must be Alcibiades.'

'Yes.' He bowed gravely. 'And you must be the sinful Aspasia.' (Impossible to reproduce the way he talked—because of a lisp it sounded like the 'thinful Athpathia'.)

'Alcibiades!'—Elpinice was horrified. 'Whoever taught you to talk like that? Say you're sorry at once.'

'Why?' He stared at her impudently. 'I heard Uncle Ariphron say it to Mother.' He walked over to me and stroked my naked thigh. 'You're much prettier than my mother. I think I like sinful ladies.'

At that moment a voice from the courtyard called: 'Alcibiades! Where are you? Come here at once!'

He patted me masterfully on the left buttock (as though he were fifty instead of five), announced grandly: 'Don't worry. I'll deal with them,' and stalked out. I collapsed with laughter and was still giggling as Andromeda rubbed me with scented ointment then helped me into the plain white wedding dress.

Elpinice frowned. 'That child is one big handful of trouble. He's a real Alcmaeonid, with too much beauty and brilliance—unlike his brother, who has neither. He's got a cruel, malicious streak too: I saw him torturing a dog to death the other day. He'll either be a great man or a complete disgrace. Or both.'

She was fussing round me, pulling and tweaking at the folds of my dress. 'You'll do. Now for the veil.'

'Elpinice!' I protested. 'I *can't* wear a veil. Really. I refuse. I should feel so ridiculous.'

'Look here, Aspasia,' she said sternly, 'if Pericles wants to pretend to marry you, he wants it as much like the real thing as possible. Real brides wear veils and so will you. Anyway, you'll find it useful —you can get a good look at people without them seeing your face. It doesn't even matter if you laugh as long as you don't do it out loud. I nearly choked at my own wedding.'

She had a point there. I meekly let myself be shrouded in the long white veil and crowned with a garland of flowers.

'I feel an utter idiot,' I said glumly.

'So you should,' she cackled. The old campaigner was having the time of her life.

While I was being dressed up in this way, you and your male relatives were making the appropriate sacrifices to Zeus, Hera and Artemis. (I should have thought Aphrodite, goddess of love, would be more suitable, but apparently she had nothing to do with weddings.) Then Evangelos came to tell us everything was ready. Elpinice took my arm and we went back through the double doors into the front courtyard, now full of people. Just to help things, there was a light drizzle falling and a cold wind.

I have never seen a more sullen-looking collection of individuals. They stood there dejectedly in the rain, about fifty people altogether, all of them related to you and all of them—except perhaps the children—convinced that this was the biggest disgrace the family had ever known. The men and women stood separately; between the two groups you were having a furious argument with someone I presumed was your brother Ariphron. He was a fat, flabby copy of you, with a high-pitched squeaky voice. (I learned later that schoolboys, whom he courted assiduously and unsuccessfully, nicknamed him 'The bestial ball'. I could see why.)

'I implore you,' he was screaming hysterically, 'before it is too late . . .'

You didn't let him finish. 'I've told you a hundred times,' you said wearily, 'my mind is made up. Now for the gods' sake calm down and be polite to Aspasia. Ah, here she is.'

You looked dashing, if a bit ridiculous, in a pure white tunic with a garland of flowers round your domed head. You took my hand, and we stood facing The Family together. Theoretically there should have been set promises exchanged between your father and my father, or at least our nearest male relatives. But I didn't have any. So the actual ceremony, such as it was, was over in a few moments as you announced in the name of various gods and ancestors that from now on I was your lawful wife. That was it— and rather an anti-climax.

But the main ordeal was yet to come. I was grateful for that veil as you solemnly led me from person to person, 'presenting' me whether they liked it or not. In the first place it kept me dry. Secondly, and more important, it meant I could see without being seen. And I was having great difficulty keeping my temper with these 'aristocratic' Athenians, some of whom were offensively rude.

I met the men first. Ariphron went red in the face and looked the other way Your eldest son Xanthippos, a mean spiteful-looking boy, sneered and muttered something under his breath. The younger son Paralos, looked too scared to say anything. One cousin, Euryptolemos I think, was reasonably civil. Elpinice's husband Callias embraced me and whispered: 'Good luck. You'll need it.' And Ariphron's son Hippocrates, a fat, unhealthy-looking boy, just picked his nose and stared.

The women were even more forbidding. Your sister Anactoria glared at me and sniffed. She was a tall, stately woman who was obviously used to getting her own way with the weak-willed Ariphron and resented the fact that she couldn't dominate you, too. Your cousin Deinomache, Alcibiades' mother, seemed rather uncertain about what to do. She had a pleasant face which would have been pretty if she hadn't looked so down-trodden. Although she couldn't have been more than thirty she had tired lines round her eyes and a perpetual worried frown. I guessed she was treated like a slave by every other member of the family and didn't know how to hit back. In fact she was the only person who had any real reason to resent me, since after her husband's death she had hoped to marry you herself. Nevertheless, after looking round in panic for guidance, she did mumble some sort of greeting. Your sister stared at her with such horror and fury I'm surprised the poor girl didn't sink into the ground.

But she had other things to think about. A small figure darted out

from behind her, reached up to me with both hands and demanded:
'Kiss me, darling.'

'Alcibiades!' There was a shocked silence as his mother pulled
him back and Anactoria slapped him, very hard. I liked your sister
less and less. The child opened his mouth and bellowed, a loud
piercing wail which went on and on (undoubtedly produced for
effect, since there wasn't a sign of a tear). This distraction, together
with the fact that it was starting to rain harder, made us rush
through the rest of the introductions. Your other women relatives
were always just a group of blurred faces to me. I never saw them
again, except at weddings and funerals.

You took my arm and led me indoors to the banquet, your
relatives following at a distance as if we had the plague. But they
didn't matter so much now, for there inside the banqueting hall
were all our friends, looking far more sober and respectable than
they had the night before. I have never been more pleased to see
their familiar faces.

You had explained to me that the wedding banquet was a con-
tinuation of the ceremony itself; it was important to have as many
guests as possible—they were witnesses that the wedding had
actually taken place. Sophocles was there, and Pheidias the sculptor
and Meidias and, of course, Socrates. Anaxagoras was beaming
benignly as he told people how he had introduced us. It didn't
seem right, somehow, without Manto, Chrysis and the other girls
who had always been at parties in my house. But at least wedding
banquets were one of the few occasions when Athenian women ate
in the same room as the men—and this created an awkward
problem.

The custom was for the women to sit silently round their own
table in a corner of the room while the men lay on couches in the
usual way. Obviously this was one custom I wasn't going to observe.
I sat down thankfully beside you, and Elpinice followed my lead,
pulling a chair up close to Callias' couch. The other women looked
confused, so Elpinice motioned to them to do the same as her. But
at that moment your sister Anactoria took charge, hustling them
all into a corner where they stayed, seen but not heard, till it was
time to leave. I noticed Deinomache looking wistfully in our direction, but she didn't have the courage to defy Anactoria.

I broke another tradition by taking the veil off—I really couldn't
sit there posing as a modest virgin in front of my old friends.
Ariphron looked scandalised. He was having a bad time of it anyway, lying between Socrates and Pheidias who appeared to be

putting him through some sort of verbal torture. We were given a lot of rather sickly cakes which I found hard to swallow but had to, since they were what one ate at weddings. And I was ceremoniously presented with a quince, supposedly a symbol of fertility. Fertility was the last thing I wanted, but I dutifully ate it.

One could tell at a glance which guests were your relatives and which were our friends. The former were stiffly silent and disapproving, visibly shuddering if anyone told a bawdy joke. Our friends, although slightly more constrained than usual, were doing their best to make things go well. The child Alcibiades had climbed up onto Socrates' couch and was listening entranced to some incredible story he was telling. Deinomache called the boy twice but he didn't move. I saw her dithering about whether to fetch him or not; she must have decided she couldn't intrude on the men's party, because Alcibiades stayed.

I suddenly felt very tired and turned to you.

'What happens now?'

'We consummate our marriage.' You smiled. 'Any objection?'

'Silly question. Let's go and do that.'

We were escorted to the bedroom by a few friends – Socrates was choking with laughter—and you went through an elaborate performance of closing the door. I simply flopped on the bed.

'Really we should have a trusted friend on guard outside the door and a chorus of virgins singing hymns,' you said. 'I thought I'd spare you that.'

'Thank you.' I sniffed. 'You smell as if you've just come from an Oriental brothel. Whatever have you got on?'

You shrugged apologetically. 'Sorry, darling. Perfumed ointment is another wedding tradition—it'll take days to wear off. You're fairly strongly scented yourself, you know.'

You threw your drooping wreath on the floor, flung off your tunic and sat naked on the bed beside me.

'You're exhausted, aren't you?'

I nodded.

'Poor love. Let me undress you.'

You undid my brooches and girdle and pulled my dress over my head. Then you carefully covered me with a blanket and climbed in beside me.

'I was very proud of you today,' you whispered. 'I'm sorry they were so awful.'

'They're not important. It's you who matters.'

I clung to you for warmth and comfort and you held me very

tight. We didn't bother to consummate the marriage after all—we were both much too tired.

I am becoming quite practised at marriages. My wedding to Lysicles last month made very little impression on me, even though it was legally more valid than my marriage to you. We went through the same rigmarole of pure water and sacrifices, ate the same cakes and the symbolic quince. It didn't rain and I refused to wear a veil at all. One big difference: far from shunning me, his relatives fawned on me as if I were the goddess Athena herself, all clamouring to talk to me, then standing speechless with confusion when they actually joined the wedding group. They are kind, simple people, overawed by my association with you. Illogically, I'd rather have your proud, insolent, erratic family even though they treated me so badly.

Alcibiades acted as my 'father'—we thought it was rather a joke. He made a sententious speech with his tongue in his cheek (everyone took it seriously), proposed endless toasts, and led the escort party to the bedroom. I might as well be truthful, and admit that my second marriage *was* consummated on the wedding night. Without love or pleasure or even pretence on my part. I just lay there and went automatically through the motions. Having married Lysicles, I can't really deny him the right to sleep with me occasionally. And I suppose I must need sex, too—I'm only 37 and still a woman.

9

LONELINESS was the worst problem during the first few
months of marriage to you. I was an outsider in a strange
house which I found uncomfortable and chilling. During the
mornings when you were out I had no one to talk to and nothing to
do. Evangelos was in charge of the housekeeping, and I didn't
want to offend him by interfering. So I lived in solitary splendour
in the front half of the house, like an unwanted guest. Everyone
else—Deinomache, the children, their nurses, tutors and slaves—
lived at the back in the women's quarters and never ventured
through the double doors. We might have been living in different
worlds, and I hadn't the courage to intrude on theirs for fear of
being turned away.

The only person I did see occasionally was your elder son
Xanthippos who thought he was too old at 16 to spend his time
with women and children. Apparently I didn't count as a 'woman',
for he didn't seem to mind spending his time with me. He was over-
familiar in a nastily patronising way—presumably he thought this
was the proper attitude to adopt towards his father's mistress. He
was one of the most mean, deceitful, spiteful, cowardly characters I
have ever met; I made a genuine effort to like him, but the more I
saw of him the more I despised him.

I soon realised your family could hardly have noticed you hadn't
been living at home for the previous two months. For even now
that you were back to your old routine of commuting between
house and office, you never saw your sons, your wards or your
cousin, never asked how they were or what they were doing, never
showed the slightest interest in their education, games or health.
Xanthippos might have been slightly more endearing if anyone
had ever cared about him.

I missed Manto and Melissa and the other girls. I missed discussions with Micon about the catering and housekeeping, and the

daily domestic dramas that always kept me busy. I missed my Pheidias frieze and my Socrates Hermes, the tapestries and cushions and ornaments that had made my house a comfortable place to live in. Your house was no different, basically—just a courtyard with rooms leading off it. But it was bleak and forbidding, furnished with only the very bare necessities of life. So I filled in time by trying to make it more cheerful. I hired carpenters, stone masons, upholsterers, sewing women; I had a fountain built in the courtyard and a frieze carved round the veranda. I converted one of the unused bedrooms into a bathroom—you had never needed one because you went to the public baths every day (Athenian women, for all their 'purity', think washing is a decadent, Oriental custom and mostly make do with a visit to the women's baths every ten days or so). It was essential for companions to be clean, and I had got used to regular baths. So, to your amusement, an enormous marble bath was installed and a special furnace built to provide heat.

One spring morning I was supervising the hanging of tapestries in the banqueting room when Evangelos appeared silently beside me (I never heard him make the slightest noise—he always appeared, and vanished again, like a ghost). He looked as gloomy as ever and stood watching the workmen as though they were nailing up his own coffin.

'May I be so bold as to make a suggestion?' he asked balefully.

'Of course. Go ahead.'

'Well, wouldn't it be simpler if the men had something to stand on. They'd get the things up much quicker.'

He was right, and in a few minutes had the whole thing organised. The tapestries went up in no time at all and when Evangelos stood back to admire the walls he was very nearly smiling.

'Beautiful tapestries, if I may say so.'

'Thank you. I had them specially woven.' I was genuinely pleased that he approved.

He went even further, saying: 'I'm not in favour of lots of decorations, mind you. Don't like gaudy trimmings.' He lowered his voice conspiratorially. 'But I must admit that when they're real quality, like the things you've done here, they can transform a place. I'd been telling the master for years it was like living in a graveyard. Now it's a real pleasure to look at.'

He grinned and vanished. I was absurdly elated.

Socrates was far more direct. He flung his arms round me one day and exclaimed dramatically: 'Darling, I have to congratulate you—I never knew you were a domestic genius as well. Before, this house was as uncomfortable as an army camp; now I'm tempted to move in permanently.'

Even you noticed the difference. 'I don't know what you've done exactly,' you said, puzzled. 'Surely a few bits of furniture can't change a house so much? It's got a warm, lived-in feeling now which it never had before. I look forward to coming home.'

In fact you were spending more and more time at home. I guessed that public appearances were as much of a strain as ever, and heard that one or two people were even refusing to speak to you after our wedding. But you wouldn't talk about it, and just spent more and more time in the 'safety' of our house.

Comfortable though it now was, however, it was still empty half the day. Most of the time I felt like a total outsider: I was neither a wife nor a concubine, neither mistress in my own home nor a guest in yours. I was cut off from the rest of the household and from my own girl friends—I didn't know who I was or what I was meant to be. I did go back to my own house every now and again to see Manto and Melissa and the other girls, but I felt like an outsider there too. And I didn't like to ask them back to see me—you would have been upset and they would have been embarrassed.

Yet you seemed so happy and relaxed I did my best not to complain. You came home early every afternoon, ate a quick lunch then lay on the veranda to 'receive' whoever called. Far more business seemed to be done at home than in your office or the market place: everyone who was anyone came to consult you about anything from foreign policy to the cost of a new statue. People came and went as they had done in my house, and many of them were the same people. The main difference was that here there were no girls.

It seemed strange at first, being the only woman in a man's world. But I got used to it, and a few of your colleagues who had viewed me with deep suspicion to begin with soon got used to me, too. The 'Pericles set' and the 'Aspasia set' became one and the same thing. People started asking my advice as well, and there were few important decisions made in home or foreign policy that I didn't at least know about. You discussed everything with me, and seemed to rely on my judgment more and more. Perhaps it was because I *wasn't* Athenian, so had a different way of looking at things. I found that many Athenians were quite blind to the impression they might make on foreigners; for them, Athens was so perfect they were convinced it must appear the same to everyone else. I would point out that their high-handed policies might look suspiciously imperialistic to other people and they would say: 'Seriously? I never thought of it that way.'

I can't truthfully say I objected to being the first and only woman to have an unofficial say in the running of the city. It was not ungratifying. Yet not even I could keep up a high-powered flow of political and intellectual conversation for ever. I missed the long hours spent chattering to girl friends about nothing at all. And it made it worse, knowing that on the other side of those double doors there was a whole world of chatter from which I was excluded, as well as a single woman—Deinomache—who might well be more lonely than I was.

'Why doesn't Deinomache come and eat with us sometimes?' I asked you one evening after we'd been married a few months.

'Deinomache? Why on earth should she?'

'She might be lonely. It seems ridiculous for her to be shut away in the women's quarters all the time.'

This had obviously never occurred to you.

'But she'd have nothing to say for herself and wouldn't know what we were talking about. Anyway, we have guests most evenings and she certainly couldn't be around then.'

'Why ever not? I am.'

'Yes, but you're not an Athenian.'

'I'm supposed to be your wife, aren't I—so what's the difference?'

'Look, dearest, I know you're being kind, but you don't seem to realise that Deinomache would be miserable in company. She'd feel embarrassed.'

I was annoyed. 'How do you know? You've never invited her.'

'I've never invited her because I've never wanted my stupid cousin sitting around looking cow-like. I simply haven't time to bother about whether she's comfortable or happy or included in the conversation. I'm trying to run a city, not a rest home for distressed widows.'

It was our first quarrel. I told you I thought you were selfish and thoughtless, and marched off to bed. When you followed soon afterwards I pretended to be asleep. But I couldn't keep it up for long—after all, it wasn't your fault that you'd been brought up to believe all Athenian women were brainless deaf mutes. I said I was sorry for losing my temper and you said you were sorry for being unreasonable and next morning you told Evangelos there would be three of us for dinner.

Deinomache looked more tired than ever, and absolutely terrified. I was afraid you were going to be proved right. We sat stiffly on either side of you as the slaves brought food in and out and you and I talked awkwardly about the new temples on the Acropolis. She didn't speak a word and seemed to be having difficulty swallowing. Perhaps she didn't even know there *were* any new temples on the Acropolis. I had to bring her into the conversation somehow, so asked how Alcibiades was—it was just too bad if you didn't want to talk about children. Thank the gods it worked: she started telling stories about his latest escapades, and even you couldn't help laughing. Deinomache turned out to be quite articulate once she got started; after a few cups of wine she and you were reminiscing and joking about your own childhoods so that it was I, if anyone, who felt excluded. But I was fascinated to hear about life in the nurseries of the Athenian nobility, and glad to see you looking so relaxed.

Socrates came in unexpectedly with a boy friend and behaved as if it was the most natural thing in the world to find your cousin sitting with us. He remembered Alcibiades from our wedding, and had served in the same regiment as Deinomache's husband, so they were soon chattering away like old friends. Socrates was marvellous with women, any women—perhaps because he treated them as people in their own right. And although he wasn't interested sexually, I think he genuinely liked women's company. Whereas with men he was the severest of inquisitors, ruthlessly rejecting loose reasoning and vague generalisations, with women he was gentle and courteous, with a knack of making any girl feel both beautiful and intelligent. He told me once : 'I adore feminine logic— if I tell Manto, for example, that there's a fallacy in her argument she simply tells me that my beard needs combing—as if that explained and settled the whole thing. What can one do?'

We drank at least two full jars of wine that evening. And when it was finally time to go to bed Deinomache looked ten years younger. She smiled, kissed me and suggested diffidently that I might come to talk to her and the children if ever I was bored. I promised to be there next morning. When Socrates asked politely if he might also call on her when he was in the house, she went back to the women's quarters positively glowing.

You were in an expansive mood too. 'I hate you,' you said, hugging me. 'You make me feel such a fool. Here I've been living in the same house as Deinomache all these months without ever finding out what sort of a person she is. And she's quite charming.'

'Just as well you didn't find out before, then. You might have married her instead of me.'

We fell into bed and made love for hours.

The next morning I did go to see Deinomache, and on my way
back I left those double doors open. When you complained that we
couldn't have children running about while you were discussing
business I begged you at least to give it a try. The doors stayed open,
and although it didn't really make much difference, I now had the
feeling that it was all one house instead of two. I went through
into the women's quarters when you weren't there, or Deinomache
came to sit with me in the front; we became good friends, and she
began to rely on me more and more. She was a very weak-willed
woman who had been ordered about all her life by her parents,
her husband, her cousins and now her sons. It had simply never
occurred to her to stand up for herself.

She ate with us quite often after that, and I tried to persuade
you to join her and the children in the women's quarters
occasionally for a change. But that was asking too much—the idea
of children put you in a panic, so I didn't insist. I also more or less
demanded that she should come through to the front in the afternoons too, pleading untruthfully that I didn't like being the only
woman among all those men. She dutifully sat in a corner listening
to what went on and saying very little. But she wasn't stupid, and I
realised from the questions she asked me when we were on our
own that she was taking a lot in.

Then one day I saw the doors were closed again. I went to look for
Deinomache to ask her why and found her in her bedroom, red-
eyed, trembling and almost refusing to speak to me. When I begged
her to tell me what was wrong she just looked frightened and
muttered: 'Nothing. Leave me alone. I'll be all right.'

I was puzzled and hurt. Alcibiades was playing in the courtyard
as I went through, so I asked him:

'What's wrong with your mother?'

He grinned. 'Guess.'

I was in no mood for playing guessing games with a six-year-old,
but couldn't drag a word out of him till I had taken him through to
the front of the house, made him comfortable on your couch and
filled him up with cakes and wine. Only then would he condescend
to tell me, with great relish, what had happened earlier that
morning.

It seemed your sister Anactoria had heard that Deinomache and I
were becoming friendly, so took it upon herself to do something
about it. She came bursting through the back door (she wouldn't
have dared come through the front) soon after dawn and sub-
jected the poor girl to a terrifying lecture on the punishment due

from the gods for consorting with whores and harlots, to say nothing of the disastrous effect it was going to have on her poor innocent children. As for her friendship with Socrates—that was a 'degrading affair' and a disgrace to the family.

Poor innocent Alcibiades was a superb mimic and seemed to remember the entire tirade word for word.

'Then she slapped mother across the face, ordered her never to speak to you or Socrates again, and marched out. By the way, what are whores and harlots?'

'All women not privileged to be born into your family,' I snapped. I was furious. Deinomache was, I knew, reasonably pious, and it would have been stupid to confuse her by pointing out that the gods didn't exist and couldn't therefore punish her.

I told you all about it when you came home and you, if anything, were angrier than I was. It infuriated you that anyone should give orders in your own house.

'I'm going to see my brother Ariphron,' you said grimly. 'And that meddling sister of mine. How *dare* they treat you like this?'

It was Deinomache, not me, they were treating badly, but I didn't expect you to see this. The important thing was to stop them interfering.

When you came back you actually went through into the women's quarters—leaving the door open—and emerged again a little while later leading a bewildered-looking Deinomache by the hand. I don't know whether you ordered or persuaded her to disobey your sister, but you called Socrates over when he came in and left them deep in conversation. I could hear her protesting : 'But Anactoria said . . .' and Socrates gently but methodically dismissing all her doubts. Whatever arguments he used they must have reassured her, for later she came over to kiss me and apologise for 'being upset' that morning.

I don't know whether public opinion was against you because of me, or whether it was just coincidence that that was a bad year for you politically. For the first time in years you weren't re-elected a general, and although you *said* you were glad of the extra time to spend at home I could tell you missed the work and responsibility. I rather suspect Ariphron and his friends did everything possible to stir up feeling against you. And it seemed the people had discovered that peacetime wasn't all that different from war, so turned against their wartime leader. You didn't say so, but I knew you were hurt that the mass of Athenians should have such short memories: you had after all been their champion for years against the conservative nobility. And as a general you had become used to doing things your own way without having to answer for your decisions and actions. (I never could understand why the Board of Ten Generals should be so much more influential than the other city officials; perhaps it was because they were elected for their ability while all the others were chosen by lot. The generals had even more power in peacetime than when we were at war, since they were all there in Athens taking a hand in government.) Objectively I thought it might do you good to be just an ordinary citizen for a year or two. But you were miserable because you felt rejected, and I suffered with you.

Once you were no longer the all-powerful Olympian, your enemies started trying to undermine your position even further. They still didn't dare attack you openly, so did it in the nastiest possible way by getting rid of your friends. Their first target was Anaxagoras, who had never harmed anyone in his life.

I was particularly upset about it because we ourselves had behaved badly to The Mind. With all the excitement of the wedding and adjusting to a very new way of life, you had apparently been forgetting to send him his monthly allowance, which he was completely dependent on. (He had once had considerable property of his own in Ionia, but had let it all run wild years before. He was no more capable of running an estate than flying to the moon.) One day we heard that he was ill in bed; you went straight round to the lodging-house where he lived and found him lying there motionless with a blanket over his head. His landlady said he refused to eat, and hadn't paid his rent for months.

You were horrified—Anaxagoras had meant almost more to you than your own father and had taught you practically everything you ever learned. You knelt beside him begging him to eat something, to give some sign of life. You more or less ordered him not to die, saying you couldn't manage without him, he was the only person whose opinion you valued, he was indispensable to Athens and to the world.

For once, The Mind wasn't dreaming at all. He let you have your say, then slowly uncovered his head, looked at you mournfully and said:

'Pericles, my boy, when will you learn? If you need light from a lamp, you have to put oil in it. If you need light from your old tutor, you have to fill him up, too.'

He stumbled out of bed and ate an enormous meal—once he was sure you'd paid the rent.

We laughed about it afterwards, but with a bad conscience—for he would have been quite capable of really starving himself to death if we hadn't heard in time. And although we didn't know it, we weren't going to see much more of him. A few months later a freak ram with only one eye and one horn was found on one of your farms and brought to you by an excited slave. People crowded round to look at the dead animal, insisting it must be an omen, and a seer called Lampon said it meant the two rival factions in the city would soon be reduced to one—yours, of course. (I don't know why you put up with Lampon around the house; he was a subservient, fawning character whose prophecies were always calculated to please his audience. I never heard him predict anything unpleasant.) I was about to protest that this was utter nonsense when Anaxagoras shuffled forward and asked for a saw. Everyone stood back in amazement as he sawed the ram's head in two then showed us, by comparing the two halves, the simple explanation for the one horn and one eye: the ram had a deformed skull.

So much for prophecy (hardly surprising *that* one did in fact come right—we could all have predicted the same thing without the help of a one-eyed ram). But although most of us there that afternoon were impressed by Anaxagoras' scientific explanation of the freak, there were a lot of religious bigots who weren't. There was talk of blasphemy and impiety, while indignant citizens suddenly remembered that The Mind's theory of the universe excluded the gods altogether. His revolutionary idea that the sun is just a mass of blazing stone and probably larger than the whole of Greece infuriated them; a crippled oracle-monger called Diopeithes persuaded the Assembly to pass a decree making it a crime not to believe in the gods, and to teach doctrines concerning the heavenly bodies.

Diopeithes was undoubtedly put up to it by your enemies. He was a venomous fanatic who played on religious superstition and should have been prosecuted himself for preaching prejudice and intolerance. The new law was obviously aimed directly at Anaxagoras, and we heard rumours that he would also be accused, for good measure, of 'collaborating' with the Persians. The basis for this invented charge was that years before he had lived peaceably in an Ionian town under Persian rule. He was such an unworldly character he probably hardly knew the Persians were there, or even that there was a war on.

After endless discussions we decided it was probably best to smuggle him out of the city before he could stand trial. Knowing him, he might well have said enough incriminating things in complete good faith to get himself sentenced to death.

So after more than thirty-five years in Athens Anaxagoras went to live in the Ionian colony of Lampsacos. His book 'On Nature' which had been hailed as a scientific masterpiece was publicly discredited, and all his writings temporarily banned. At least he became a local celebrity in his new home, where you went on sending him his allowance. (Last month I was going to send his money myself, then I heard he had died a few months before, aged 72. When he fell ill, the city authorities at Lampsacos asked their most distinguished citizen what sort of memorial he would like; typically, he asked for the anniversary of his death to be kept as a school holiday for ever.)

Another close friend who was exiled was your music teacher Damon, the man who probably did most to make you enter politics as a radical democrat. Unlike most of your friends, he didn't belong to the circle of great political families, and it was he who opened your eyes as a young man to the realities of the big wide world. The conservative aristocrats had always resented him: they accused him of being responsible for most of your 'progressive' legislation, such as introducing payment for jury service and other public jobs. In their opinion this was bribing the people with public funds. In yours and Damon's it was the only way of making sure that even the poorer citizens could afford to take a part in city business.

Damon wasn't prosecuted—he had committed no crime. He was simply ostracised. This procedure whereby anyone can be banished for ten years, for no reason at all, if more than six thousand citizens write his name on a piece of broken pottery is to my mind completely unjust. It was originally intended to safeguard democracy, if any one politician seemed to be getting too powerful. But in Damon's case it was a political manoeuvre to discredit one of your friends. The ostracism ceremony was called with him in mind, and for days beforehand your enemies were campaigning all over town 'helping' write the name. They got their six thousand votes, and Damon had to go.

Another ostracism was called soon afterwards with the aim of exiling you, too. But your enemies had underrated your personal popularity—whether through loyalty or fear, Athens was not prepared to banish her most eminent citizen. Only a few people dared write your name, while the others voted to ostracise your friends, your relatives, your supporters—anyone who was close to you. Fortunately, however, organisation had slipped up somewhere; there were too many names and not enough votes against any single one.

You tried to be philosophical about it. After all, you had put power in the hands of the people, so you had to accept their decisions. And your faith in them paid off, for by the next year you were their idol again. Your enemies called yet another ostracism in a desperate bid to get rid of you, but it was very badly timed: instead of voting against you, the people banished your one serious rival, Thucydides (the son of Melesias, not the Thucydides who is writing a history of the war).

After that you really did become supreme. You were re-elected general, and the law was changed so that one general each year was chosen by 'all the Athenians'. From then on you filled this position of 'General-in-Chief' with monotonous regularity—the yearly election was little more than a formality. You liked to think that during your year out of office the people realised they had made a mistake. And although conservative politicians, backed by the comic playwrights, accused you of being a virtual tyrant, you pointed out rightly that you could have been suspended by the Assembly at any time. The reason you stayed in power was that you were the best and probably the only man for Athens at the time.

Not that I admitted this to you. I was probably your severest critic, lecturing you severely when your policies failed to match up to your personal standards of perfection. You tried almost too hard to be fair and just, but you were over 50 and set in your ways. However much you prided yourself on being reasonable, you would listen patiently to someone else's argument, agree that he had a valid point, and proceed to take very little notice. Your way of doing things had brought peace after fifty years; it had made Athens the greatest city in Greece; it had provided employment for thousands of citizens and changed the face of the city. It must be right. It was hard to make you see that although it was probably the best, there were still a lot of things wrong with it.

You were childlike in your enthusiasm for the new temples. Pheidias and the architects working under him were doing a magnificent job and you couldn't resist climbing the Acropolis nearly every day to 'see how they were coming on'. We often went up there in the early evening, a group of five, ten, twenty people who had been at the house during the afternoon and were then urged to come and visit 'your' temples. We would sit on the huge blocks of marble, talking politics or philosophy or literature, watching the builders and masons chipping away as the sun went down and bathed everything in a warm pink glow. I was always amazed at the perfection and precision with which every lump of stone was cut and chiselled; Pheidias explained that in order to make the temples *look* symmetrical, every line and every pillar had to be slightly rounded or tapered. He really was a perfectionist, never satisfied till something was exactly right. Even then he would shake his head gloomily, muttering, 'It looks like a Spartan barracks,' as you stroked the marble and ran your fingers down the fluting, bursting with pride in 'your' achievement.

Your house gradually began to feel more like a home. The double doors were never shut again after Anactoria's visit, so little by little I got to know the slaves and the children and become an accepted part of the household. Evangelos started asking my advice about domestic problems and I often gave him a few drachmas to help with the housekeeping; expenditure had gone up now there were so many more people around, and I didn't see why we shouldn't live comfortably. I gave Deinomache presents, too—clothes, perfume and jewellery. She had money left by her husband, but Ariphon was in charge of it and made her account for every obol.

It wasn't that you were mean—you were so indifferent to money you didn't want to be bothered with it (coming from a wealthy family, you had never had to worry about not having enough). This was a great advantage to you as a politician, for it meant you were completely incorruptible. By the time I met you people had given up even attempting to bribe you. You spent a lot on providing public entertainment—games, chariot races, public banquets and so on—and I argued that this was bribery the other way round. But you smiled your 'I know best' smile and asked why the people shouldn't be entertained if they enjoyed it.

At home, however, your attitude to money caused a lot of friction. You had large country estates inherited from your father which made you a fairly wealthy man, in theory. But you didn't follow the example of other landowners who supplied their own homes, lavishly, from the estates, then sold the surplus produce. To save trouble, you sold a whole year's cultivation. And Evangelos bought everything for the house in the market. It was much more expensive, but you found it easier.

The trouble was that Evangelos was on a fixed budget, the boys were on small allowances and Deinomache was given nothing at all —you didn't think women needed money. I was very glad I had kept my own finances separate. Whenever I suggested you might be a bit more generous towards the family you immediately offered to give me an allowance of my own, which wasn't the point at all. You simply had no idea what things cost; Evangelos managed everything for you, and he was determined not to spend one more obol of your money than was absolutely necessary.

Your eldest son Xanthippos was as extravagant as you were tight-fisted. He belonged to a set of young men who spent their time drinking and gambling and seemed to get unlimited funds from their fathers. Xanthippos just couldn't keep up; he was always in debt and you refused to pay his creditors. About the only conversation you ever had with him seemed to be rows about money.

He sidled up to me one morning, looking sly, and pulled a chair up close.

'You're looking very beautiful.'

'Thank you,' I said curtly. I could guess what was coming.

'That dress must have cost a fortune—a mina at least?'

He fingered the material, stroking my thigh as he did so. I pushed his hand away. He really was a repulsive youth.

'What's the matter?' he asked with a leer. 'Don't you like me touching you?'

'No, I don't.'

'I should have thought you'd be the last person to object. After all, in your profession . . .'

'That's enough,' I said sharply. 'What do you want?'

He wouldn't come to the point, but whined on and on about how all his friends had allowances of at least ten minas a month while he only got two, how he'd had a run of bad luck lately but knew it would change—and if I could only help him out he swore to pay me back within the month.

I sighed. 'Tell me the truth. How much money do you actually owe?'

'Well . . . I think it's about thirty minas.'

'Xanthippos!' I was horrified. 'That's half a talent, enough to keep the whole family for a year!'

'Not any family that lives properly.' He sneered. 'It wouldn't even buy a decent racehorse. Anyway I could pay you back, I promise, in the best possible way.'

I should have understood what he meant from his ghastly grin, but I wasn't thinking too clearly that morning.

'What do you mean—the best possible way? Don't tell me you'd win it back gambling, because you know perfectly well you wouldn't.'

He edged his chair closer.

'Oh, come on, Aspasia, you know what I mean. After all, I'm only five years younger than you and I've been doing it for years. You need someone like me—Father's much too old to be any use to you.'

I was still lost. But then he grabbed me with one hand and pulled his tunic up with the other, to demonstrate how 'manly' he was.

I slapped him across his face.

'Get out of my sight. Now. And never come near me again.'

He spat on the ground. 'You filthy slut. How dare you hit an Alcmaeonid? I'm going to make sure you get sent back to the brothel where you belong.'

I picked up a chair to hit him and he slunk back, cowering.

'If you don't give me the money, I shall tell Father you seduced me. I shall tell him you have a string of men in the house every morning.'

Xanthippos was even more vile than I'd thought. I took a deep breath:

'You can tell him what you like. Now get out.'

I knew he was too much of a coward to try telling you any of these lies—you would simply have thrown him out of the house. But he did spread stories round Athens for a few months. Then he went off on his two year military service and I gave a sigh of relief. The house was a happier place without him.

I never told you about this scene. It would just have upset you. And whether you liked it or not, Xanthippos was, after all, your eldest son, the man who would be carrying on the sacred family name.

Paralos, your other boy, was in his early teens and going through a very difficult stage. Although he hero-worshipped you, he was always being bullied by his brother, who hadn't a good word to say for you. So he got very confused and retreated into moody silence. I tried to be kind to him but he looked scared and suspicious, as if there were a trick somewhere.

Then there were Deinomache's sons, Cleinias and Alcibiades. Cleinias was an idiot: at the age of eight he still had the mentality of a child of two, and although he seemed quite good-natured there was little we could do for him. Alcibiades made up for it, however. He was an extraordinary child; by the time he was six he had everyone in the house, from his mother to his nurse to his tutor, eating out of his hand. He was capricious, charming and cunning;

he could be sweet as honey or cruelly malicious; oddly enough, the only person who could manage him at all was Socrates. The little boy would spend hours sitting on his knee playing word games or listening to myths and legends which they systematically demolished together.

A few months after Alcibiades started going to school, his teacher complained that he refused to learn the flute. Deinomache—who was totally baffled by her infant prodigy—couldn't find out why, so asked me to try.

'Why won't you learn the flute, Alcibiades?'

He sucked his thumb and looked coy.

'Come on, you must have a reason.'

'It's too ugly.'

'Nonsense, flute music is beautiful.'

'No, no, no—not the music.' He sighed impatiently. 'It makes your *face* look ugly when you blow into it.'

'That's not the point. You don't look at a musician's face, you listen to what he's playing.'

'But the goddess Athena herself threw away her flute when she looked in a stream and saw how ugly it made her. If she wouldn't play it, nor shall I.'

I cursed Socrates, who had undoubtedly taught him this fable. And needless to say, Alcibiades never learned the flute. Not only that—all the other boys at his school followed his example. And nowadays flute playing is not taught at all to young Athenians. Even as a six-year-old, Alcibiades knew how to sway the mob.

I sometimes thought the mob needed to be starved rather than swayed. You would lecture on about democracy, and how wonderful it was that every single citizen had equal rights, duties and responsibilities in the government of his own city; I would reflect gloomily that ninety per cent of the citizens weren't fit to rule a farmyard, let alone a city. (In any case, Athens was far from being a true democracy. She was ruled by you and, to a lesser extent, the other nine generals. And the privileged citizens who 'governed' her were outnumbered by the women, slaves and resident foreigners who had the same duties and responsibilities but practically no rights at all.)

I was disenchanted with the mass of Athenians because of some of the stories circulating at the time. They had temporarily lost their taste for inventing scandal about me—after all nobody tried to deny I was an ex-companion with a dubious past, so nothing they said about me could have full shock effect. Instead, they started on you. I could hardly believe my ears when I heard there was a rumour going round that your real reason for visiting the temples every day was to keep secret assignments with free-born Athenian women procured for you by Pheidias. You of all people—it was absolutely ludicrous. As was the idea of melancholy Pheidias acting as go-between. I suppose the implication was that you had got tired of your vulgar Milesian whore and wanted real 'ladies' as a change. (Also, it is a serious crime to seduce an Athenian woman; sex with citizens' wives and daughters is considered both immoral and illegal.)

I asked you if you'd heard the story and you nodded miserably.

'Yes. I'd hoped it wouldn't reach you.'

'Why ever not? You can't think for a moment I'd believe it?'

'Well, no, of course not.' But you looked relieved. 'I can't imagine why they invent such lies.'

I laughed. 'Last time you broke your famous daily routine it was because you were going to see a woman. I suppose they think you're doing the same thing again.'

There was another ridiculous story about some rare birds called peacocks which a friend of ours brought back from a visit to Persia. He gave me one for the courtyard and distributed the others among the wives of several leading politicians, including Elpinice. They really were beautiful birds and we all wished he'd brought more. Then a few days later the rumour went round that the lucky women who had received them were all Pericles' mistresses! You had never seen most of the wives, let alone spoken to them.

It was maddening, but there was nothing we could do. And as Elpinice had predicted, after a while the gossip died down—when people got bored with it or found someone else to talk about. It flared up every now and again, undoubtedly fanned by some member of your devoted family. But little by little Athens accepted the fact that I lived with you and was going to go on living with you. One of the few true stories that went the rounds was the report that you kissed me before you left the house each morning and when you came back in the afternoon. It wasn't considered exactly immoral—but it was unusual enough to talk about.

I may have become a bit confused about exactly when some of these things happened. They all took place during the first two years I was living in your house, and *before* the Great Panathenaic Festival when you inaugurated the concert hall. This is a month I shall never forget. Everything that happened before seems slightly unreal, looking back, as though we were just playing at being man and wife, at being in love even. It was too easy, too idyllic. Afterwards life was different. We were less starry-eyed. But we were also, in a way, very much closer.

E

10

THE Great Panathenaea—the four-yearly festival in honour of the goddess Athena—was very important to you that year because the first of 'your' new buildings, the Odeon, was finished. It had been entirely your idea to have this concert hall built below the Acropolis, next to the theatre, and it did look very impressive, with a shining marble façade and a high, conical roof. You wanted to find a use for it as soon as possible, so suggested that musical contests should be added to the games and races already held at the festival. The Assembly agreed, and from then on lyre-playing, singing and flute-playing (despite Alcibiades) became a regular part of the Panathenaea. You were on the board of organisers, so personally drew up the regulations for the musical contests. It made a change from politics and finance, but meant you were even busier than usual. For, being you, you had to be sure that the rules were absolutely fair, the judges fully qualified, the contestants all worthy to compete. Neither you nor I was very musical so it wasn't easy—particularly since your former music teacher, Damon, was in exile.

I can never understand why the tiring six-day festival is held at the height of summer. The most stifling month of the year is anything but the best time for athletics, races and that never-ending procession up to the Acropolis to give the goddess Athena her new dress. That summer had been exceptionally hot; you were out all day and came home utterly exhausted, often too tired even to eat or do anything but flop into bed and toss and turn.

So you didn't notice that I was nervy and irritable. At first I thought it must be because of the heat. But the days went by, and I started feeling sick in the mornings. By the first day of the festival I knew I must be pregnant.

It was hardly the moment to tell you—you had a hundred other things to worry about. And I wasn't sure how you were going to react. I had told you soon after we first met that I thought I might not be able to have children—it seemed likely, since in eight years I had never got pregnant—and you looked pleased, saying 'Good, that cuts out a lot of problems.' The Aspasia you had fallen in love with was a slim, beautiful, intellectual girl, different from other women because she didn't talk about clothes and babies. You might be repelled by a pregnant Aspasia, you might even resent sharing her with a wailing infant. Although I knew you cared about your sons because they bore the family name and would have to carry on all those meaningless traditions like tending your ancestors' graves, you seemed quite indifferent to them as people, and certainly never showed any sign of loving them. Admittedly it would have been difficult to love Xanthippos; but perhaps he had turned out so badly *because* you had never taken any interest in him.

Personally, I was thrilled. Although it was exciting and stimulating to exercise my mind with the best brains in Athens, I had begun to feel there was something missing, and secretly envied Deinomache, sitting placidly among her children. From now on I would have that, too. And, for the first time, a family of my very own.

If the child was a boy he couldn't be a citizen, thanks to your citizenship law. But he would be free-born, would be a full member of the family, could serve in the army and do practically everything a citizen can—except hold public office and vote in the Assembly. He would have the same status as a foreign resident, many of whom are highly respected and very prosperous. If it was a girl there would be no citizenship problems. And I myself would make sure she had the best possible education.

Even foreign women were allowed to watch the Panathenaea, but I simply couldn't face it in that heat. I was feeling sick most of the time by now and didn't want to leave the house for anything at all. So when on the second day you asked if I was coming, I said I had a headache. You looked at me closely for the first time in days.

'You don't look at all well, my love. Are you sure you're all right?'

I shrugged. 'I expect it's the heat. I'll feel better as soon as it gets cooler.'

'I expect that's it. Take care of yourself.' You kissed me and were gone.

I wanted to wait at least till the Panathenaea was over before telling you. But you started worrying once you noticed there was something wrong, and on the evening of the fourth day you brought the subject up again.

'You look terrible, dearest. It can't be the heat—it's been much cooler today. I think you should see a doctor.'

'No, really—I'll be all right.'

'But you *can't* be all right. Your face is grey and you've got rings under your eyes. I wanted you to come to the festival tomorrow—it's the most important day—but you obviously can't go out in that state. I shall send a doctor to see you first thing in the morning.'

'No, darling, please don't. It's nothing, I promise you.'

You were tired and irritated. 'Aspasia, for the gods' sake be reasonable. If you're ill you must see a doctor. I shall send one whether you like it or not, and get him to report to me at the Odeon. Don't you understand that I'm *worried* about you?'

There was nothing for it—I had to tell you. Any doctor could have seen what was wrong with me immediately, and I preferred to tell you myself.

'A doctor isn't necessary. If you really want to know, I think I'm pregnant.'

'Oh *NO!!!*' You looked absolutely horrified. 'You *can't* be!'

'Why ever not? You didn't exactly avoid me last month.'

'But I thought you couldn't have children.'

'Well, obviously I can. I'm twenty-four days late, feeling sick all the time and already getting fatter. I must be pregnant.'

'But it's appalling. Just when everything was going so well ...'

I was amazed at the violence of your reaction.

'Come on, darling, it's not as bad as all that. I'm very happy about it—I want to have your child.'

'What's the point, when we'll have to expose it?'

It was my turn to be horrified. '*WHAT?*'

'I said what's the point, when we'll have to expose it?'

I could hardly speak. '*Expose* it? Do you seriously think for a moment that I'd let any child of mine be exposed? You must be mad.'

You were tight-lipped. 'On the contrary, I'm being sane and reasonable. Do you seriously think I could be father to any child which wouldn't be an Athenian citizen?'

'You *can't* mean it.'

'I do mean it. Our family has a long tradition to uphold. It's unthinkable that any member of it could be an outcast. My sons must not only be citizens, they must be distinguished citizens.'

I had never known you so pompous, and was struggling to keep my temper.

'What if it's a daughter? She couldn't be a citizen anyway.'

You shrugged. 'Who wants daughters? You spend fifteen years bringing them up, putting up with nurses, screaming, illnesses, tantrums, children under your feet all the time, then in the end you have to pay an enormous dowry to get rid of them. Better to expose them in the first place.'

Your cold reasoning was frightening. I stared at you blankly and saw an inhuman monster, relentlessly destroying my child. I couldn't believe it was you; if it was, I couldn't believe I had ever loved you.

'What about me? You don't seem to have taken *my* feelings into account.'

'Look here, darling'—you were smoothly patronising—'you know you don't really want a baby. It's just a whim, like getting a dog or a peacock. You're such an exceptional woman you'd be wasting your talents in the nursery. And you'd get bored with it almost immediately. Come on, be reasonable. I'll buy you a dog if you like.'

I couldn't bear it. 'What on earth do you think I am,' I screamed, 'a talking statue? For your information I am a woman, one of those inferior beings whom you treat worse than slaves. If you had ever taken the trouble to find out anything about them, you would know that women want children and love their children and fight for their children. It's a natural instinct. You always remember I'm a woman when you feel like sex. Now just get it into your head that I'm a woman all the time, not a freak boy!'

'Perhaps you're too much of a woman,' you sneered. 'How do I know it's mine?'

'How dare you?' I was shaking with anger. 'How *can* you say a thing like that? I suppose you've been gossiping with your girl friends on the Acropolis.'

'Shut up!' you roared. 'Let me make this clear once and for all—I will *not* have my life ruined by any damned baby. You belong here with me, not fussing over the cradle of a screaming infant. That's what I married you for.'

'You, you, you! You never think about *me*. Well, let *me* make it clear that if you want to stay married to me, you'll have to accept the baby.'

'But I told you—it couldn't be a citizen. I'd be ashamed of it.'

'Pericles'—I could hardly trust myself to speak—'if you're ashamed of my child, you're ashamed of me, too. *I* don't even have one Athenian parent, remember? Either we keep the child and you make an effort to be a real father to it, not like you were to

Xanthippos and Paralos, or I shall leave you and take the child with me.'

'You can't!'

'Why not?'

'You're my wife.'

'So what? Since I'm not Athenian I'm not bound by your ridiculous marriage laws. And I've plenty of money of my own.'

'I won't let you! I forbid you to!' You were becoming hysterical.

'If you talk to me like that I shall leave here and now and not come back. I'm not your slave, GENERAL, and I don't take orders.'

'You're completely impossible! How dare you spring this on me when you know how busy I am? We'll talk again when you've come to your senses.' You picked up your cloak and stalked out. I went to bed and cried.

You slept in another room that night and for two nights afterwards. You were out all day at the festival and came home late in the evening. We hardly saw each other, and when we did we didn't speak. I was utterly miserable and didn't know what to do. If you really refused to keep the baby, I should have to leave you before it was born. I remembered how my father had cold-bloodedly removed babies the moment they were born, while their mothers were still too weak to stop him. You might even be capable of that. Yet I couldn't believe you were really so inhuman, that you could be so cruel. And I didn't want to leave you. Even while I hated you, I still loved you: it hurt me to see you looking strained and unhappy, and I longed to take you in my arms and comfort you. It made it ten times worse to know you were unhappy because of me, but there was nothing I could do about it. I was determined not to give in; our quarrel had made me realise how very, very much I wanted the baby. I wasn't going to lose it, even if it meant losing you.

The day after the Panathenaea ended you came home as usual at lunch time. We sat on the veranda in stony silence as I hoped and prayed someone would come in and force us at least to pretend to be normal. Of course nobody did, for the first time in months. I longed to say I was sorry and make it up. But sorry for what? Sorry I had lost my temper? I was. But I certainly wasn't sorry I'd said I wanted to keep the baby. In the end it was you who broke the silence.

'Have you seen Sophocles lately?'

'Not since before the Panathenaea. Why?'

'I wondered when he's going to deliver his plays. It's almost time for the selection committee to meet.'

'I know he's finished all four of them. In any case surely it's only a formality—he's bound to be one of the three playwrights chosen for next year's drama festival.'

'Not at all,' you snapped. 'Why must you always assume these things aren't done fairly? The selection committee is there to *choose*, and if there happen to be three better entries than Sophocles', his won't be chosen. You never know—what about that young man who won this year? What was his name . . . ?'

'Euripides,' I ventured.

'That's right. A useless idler, I gather. Well, supposing he does it again? How many times must I tell you that this is a democracy in which *everyone* has a fair chance?'

There was another long silence until you said, in a different, gentler tone:

'I'm sorry, Aspasia. I can't keep this up any longer. I suppose you haven't changed your mind?'

'No. Have you?'

'No. But just to show you how reasonable I am, I'm willing to come to a compromise.'

I suspected a trap. 'Go on.'

'Well, I'll agree to let you keep the baby—if it's a girl. It will be most inconvenient, but at least there won't be citizenship problems and I'm sure we could find her a good husband somehow.'

'And if it's a boy?'

'We expose it.'

I sighed. 'Absolutely not. I'm sorry, but my mind's made up.'

'But, but what if it has two heads or only one arm or a humpback?'

'That's different. I suppose I'd consider it then.'

'Please, darling'—you were pleading with me now—'can we at least behave like two sensible adult people and agree to discuss it reasonably once the child's born? After all, we shall have ten days to decide one way or the other before I have to present it to the family.'

I thought about this. 'I suppose so—but on one condition: that you promise on your word of honour, or by the goddess Athena, or on your father's grave, anyway you *promise*, once it's born, not to touch it without my agreement. *We* shall make a decision, not you on your own.'

'All right,' you said wearily, 'I promise. Now come here.'

I walked over to you and you pulled me down beside you, hugging me so hard I thought you would stifle me.

'Darling,' you whispered. 'My darling. It's been murder. Don't ever leave me. I can't live without you.'

I felt nothing. Just numb detachment. And although we made love that night and you clung to me, sobbing, it was like being in bed with a stranger.

I don't know how we survived the next seven months. We hardly referred to the baby again, yet we thought about it all the time, separately. It was an unspoken barrier between us. I was fairly sure you would give in, in the end. But you would probably hate the child for the rest of its life. And if you didn't give in, I would have to leave you. It was ironic, I thought, that I of all people should be in the same situation as my father's wives, dreading giving birth to a boy.

I began to feel better physically, but as I got bigger we couldn't *help* being reminded of the baby all the time. We agreed to tell friends we were going to decide its fate when it was born. We didn't tell friends that I was going to keep it regardless, even if it meant leaving you. And I don't think you were really convinced I was serious about this — or you preferred not to believe it. I knew I was serious, and dreaded the battle ahead. I had to think about the practical implications of leaving you, and plan where I would go and what I would do. As a result I felt as if I'd half left you already.

It wasn't made any easier by the fact that you were kind and sweet and considerate, fussing about my health, begging me not to overtire myself. What on earth was the point, if you wanted to kill the baby once it was born? You were shocked at first because I didn't hide myself away as soon as the pregnancy started to show.

'Surely you feel embarrassed? I mean, other women don't appear in that condition.'

'Other women don't appear. Full stop. You've never been sociable with a pregnant woman because you've never been sociable with any women. I feel absolutely fine and see no reason to change my way of life — unless, of course, it embarrasses *you*?'

'No, of course not. I suppose you're right.' You were unexpectedly meek, and, I think, agreeably surprised to find that pregnancy didn't mean six months' mysterious isolation. Also, despite the fear that I might have to leave you, I was more even-tempered than usual. In my more optimistic moments I reasoned that whatever happened I would love the child, and since the child would be yours I should still have at least a part of you.

Socrates was enchanted with the idea of the baby and had already decided it would be called Apollo or Aphrodite. When I pointed out that it was illegal to use the gods' names he just laughed.

'What could be more godlike than the child of Pericles the Olympian and Aspasia the Star of Athens? I wonder if it will have your beauty and his brains? Or his vast skull and your illogicality? Will it count as an Alcmaeonid?'

'Yes, I think so. If it's a boy he can't be a citizen, but he's still a member of the family.'

'Well, beware the curse of the Alcmaeonids. You know about it, of course?'

'Yes. Because an ancestor killed someone on holy ground two hundred years ago, they're all fated to come to a bad end.'

'That's right. But not until they have proved they're best at everything they try. Incidentally, I presume you haven't the slightest intention of having this baby exposed?'

Socrates understood me better than you did. I explained the whole thing to him.

'Hmmm. I can't think what you're worrying about. He'd rather be banished from Athens than parted from you. And he'll probably like the baby because it's yours.'

Socrates was generally right. I hoped this wasn't going to be the one exception that proved the rule.

I dreamed a lot, during those seven months. And became irrationally obsessed with the curse of the Alcmaeonids. At times I almost believed that if the child was predestined to a life of disaster it really might be better to expose it as a baby. Then I had to pull myself together firmly and remind myself that I didn't believe in curses or omens or the vengeance of the gods. There were many Alcmaeonids who had led normal lives and died natural deaths. You, for one, had so far appeared to be favoured rather than cursed by the gods (unless I was your curse, and in that case I hoped my child *did* inherit it). The whole thing was a ridiculous superstition, kept alive for political convenience; Aspasia of Miletos should be the last person to take any notice of it.

And yet . . . I went on dreaming and worrying, feeling increasingly lonely and afraid. In the past I had discussed everything with you, but now, when I needed you most, you were the last person I could talk to about my silly fears. I couldn't mention them to anyone else—it would have been a shameful confession of weakness. And I refused to admit to myself that pregnancy was affecting my mind as well as my body.

Involvement with one of Sophocles' plays made me even more confused emotionally. He had, of course, been selected as one of the three contestants at the spring drama festival, and was almost certain to win it. But Athens' most celebrated playwright was anything but confident; right up to the last moment he was trying to improve the four plays, and for one of them in particular he came to me for advice.

I had read the first draft of 'Antigone' years before and told him I thought it was the best thing he had ever done. Encouraged by this, he had followed some of my suggestions, with the result that his female characters now resembled real people instead of lifeless dolls. More than that, he had written a play about women, for women, in defence of women—or so it seemed to me in my exaggeratedly womanly state.

I was especially susceptible to the Antigone story because the curse of the House of Oedipus reminded me of the curse of the Alcmaeonids. And neither Sophocles nor any other playwright was allowed to stray from the legendary story, which in this case was even more incredible than usual. Starting with poor old Oedipus himself who in all innocence killed his father and married his mother, thereby bringing down the wrath of the gods on the entire family—even though neither Oedipus nor his mother-wife Jocasta knew what they were doing. It's a hard story to believe, yet one can be charged with impiety for questioning it. (Oedipus had been exposed, then rescued by a soft-hearted shepherd. I didn't bother to point out to you that if we exposed our son there was the risk he might kill you and marry me. In any case Apollo had pre-arranged the whole Oedipus disaster from the start, presumably for his own amusement.)

We are asked to believe that Jocasta hanged herself and that Oedipus blinded himself, before going into exile with his daughter Antigone, a girl who had always seemed to me to be insufferably devoted and pious. Oedipus finally disappeared into the ground in a clap of thunder. So Antigone went home to join her sister Ismene in Thebes, now ruled by their uncle Creon. She became engaged to his son Haemon and they might have lived happily ever after.

But Antigone's two brothers had just killed each other fighting on different sides during an unsuccessful attack on the city. Creon ordered the body of the one who had led the attack to be left unburied. God-fearing Antigone thought this was sacrilegious, so tried to bury the body. Creon ordered her to be starved to death in a walled-up cave, where she hanged herself. Creon's son Haemon killed himself when he found out, and Creon's wife followed suit when she learned of her son's death. One hopes Apollo had a really good laugh.

I had always thought it would be impossible to make a sympathetic figure out of the righteous Antigone, yet Sophocles managed it. I found it difficult to feel sorry for a girl who made such an issue out of a burial rite—after all, once the man was dead he was dead, and the body would rot just the same above or below ground. (I realise I could be sentenced to death for this blasphemy: burial is far more sacred to most Athenians than birth or life, and one of the main reasons for raising a family is to ensure there will be someone to look after the ancestors' graves.)

But in Sophocles' version I identified almost too much with Antigone—her conflict with Creon seemed similar and parallel to my conflict with you. For although Sophocles stressed the importance of respect for the gods, basically the play was about two strong-headed people who were both passionately convinced they were right in principle, and both blind to the other's point of view. Creon insisted on obedience to his own authority, at all costs; Antigone obeyed only her own conscience.

Sophocles' Antigone is a strong-willed, stubborn girl determined to fight, and die if necessary, for what she believes is right. She embodies the principle that one should stand up for one's beliefs— and it didn't matter to me that I didn't share the beliefs in question. Her sister Ismene is a complete contrast, a scared, submissive, ordinary type who wails: 'We are women, it is not for us to fight against men.' She reminded me of Deinomache.

I was living with the play day after day—Sophocles refused to be satisfied till we had gone over every verse, till every line had my seal of approval. He was as charming as ever during those months, but his eyes had lost their mischievous twinkle. He was no longer chasing girls, and he spent so much time with me he can't have been paying much attention to city business either—unusual, since he took his civic duties very seriously and had been city treasurer only the year before.

You seemed pleased to see me spending so much time with Sophocles. You thought it would help distract me, and not even you could be jealous about literary discussions between your pregnant wife and your oldest friend. You didn't realise, however, that in my confused emotional state I was almost turning into Antigone —it was a way of forgetting Aspasia. And more and more I began to see you as the overbearing, bullying Creon.

Looking back, I realise it was quite unfair; Sophocles, who was very fond of you, would have been horrified if he'd known what was going through my mind. Creon was an absolute dictator and a bully; he stood for the principle I most detest—of blind, unquestioning obedience to authority just because it is authority. Like most men with too much power, he let it go to his head. You, on the other hand, ruled by the will of the people, not because you were distantly related to a royal house. You could be summoned before the Assembly at any time to answer for your actions, and be deposed by a simple vote. The only real similarity with Creon was that you were about the same age and, at that time, apparently deaf to my reasoning and impervious to my feelings.

Yet Creon's justification for walling up Antigone in the cave with just a little food, instead of having her killed outright, seemed very like the Athenian excuse for the practice of exposure. He does it 'to acquit ourselves of blood-guiltiness', and announces pompously: 'her blood will not be on our hands'. In the same way, exposing a new-born baby is not considered to be murder since, even though it dies of cold and starvation, nobody actually kills it. And there's always the chance that it will be rescued and sentenced to living death in a brothel or silver mine.

I have no pity whatsoever for Creon and regret that he didn't die as well. Yet Sophocles makes him alarmingly lifelike: there are dozens if not hundreds of Creons in Greece today who believe, like the king of Thebes, that 'there is no more deadly peril than disobedience'—as long as it is they who are giving the orders. Even democratic Athenians are Creons in their own homes, and would whole-heartedly agree that it is 'better to be beaten, if need be, by a man, than let a woman get the better of us.' The Assembly would cheer any orator who declaimed: 'We'll have no women's law here, while I live.'

I still know most of the play off by heart. And it is still, in a way, more real than any of the dozens of tragedies I have seen or read since then. It wouldn't be fair to Sophocles to say I feel I wrote it— although I do write poetry, I would never presume to mix mine with his. I just told him what sort of thing I thought Antigone or Creon would say, and he found the right words to express it. I like to think I was responsible for humanising Antigone a bit; her spite and scorn towards her weak-willed sister, her self-pity as she goes off to her death, are there at my insistence. They certainly don't make her any more likeable; they do make her less perfect and therefore more credible.

Creon changed his mind (too late) when he was frightened by a prophecy. But I knew no forecast of doom could make you change yours. You were not a coward, and you didn't believe in the gods and their punishments. At least you *said*, to me, that you didn't believe in them. In fact I always suspected you were secretly far less of a rationalist than I was, not entirely convinced that Zeus and Apollo and the rest of them might not be meddling in our lives and fates. I couldn't blame you—the gods had been an accepted part of your life and thinking since you were a tiny child, and not even Anaxagoras' influence could get them out of your system. I personally have never believed in the gods at all. It seemed to me, and still does, that every human being is fully responsible for his or her own actions and answerable to himself or herself alone. Organised religion is obviously necessary for many reasons, and it is even arguable that everyone should pay lip service to it. But one should at least be free to disbelieve in private, among one's friends. I have never tried to force anyone to think the way I do; in return, I expect freedom to hold my own personal opinions. My total rejection of the gods has always been considered shocking— all the more so, for some reason, because I am a woman. And, coming as I did from a godless home, I was shocked at first to find what an important part the deities played in the life of Greece's most civilised city.

In fact I think I was the only genuine disbeliever left in our group of friends. Anaxagoras had been my great ally; once he was exiled I was on my own. There were many others who didn't believe for a moment that there really were a bevy of squabbling gods and goddesses sitting on Mount Olympus planning bad jokes to play on mankind. But, like you, they were incapable of shedding all their inborn superstitions. Just in *case* there was something in it, it was better to play safe and be apparently respectful.

There were also people, like Sophocles, who were truly pious. Yet his concept of the gods was of a single supernatural power rather than a family of deities with human characteristics. And even Socrates believed in some sort of god. He was convinced there must be *some* divine purpose in life to account for the many things we can't explain scientifically. I was equally convinced there was a scientific explanation for everything, if only we knew how to find it.

11

I DIDN'T see 'Antigone' performed in the end. I had wanted to, desperately, and had even convinced you there was nothing wrong in a woman who was eight and a half months pregnant going to the theatre. But early in the morning on the first day of the Dionysia drama festival the birth started, and that was that. I sent Sophocles a hurried note and a lucky charm (his plays were due to be shown on the second day), then retired to the women's quarters.

In spite of my disappointment about 'Antigone', I was rather relieved that the baby chose that moment to arrive. It meant you would be out of the house for four days instead of fussing and worrying and getting in the way. You wouldn't be fretting because I wasn't around, or blaming the poor child for upsetting our normal way of life. I couldn't have sat with you in the theatre anyway—men and women were strictly segregated, and the women in their turn were divided up into Athenians and 'others'. We 'others' were always far more elegant.

The women slaves had everything ready for me and were beside themselves with excitement—it was the first birth in the house for about fifteen years, and from the way they fussed one would have thought I was about to produce a demi-god at least. Amycla, Alcibiades' nurse, appeared to be in charge. She installed me in a vast bed in the room where I had dressed before the wedding, delivered a string of instructions about how I shouldn't move, speak, eat, drink (she hardly tolerated my breathing) and surrounded me with a bewildering array of buckets, jugs and basins.

Nothing much happened that day, so I disobeyed all Amycla's orders. I ate a light meal, drank two cups of wine and wanted to sit in the sun in the courtyard—it was beautiful spring weather. But the old nurse was horrified.

'Really,' she scolded, 'what will you think of next? Don't you know the baby could be born with five arms or something if you do that? It's disrespectful to Apollo.'

I laughed, thinking of Chloe and wishing she were there. Though Amycla wasn't unlike her, being both superstitious and Spartan. For some reason all the best nurses come from Sparta—they have a reputation for being 'good' with children. Perhaps it is because once away from the barracks-like life of their own city they enjoy spoiling other people's offspring in a way that would get them severely punished at home. Amycla could be strict when she wanted to, however, and I had noticed that she at least had some control over Alcibiades. Unfortunately now he was going to school she didn't see much of him.

The pains began late that evening, and as they came faster the room filled up with people—Deinomache, who sat silently holding my hand, the midwife, Amycla, all the women slaves. I thought I saw Alcibiades peering round the door once or twice. It seemed that half the women in the room weren't *doing* anything at all—they were just there to enjoy the show, give contradictory advice and get in each other's way. Then Elpinice arrived, sane and practical, and drove half of them away. During the night someone wrapped in a dark cloak slipped in and sat down silently in a corner of the room. I was too weak to ask questions.

Amycla told me it was a difficult birth, but not unusual for a first child. I know that night seemed to go on for ever. And as I struggled and screamed I vowed that never, never again would I go through such torture. A vow that every woman makes, and forgets the moment it is all over.

My baby was born in mid-morning, on the second day of the Dionysia festival, at just about the time that the rest of Athens was watching Sophocles' 'Antigone'. I was semi-conscious for some time after the birth, lying there in a daze listening to muffled sounds of whispering and splashing water. As I gradually attuned to the different noises I heard the unmistakable, relentless wail of a baby crying.

'Is it a boy or a girl?' I whispered.

'A beautiful boy. The image of the master.'

Amycla's voice sounded very loud and very close. I couldn't possibly have heard wrong. I kept my eyes shut, unwilling to come back to life and face the struggle ahead.

When I finally opened them the sun was streaming in the door. Amycla was standing beside me cradling a tiny bundle wrapped in swaddling clothes. She bent down and lifted my arm away from

137

my side, then reverently laid the bundle beside me, its head resting on my shoulder.

He didn't look a bit like you. He was red and wrinkled and apparently very angry. His miniscule face was screwed up in an expression of impotent fury and outrage at the indignities he had just suffered. He was absurdly small and helpless. He was beautiful. He was perfect. I closed my arm round him to prevent anyone taking him from me, ever. Then I began to shiver uncontrollably, and burst into floods of hysterical tears.

I became aware of Deinomache kissing me and comforting me, and the sobbing stopped as suddenly as it had started. I was no longer cold. I took another long, incredulous look at my baby. He was still there. He hadn't changed. I raised my head and smiled.

'I want to sit up. I'm hungry.'

A dozen hands brought pillows and eased me up onto them. Elpinice was beaming with pride, as though it were she who had just performed the remarkable feat of having a baby. I picked him up and cradled him in my arms—it was amazing how I knew by instinct how to hold him. At that moment I didn't want anyone else ever to touch him. I sat there grinning inanely, nursing my baby, the sun blinding my eyes. I was ecstatically happy.

The cloaked figure in the corner got up and came over timidly to the bed.

'Chrysis! Look—just look at him!'

She leaned over and kissed me. 'He's beautiful. I envy you.'

Deinomache was explaining: 'I hope you don't mind, Aspasia—I knew Chrysis was your greatest friend so I sent her a note saying I thought you'd like her here. You know how it is, one needs friends around at these times and you haven't any relatives in Athens ...'

I was amazed that Deinomache should have been so enterprising, and delighted that Chrysis was there. Although we had seen very little of each other over the past few years she was one of those people with whom you feel completely at home no matter how long you've been parted.

After a bit the women left us alone together—with the baby, of course, and strict instructions that I wasn't to tire myself out. I felt immensely empty (hardly surprising) so asked them to bring some bread and cheese and grapes. We sat there almost silently, nibbling the food and worshipping the sleeping child.

'How does Pericles feel about it?' Chrysis asked.

'Well ...' I didn't want to break the spell and face up to reality. But Chrysis was a friend and a probable ally, so I told her everything. I didn't see how anyone could dream for a moment that I would ever leave the helpless baby in my arms to starve to death on a hillside.

'I see. Does he mean it, do you think?'

'I honestly don't know. Socrates thinks he'll back down, but he'd have to swallow an awful lot of pride. And he's not good at that.'

'From what I've heard, the Olympian would go into exile rather than give you up. But you know how people talk. Incidentally, I hope he's not going to mind too much when he hears I've been here.'

'Too bad if he does,' I said grimly. 'You're going to come here a lot more—provided I'm still here, that is.'

Chrysis was thinking. 'Titormos is away for a few months so I could look after the baby for a bit—I'd love to. But I can see from the look of you that you're not going to be parted from him. No, if the worst comes to the worst you'd better both come to me—it's peaceful at home at the moment and you'd be better off there than with Manto and the girls.'

I was very grateful to her. Chrysis was always calm and practical. She *did* things instead of just talking.

'We'll know one way or other within the next five days. I'll send you a note. I just hope it isn't asking you to prepare for the invasion of a refugee mother and child.'

She smiled comfortingly. 'It'll be all right. You'll see. I doubt if Pericles realises you meant what you said.'

'Well, he's going to find out now.' We both looked lovingly at the baby, struggling inside his tight swaddling clothes. Whatever happened, things weren't going to be too bad after all.

Late that night I had just fed the baby, and the women had insisted on taking him away so I could get some sleep, when a shadow appeared in the doorway.

'Aspasia?' you whispered.

'Darling! I'm here.'

You lurched forward, tripped over the bed and practically fell on me, smothering me with kisses.

'I didn't know where to find you . . . I'm not used to this part of the house . . . I didn't know if they'd let me in . . .' You were babbling incoherently and had obviously been drinking.

I held you tight—like the big baby you were—as you asked, urgently: 'Are you all right? Are you *sure* you're all right? I was worried . . . it went on so long . . . I thought I heard you screaming . . .'

139

Trust you not to know that women generally scream during childbirth—if they don't, they're probably dead.

'Yes, yes, my love. I'm perfectly all right. It's all over now. Tell me about what you've been doing, tell me about the festival.'

'But shouldn't you be sleeping or something? I mean . . . you must be tired.'

'No I'm not, I'm wide awake,' I lied. 'Come on, lie here beside me and tell me all about it.'

You relaxed a bit as you lay there in my arms telling me about the two days' plays. Sophocles' four entries had been a triumph and you were certain he would win. A crowd of people had come back to our house that evening to celebrate—which explained why you had been drinking.

'We missed you,' you murmured. 'It didn't seem right without you.' You added, awkwardly: 'They all send their love—and congratulations.'

That was the only veiled reference you made to the fact that you had a new son. I was glad in a way—it seemed too early to start the inevitable fight. And I loved you so very much I was overflowing with enough maternal instinct for a dozen babies and you as well.

You were chattering drowsily on when you suddenly stopped short, sat up and swore.

'Oh *no!*'

'What on earth's the matter?'

'Oh darling, I'm sorry. The last thing I meant to do was this . . . I suppose it's because I've missed you so much. I'd better go . . .'

The shape of your body was silhouetted against the doorway and I could see what was troubling you. I stifled my laughter and pulled you closer to me.

'Don't be a fool. Come here, closer. That's right.'

I took you in my hand. Then you sank back on the pillows, exhausted (anyone would think *you* had just had a baby).

'I didn't know, I never imagined, that a woman could be like this so soon after . . . I love you, I love you . . .'

You fell fast asleep, snoring, and were still there some time later when a slave poked her head round the door to see if I was awake and she could bring the baby for his feed. She retreated hurriedly when she saw you, but Amycla was not to be deterred by a mere man. She came storming in, brandishing a lamp, and delivered a fearful lecture about the dangers of wearing me out, inducing 'complications', sapping my strength and the gods know what else (she'd have had a fit if she'd known what we'd actually been doing). You

140

slunk away shame-faced to the other part of the house, pausing in the doorway to ask wistfully:

'You'll come back to our bed soon?'

'Very soon.'

'Promise?'

'Promise.'

I blew you a kiss and you went obediently away. I think you realised they were going to produce the baby, and you didn't want to see him, to accept the fact that he really existed.

You came to see me the next two nights, too, rather more soberly. We talked about the day's plays—Sophocles had, as expected, won the tragedy prize—and echoed your indignation about the way the comedy writers, on the last day, had all made jokes at our expense. Secretly, I thought them quite funny. It seemed to me a healthy sign that the city's leaders could be openly ridiculed in front of an audience of thousands. You were oversensitive about it, however, particularly when there were references to me being a prostitute, a brothel-keeper and so on. And I must admit that I never actually *saw* any of these plays—women weren't allowed in the theatre on the last day of the Dionysia when the comedies were shown.

As you left my room on the third evening you said stiffly: 'Tomorrow we'll have to talk, I suppose.'

I knew what you meant. The truce couldn't go on for ever. I had been questioning the slaves about traditional procedure and discovered that on the fifth day you were expected to announce formally to the household whether you were going to keep the child or not.

'I suppose we shall. Will you be going to your office as usual?'

'Yes. I'll be home at lunch time. Goodnight, my darling.'

'Good night.'

To Amycla's dismay I insisted on getting up the next morning. I still felt weak, but well enough to walk slowly over to the other side of the house, where Andromeda helped me wash, do my hair and make up my face. I put on one of my prettiest dresses—it was wonderful to feel relatively slim again—then lay down on a couch on the main veranda and demanded that they bring the baby.

Amycla was aghast. 'You *can't* have the baby in this part of the house.'

'Why ever not?'

'It just isn't done. What if he cries?'

'If he cries, he cries. I want him here and I want him with me, so please go and get him.'

She fetched him very unwillingly and deposited him on the couch beside me, shaking her head as if to say this would be the end of both of us. Apollo obviously disapproved.

So you found me lying there with the baby in my arms when you came home for lunch. You looked panic-stricken for a moment, then pulled yourself together and came over to kiss me, studiously ignoring the child.

'Hello, darling. It's good to see you up. Are you sure it's not too soon?'

'No, I'm fine. Meet your son.'

You eyed him nervously. 'Hmmm. Is it healthy?'

'Perfectly. And he looks like you.'

I pulled back the clothes from his head to show that he did indeed have a tiny domed forehead. You looked both fascinated and repelled.

'Are all babies as . . . as crumpled up as that?'

'Yes, I suppose so. Haven't you ever seen one before?'

'I don't think so. No, I'm sure I haven't. How could I have done?'

You flung yourself down on a couch and began to talk about the day's business, asking my opinion and advice about things which had come up during my four days' 'absence'. We managed to talk almost naturally, ignoring the baby who fortunately went on sleeping quietly. There seemed to be a lot to talk about—or perhaps we were both putting off the moment of truth.

When the time came to feed him I simply slipped my dress off my shoulders and held him to my breasts, still carrying on our conversation. You looked away at first, embarrassed. But then you broke off what you were saying to exclaim, almost with awe in your voice: 'By the gods, you're beautiful. I've never seen you look so radiant. You're a different woman . . . fantastic . . .'

I think we both knew then that there wasn't going to be any fight after all. The only problem was—how were you going to concede defeat without feeling too humiliated? I couldn't resist teasing you a little, so got up slowly, picked up the baby and held him out to you.

'I've got to go inside for a moment. Hold him for me, would you?'

You were appalled and shocked. 'Me? But I can't! What if I drop it, what if someone comes in and sees me, what if it starts to cry?'

'You won't drop him. Here, hold him like this.'

I left you gingerly clutching the small bundle, looking more scared than if the whole Spartan army was outside the front door. When I came back you were rocking him frantically to and fro, and I'm almost sure I saw you whispering at him. Evangelos had appeared silently on the other side of the courtyard and actually had a smile on his mournful face.

'It hiccoughed or something,' you said accusingly. 'I thought it was going to choke.'

'That's nothing to worry about. He always hiccoughs after his feed.'

I was feeling worn out by this time, so as soon as people began to drift in I went back to the women's quarters and slept. But I was determined not to stay there—my 'behave normally' tactics seemed to be working well and I had to keep them up. I joined you, Sophocles and Pheidias for dinner, and we dissected every play that had been performed at the Dionysia till late in the evening. I was glad that 'Antigone' had been the biggest success of all.

When the others had gone you stretched out beside me and squeezed my hand.

'Tired?'

'A bit.'

'Poor darling. I think you're magnificent. Do you know, I never dreamed, I could never have guessed that you'd be, well . . . *normal* like this so soon. I thought it took months to get over having a baby and that even then I'd hardly see you. If you kept it, that is.'

I kissed you. 'It just goes to show how little you know. The baby makes no difference at all.'

'I wish I could really believe that. Certainly you don't *seem* any different—except more beautiful.'

There was a long silence before you asked hesitantly: 'Did you really mean what you said about leaving me if I insist on having it exposed?'

This was it. 'Yes, darling. I did and do. I've arranged to go to Chrysis tomorrow if necessary.'

You gulped. 'Well, actually, you needn't have arranged anything. You see, it hadn't occurred to me that the baby might *look* like me. It's unmistakably an Alcmaeonid. If we exposed it, a childless couple might take it, or it might get brough up in a brothel or even sold to the mines. It's unthinkable that a recognisable Alcmaeonid should end up like that. So I'm afraid we'll have to keep it.'

I breathed a long, silent sigh of relief. You had thought up your own way out of the dilemma without losing face. You have even made it look as though *you* were having to persuade *me* to keep the child. I wanted to burst into tears of joy, relief, gratitude, but held them back.

'Yes, I'm afraid we shall,' I agreed. 'What shall we call him?'

'Pericles. Alcmaeonid boys are generally called after their grandfather, but we've already got a Xanthippos. The only other possibility is Ariphron, and I don't think we want a constant reminder of my brother?'

'Certainly not.' I would have agreed to any name you suggested, I was feeling so relieved. And it *was* supposed to be the father's prerogative to choose the name. I was pleased you were not too ashamed of your son to give him your own name, and thanked the gods you were so unknowledgeable about babies—otherwise you might have realised they nearly all have protruding skulls.

'Good. That's settled then. Pericles it is. Tomorrow we'll have the fifth day feast and I'll announce that we're going to keep it . . . I mean him.'

It was time for young Pericles' feed. I said wistfully: 'I'd like to come and sleep with you, darling. But it would mean getting up again later on—he has to be fed regularly.'

'Well, why don't you go and feed him now, then bring him back with you? I want you with me, and I don't like you wandering about the house in the middle of the night in your weak state.'

I could hardly believe my ears, and was half way to the women's quarters before you could change your mind. Amycla, needless to say, found the whole idea scandalous. But the outcome was that you, your son and I slept in the same bed. He had rather a meagre feed because you insisted on sharing it. And the wonderful child didn't cry once, all night.

The women who had been present at the birth were all supposed to attend the fifth-day feast as witnesses that it had really taken place. I would have thought the evidence was undeniable, though there is always the possibility that a couple might try to pass off someone else's exposed infant as their own. So early next morning I wrote Chrysis a note:

'All well. Your sleep won't be disturbed by howling baby after all. Come and celebrate this afternoon—it's a family affair which might amuse you. Go to the back door and ask for Deinomache. And dress soberly!'

I was undecided about whether or not to tell you Chrysis was coming. I didn't want to upset you again when you'd been so magnanimous, yet it might be worse still if you just found her there. You left for the office before I'd made up my mind, so I simply asked Deinomache to look after Chrysis when she arrived —they seemed to have made friends—and hoped for the best.

Fortunately you were in a good mood. It was a glorious spring day, you had just heard that the Parthenon would be finished for the next Great Panathenaea, and secretly I think you enjoyed the prospect of presiding over this informal ceremony. It only included people who actually lived in the house or had helped with the birth, so we didn't have to worry about your hostile relatives. By the time you got home there were garlands hanging on the front door and a strong smell of cooking cabbage—for some reason the traditional delicacy for the fifth-day feast.

The door porter had been told to keep everyone away that afternoon, and there was a flurry of activity between the two halves of the house. Evangelos and Amycla were jointly in charge; they knew exactly what was supposed to happen, so you and I resigned ourselves cheerfully to doing what we were told. We sat in the sunshine as you ate your lunch and I gave little Pericles his—then the women took him away to dress him up for the occasion. You looked happier and more relaxed than I had seen you for months.

Deinomache came timidly into the main courtyard leading Chrysis by the hand. I took a deep breath.

'Darling, you remember Chrysis, don't you? They called her when the baby was born, so I thought she'd better be here today.'

For a moment you looked furious, and I felt bad about having tricked you. For I knew, and you knew I knew, that you would never be rude to a woman in your own house, whoever she was. But one glance at Chrysis reassured you. She looked so demure, so respectable, so innocent that nobody could have accused her of being a 'loose woman'.

You gave me a quick look, half reproachful, half amused, then smiled at Chrysis.

'How are you? Yes, we met at Aspasia's old house. It's a pleasure to see you again.'

From then on you positively oozed charm all afternoon. You were courteous to Chrysis, friendly to Deinomache, almost flirtatious with Elpinice. You joked and laughed with the women slaves, appealing to me when you couldn't remember (or had never known) their names. When you saw your son Paralos standing awkwardly in a corner you called him over, took his arm and kept him with you 'as an ally against all these women'. The boy glowed with pride and pleasure.

Of course your only serious rival for feminine attention was Alcibiades. He was everywhere, showing off, playing the fool, asking precocious questions.

He asked me in a loud voice: 'Will you let me know next time you two are going to make a baby? I'd like to learn how to do it.'

There was a general horrified gasp of 'Alcibiades!' as you saved the day by saying, without the trace of a smile: 'You can't learn to do it till you've got the equipment to do it with. By that time you'll be only too eager to teach yourself.'

This silenced him. He thought it over, then vanished mysteriously for a few moments. Knowing him, I would guess he was examining his equipment to try and find out what it lacked. He was slightly in awe of you, and didn't dare provoke you any further.

It was a silly, idiotic, happy afternoon. The ceremony itself was a big joke: Amycla, followed by a small procession, solemnly carried the baby round the house introducing it to him and him to it. Then everybody gathered in the main courtyard to hear you make a little speech: 'I, Pericles, son of Xanthippos, declare that this child is my son, born to me by my wife Aspasia. He will be brought up in my house and accorded all respect due to a member of my family.'

I didn't know whether to laugh or cry as Amycla respectfully handed the baby to you and you stood there holding him gingerly, not sure what to do. I took him from you and grinned. 'You make a handsome father.'

'You make a beautiful mother.'

Then we all, men, women and children, went in to eat the ritual cabbage. You were so mellow you even condescended to tell Alcibiades and his brother Cleinias the stories of some of the plays you'd seen at the Dionysia. And you promised to take them up to the Acropolis with you one evening. Elpinice, who was enjoying herself immensely, caught my eye and winked. The Olympian was almost unrecognisable.

We soon found it was extremely confusing have two people called Pericles in the house, even though one of them had nothing to say for himself as yet. And much as I loved the name it seemed rather too weighty and dignified for such a comic small creature. The problem was solved when I went to see Manto to brag about the joys of motherhood. She couldn't resist abbreviating names, referring to 'Asp', 'Chrys', 'Tito' (Titormos) and, appropriately,

'Tease' (Socrates). She immediately named the baby 'Peri', which sounded just right for a week-old infant. Peri he became, and Peri he has been ever since.

It wasn't easy during those first few days and months to keep up the illusion—for you—that the baby made very little difference to life. But I did my best. I wanted you to love your son, so whatever happened you mustn't resent him, mustn't feel he was taking me away from you. Thank the gods he was an exceptionally well-behaved baby who hardly ever cried. I kept him with me as much as I could and you soon got used to him. Little by little you even started playing with him, asking questions about him, actually *talking* to him in rather self-conscious baby-talk. He didn't realise what an unprecedented honour this was.

You had wanted me to hire a wet-nurse—it was the accepted thing to do if one could afford it, which we could. You thought, perhaps rightly, that it would be less tiring for me if I wasn't feeding Peri myself. But I *liked* nursing him; why pay a substitute mother when there was a perfectly adequate real one on the spot? So when his feeding times arrived I simply fed him without any fuss, and regardless of who was there. I didn't see why I should retire modestly to the women's quarters to feed my son, as long as you didn't mind your friends seeing my breasts. I think secretly you were rather proud.

It was taken for granted that Amycla would stay on with us as Peri's nurse—provided she could bring herself to tolerate what she called my 'goings-on'. If she had had her way he would have been shut away in the nursery, to be produced for my inspection once a day. She never stopped lamenting the fact that I kept him with me, that he and I both spent most of our time in the front of the house 'where babies don't belong,' and above all that I insisted on having him there even when, as nearly always, we had visitors. When I asked what was so wrong about this she retaliated firmly that it simply wasn't right. And whenever it was time to wash or change him she came and whisked him away with a look of offended triumph, as if she were rescuing him from a den of iniquity.

I did let her look after him at night; it would have been too much to ask you to let him sleep with us all the time. And infatuated though I was with the baby, even I was glad to be free of him for a few hours. You were thoughtful and solicitous and loving and still amazed that I could apparently be a mother, wife and companion all at the same time. I was calm and placid and content. We were both very happy.

We had even survived the formal ceremony on the tenth day after Peri's birth without too much trouble. It reminded me of our wedding—the same ritual sacrifices followed by a banquet, the same feeling of being on stage in a meaningless play. Yet it was necessary, as legal proof that a child was recognised by its father. And, as with the wedding, the more friends and relatives who heard you inform the gods of your intentions, the more legal they became. Fortunately most of your family refused to come—they were probably busy writing scandalised letters to each other about the shame of rearing a bastard. I was glad—it would be several years before Peri's mixed parentage caused any real problems. And there were more than enough friends at the banquet to witness the fact that you recognised your son.

Everyone brought presents: gold and silver trinkets, rattles, little clay dolls, perfect models of athletes, soldiers, charioteers. The household slaves had realised this was a baby who was going to move about the house instead of living in the nursery, so made him a tiny bed on wheels. I had never seen anything quite like it; it proved to be the most useful piece of furniture ever invented (I think it was Evangelos' idea). The women had made cushions and covers for it, and it even had a sunshade for the summer. Manto, Melissa and the other girls at my house sent a silver cup inscribed 'To Pericles, from his aunts'. His real aunt sent nothing. Chrysis brought lengths of the purest Milesian wool in all the colours of the rainbow (shades which might be considered 'immoral' for a woman but were simply 'cheerful' for a child). Socrates had made a grinning stone dog, almost life-size, which he pointed out would be far less trouble than a real one. And Sophocles had written a full-length play in which all the characters were children or child-gods and nobody came to a tragic end.

You and I were expected to produce gifts, too, even though Peri was quite oblivious to all this generosity. To my amazement you decided to give him your grandfather's gold signet ring with the Alcmaeonid crest, which you had always said you would never part with. 'He's going to have a difficult life,' you said wryly. 'It may bring him luck.' And I had a beautiful gold chain, inherited from my father, which was too heavy for a woman to wear. We hung the ring on it and laid them out with the other presents in front of the shrine to the household gods.

You made a longer speech this time, invoking all the deities who were supposed to protect the child. Then you announced his name and we all thankfully trooped in to the banquet. Deinomache,

Elpinice and Chrysis were the only other women there; we soon forgot babies and were immersed in politics.

Your family waited till several months after Peri's birth before launching their attack on your latest example of 'immoral' behaviour. And then they used Alcibiades, of all people, as their excuse.

He had been behaving very strangely since Peri was born, sulking, crying, almost refusing to speak to me. I supposed he missed being the baby of the house and was jealous of the attention that even his own mother, Deinomache, paid to Peri. He became more disobedient than usual, wouldn't listen to a word his tutor said, and was described by his exasperated teacher as a 'disrupting influence' at school. Amycla would probably have given him a sound spanking, but she was too busy with Peri to take much notice of him and he was careful to keep out of her way. It was only when Socrates came that he seemed to be his normal lively self—but Socrates could hardly spend hours every day humouring an 8-year-old child.

He spent more and more time playing in the street with a group of boys from the carpenters' district. You disapproved, but I didn't really blame him—it wasn't much fun for him at home with the women, and Amycla refused to allow his 'low class' friends into the courtyard. I suspect he treated the other boys worse than slaves and realise now that it was probably very bad for his already exalted sense of self-importance.

One day they were playing knucklebones in a street near the market place, when a loaded waggon wanted to get past. Alcibiades had just thrown the dice, and 'commanded' the driver to stop while he finished his turn. The man naturally took no notice—Athenians do not take orders from eight-year-olds. Whereupon Alcibiades threw himself down in the dusty street right in front of the horses, and the panic-stricken driver had to pull them up with a jolt. People rushed to see if he was hurt, but he stood up with an insolent grin, saying: 'That will teach people to obey Alcibiades.'

You were furious and gave him a thrashing which seemed to do some good. His behaviour improved slightly, and we would probably have forgotten all about the incident. But the angry driver had lodged an official complaint, the story went all round the city and a few days later you received a pompous letter from Ariphron.

It went on and on about the corrupting influence our depraved household was having on two innocent young boys—Alcibiades and his elder brother Cleinias. The business with the waggon was, according to Ariphron, a direct consequence of the fact that we had dared to conceive and keep 'a shameful bastard'. He made it sound as if Alcibiades had been the most well-behaved child in the world before entering an atmosphere of 'whoredom and harlotry'. If Alcibiades was already past redemption, he wrote, surely conscience should prompt you to think of 'that sweet boy Cleinias'. As joint guardian of the two boys he felt it his duty to beg you yet again to throw me and my bastard out of the house, if the great name of the Alcmaeonids was not to be for ever stained and sullied.

Once you had stopped cursing your brother, I made a suggestion: 'If he cares so much about "that sweet boy Cleinias" why doesn't he remove him from our sinful influence? After all, Ariphron is as much the boys' guardian as you are, and he's never offered to do a thing for them.'

You frowned. 'Hmmm . . . I wouldn't want a son of mine to go anywhere near Ariphron's house. He'd learn nothing but pomposity and prejudice. But I suppose with Cleinias it wouldn't make much difference—the boy's an idiot. At the age of ten he can't read a line or write his own name.'

It was true. The poor child was very backward and seemed quite unable to learn. One of the reasons I suggested that Ariphron took him was because I knew it irritated you to see him standing about staring vacantly into space. It might just help him not to be continually compared with his brilliant brother Alcibiades.

We consulted Deinomache, who seemed to welcome the idea. Although she was fond of Cleinias, it upset her to have the big boy following her about silently all day like a reproachful dog (after a few days at school we had realised it was a waste of money and stopped sending him). Alcibiades' tutor, Zopyros, patiently tried to teach him to read, but all he could ever learn was nursery rhymes. He did have a feeling for music, however, and played the lyre extraordinarily well.

So we wrote briefly and coldly to Ariphron, saying that since it might be good for Cleinias to be away from Alcibiades' influence we suggested that his joint guardian should take him over. Ariphron agreed unwillingly, so Cleinias went to join a family that consisted of Ariphron, his son Hippocrates and the formidable Anactoria (Hippocrates' mother had died in childbirth, so your sister ruled the house).

I suppose he was there about three months. I had heard from the slaves, who heard it from Ariphron's slaves (family feuds didn't apply in the kitchens) that he appeared to be more miserable than ever. In our house at least we had tried to be kind, but in Ariphron's he was either screamed at or ridiculed. He wasn't allowed to play his lyre because Hippocrates was jealous of his talent. He was mercilessly teased and bullied by Hippocrates and his friends, who were all a few years older. And the result was that he became so terrified he wouldn't even speak the few words he did know.

Things came to a head when Ariphron 'the bestial ball' tried to seduce the backward boy—or at least I imagine that's what happened. I heard from the slaves that the old fool was scratched and bruised as if he'd been fighting a wild animal. And the same day we got a letter saying that since Cleinias was a wicked, depraved character who might corrupt his cousin Hippocrates, Ariphron was sending him back at once to the brothel where he belonged.

I was amazed and touched when Cleinias flung himself into my arms, sobbing with happiness to be back. After a few days he stopped looking scared and began to smile more than he had ever done before. He formed a great attachment to Peri, to whom he became a devoted watch-dog. And although he never developed beyond the mental age of about five, he seemed perfectly happy to carry on his limited life in the women's quarters, pouring his heart out on his lyre and glowing with pleasure when anyone took the trouble to be kind to him.

Writing about Cleinias worries me—how should I feel if I ever had a child like that, physically normal but mentally deformed? There's no way of telling when it's born. It matters particularly now that I am pregnant by my husband Lysicles. Cleinias, of course, was an Alcmaeonid, and more and more members of your illustrious family seem to be giving birth to imbeciles. A physician I was talking to the other day has the interesting theory that it's because you intermarry whenever possible, so as not to 'taint' the stock with outsiders.

How I hope this new child won't be too much like Lysicles. He's a considerate husband, he doesn't interfere in my private life, yet after a day spent listening to Socrates or Sophocles I can hardly bear to spend the evenings with him and his noisy, boisterous friends. He wants me to be there, of course, to show me off. And he's delighted about the baby—no problems this time about whether or not it will be exposed. I shall use the pregnancy as an excuse for being unsociable. Lysicles has just been elected a general, and is unbearably excited about it since he's the first tradesman ever to achieve this position. I think he sees himself as a second Pericles. How I wish he were.

12

As Peri got older and more demanding it became increasingly difficult to keep him in the background. A baby who just eats and sleeps and smiles is one thing; an infant who crawls round your feet, pulls your beard, beats on your helmet and wails for attention in the middle of a complicated financial discussion is another. Peri was good, but he was lively and curious and interested in everything. I refused to let Amycla keep him in the women's quarters all day, so had somehow to solve the problem of carrying on our usual social afternoons with an active baby around. Evangelos made a sort of wooden pen for him which helped a lot. but it was just beginning to become too much of a strain when an international crisis temporarily solved the problem—by taking you away.

The 'Aspasian War' began soon after Peri's first birthday and looked as if it wouldn't last more than a month. Needless to say, it had nothing at all to do with me. But since my home city of Miletos was involved, half Athens was convinced that I had started it.

Miletos was having a silly squabble with the nearby island of Samos, her traditional enemy, about possession of a small town in the Ionian area, and nobody expected the big powers to interfere. But both Miletos and Samos were members of the Athenian alliance, and when the Milesians started to get the worst of it they sent a delegation to Athens complaining that Samos was planning to defect from the alliance.

At this point I am supposed to have implored you to send help to my home city against the hated Samians—hence the 'Aspasian War'. In fact I did exactly the opposite. I pointed out that it probably wasn't even true that Samos was planning to leave the Athenian alliance—it might just be a trick by Miletos to get help in a private war which was none of our business. If we once became involved it really *could* lead to rebellion all along the Ionian coast, the

Persians would welcome the opportunity to help the rebels and the rest of Greece would join in. Even if it was restricted to Samos, the island had a fleet of seventy ships and we only had sixty ready to put to sea. It seemed much more sensible to keep on good terms with Samos by refusing to interfere at all.

I think you secretly agreed with me—you hated the idea of wasting time and money which could be used for the building programme at home. But common sense was outvoted in the name of 'democracy'. For Samos was one of the few remaining members of the alliance still governed by a handful of conservative aristocrats, and the majority of Athenians were persuaded that it was our duty as head of the alliance to impose a 'free' democracy there. I thought it was outrageous—we certainly had no right to meddle in the island's internal affairs even if the aristocrats were less reliable allies than democrats would be. It could only cause major trouble. And of course it did.

As a formality, Samos was ordered to break off her war with Miletos. And, as expected, she took no notice. So the Assembly passed a decree authorising an expedition to Samos on the grounds that she had disobeyed Athenian orders. Nobody would admit that this was an unjustified invasion of Samos by Athens; it was referred to piously as 'the suppression of a revolt by an ally'.

As General-in-Chief you obviously had to lead this shameful expedition, and duly set sail with sixty ships. It was the first time in five years that Athens had been involved in a war, the first time since our wedding that we had been separated for more than a few days.

It was a relief at first, not having to worry about whether Peri was irritating you, whether you thought I was giving up too much time to him. Life went on much as usual: the same people congregated in our courtyard in the afternoons, our house still seemed to be the focal point for everything going on in the city. Perhaps it had become a habit. Or perhaps I was the main attraction anyway. I was surprised that one or two of the other generals kept on coming, ostensibly to ask me what I thought your opinion would be on various problems that had come up. But after a few days they simply asked my opinion. With you out of the way I didn't care how much of a nuisance Peri was—if people objected to him being there they were free to go somewhere else.

I think some of the more old-fashioned politicians were encouraged to come by Sophocles, who was a general himself that year. It always amazed me that Athenians could be so versatile.

Sophocles, for example, had been city treasurer one year, produced 'Antigone' the next, and was now one of the ten generals. He cared more about being a good citizen than he did about his writing, even though you often told him he was a hopelessly incompetent soldier and should stick to the one thing he did superbly well. I suppose the thing that made Athenian democracy work in those days was the way that everyone was so eager to serve Athens and put city business before his own. Thank the gods Sophocles did at least find time to write his plays.

He arrived one afternoon arm in arm with a man I didn't know who looked as if he wanted to turn tail and run. He was in his mid-forties, tall, slim, with a long thin face and intense brown eyes.

'Aspasia, my dear,' said Sophocles, 'here is someone you're certain to approve of. For while I create characters as they ought to be, he describes them as they really are. You two should have a lot in common. His name, in case you hadn't guessed, is Euripides.'

Of course I had heard of Euripides—he was the most talked about playwright in Athens. He had been writing for about fifteen years, had won the prize at the annual Dionysia drama festival only once, and was generally regarded as shocking, exciting and blasphemous. He was extremely unpopular; nobody had a good word to say for him; yet everyone flocked to see his plays.

I had been curious to meet him for a long time, but although you knew him slightly you despised him because he shirked his city duties. Once when I suggested you brought him to the house you declared pompously that he was a subversive influence. I had read all his plays and thought he was a genius. He was reputed to live like a hermit in a cave on the island of Salamis opposite the port of Athens, to be thoroughly anti-social and to hate all women.

So I was surprised and intrigued when Sophocles brought him that afternoon. And it only took a few moments to realise that the rumours, as usual, were pure invention. He wasn't anti-social; he simply wasn't interested in trivialities. He *was* interested, fascinated even, by other human beings, and gave one the sensation that those extraordinary eyes were probing one's intimate feelings, penetrating something deeper than the mind itself. He didn't speak much, but just stood there observing, sometimes smiling sadly as if at a private vision of grief or suffering. It was disconcerting and provoking; I longed to find out more about him.

Sophocles and I discussed the latest war news—you had dealt easily and firmly with Samos and would soon be sailing for home.

Then he went bustling off on an 'important errand' (probably young and female) leaving me with Euripides.

His face broke into an unexpected smile.

'So . . . this is Aspasia. I'm overwhelmed. You've upset my preconceived ideas.'

I motioned to him to lie down. 'What were they?'

'I expected you to be a shallow, brittle, garrulous companion—the sort of girl who makes me nervous because she is incapable of passion. A decorative butterfly, like Sophocles' mistresses. I know I'm supposed to hate women, and it's true that I do hate artificial puppets masquerading as women. But I adore real women, women who love and hate and fight and suffer. They may be dignified old slaves, they may be barbarian princesses. They may be illiterate, they may—like you—be lucky enough to hold their own, intellectually, in a man's world. What they have in common is a capacity for passion and understanding and resignation and suffering . . .'

He was talking half to himself, explaining a vision of womanhood I had never expected to hear from any man, let alone an Athenian. Then he shook his head abruptly and blinked, as if coming back to reality and the spring afternoon on our veranda.

'Of course I should have known you'd be different. There had to be something exceptional about you if Socrates dotes on you, Sophocles takes your advice, Pericles practically risks his career for you. I didn't realise you are a mother, too—lying there with the baby you are wonderfully serene, with a maturity that only comes through suffering. I used to be quite an accomplished artist; I wish I could paint you as I see you now.'

'I've been lucky enough to be able to fulfil myself both as a woman and as a person,' I said. 'Or the gods were kind to me, if you prefer me to put it that way—but I don't somehow think you do.'

We both laughed and settled down to a passionate discussion of woman's right to be treated as a human being. Euripides was a remarkable man—I felt as if I had known him all my life, as though we spoke our own private language based on a series of assumptions that we alone recognised as truths. Although we had only met that afternoon, he was already an old friend.

Socrates came in, saw us together and groaned.

'Oh no! I can't bear it! The combination of Aspasia and Euripides is more than mortal man can tolerate. Between the two of you you'll have the whole of Athens worshipping the goddess Woman. I think I'll emigrate to Sparta.'

He had brought a present for Alcibiades, and came back later

F

with him and Deinomache. We all had dinner together, arguing fiercely about the message or meaning behind myths and legends we all knew. It was the most stimulating evening I'd had for months, yet I was puzzled: Euripides and Socrates were obviously close friends and had had the same arguments many times before. So why had Socrates never brought the poet to our house, and never referred to him as anything except a vague acquaintance?

I puzzled over it as I tried to get to sleep, and came to the conclusion they were jealous of each other. It was odd, since Sophocles, if anyone, was the person one would expect to be jealous of the younger, controversial playwright. Yet Sophocles seemed to have nothing but affection and admiration for him. Socrates, on the other hand, had no reason to be antagonistic. But there was an underlying tension between him and Euripides, as if each man was too brilliant to be really happy in the other's company. They did admire each other immensely: Socrates refused to go to the theatre unless there was a play by Euripides being shown, and had even been known to endure the two-hour walk down to the port of Piraeos to see a Euripides play performed at the theatre there. And Euripides was often accused of stealing most of his 'shocking' ideas from Socrates. When they were together, however, they behaved like spoiled children.

I think perhaps Socrates wanted to protect me, too. He was deeply fond of me and may have guessed that I would be instantly attracted to Euripides—as indeed I was. This, he reasoned, could create problems and unhappiness. And since, unlike Euripides, he didn't believe in the inevitability of suffering, he did what he could to prevent it. (Once we had met, he was even more worried, particularly since you were away. But however hard he tried to look after me, he couldn't end the 'Aspasian War'.)

I had to admit to myself that I was very disturbed by Euripides. I couldn't get those piercing brown eyes out of my mind, couldn't help comparing his sincerity about things that mattered—at least to me—with the average Athenian's imperviousness to human feelings. I hoped you would come back soon, to reassure me and bring me back to normality.

Euripides came again, a few days later. We talked for hours as he told me about his boyhood on the island of Salamis, his triumphs as an athlete, his ambitions as a painter. I was surprised to find he had been a friend and pupil of Anaxagoras—something else we had in common. It was hardly necessary to explain my thoughts or reasoning to him; he knew them already and was even ahead of me.

He described his cave on Salamis, lined with books. He didn't live there, but used it as a refuge when he was writing. 'It's not my wife's fault that I can't work at home—she keeps out of the way and makes sure I'm not disturbed. It's just that when I'm writing about real people with real passions I can't bear to be surrounded by reminders of our so-called civilisation. I need to forget the polite conventions of society and strip everything of the "moderation" that is so admired as a virtue nowadays. I can't do that in a comfortable house in Athens.'

I understood. 'I should like to see your cave—that is, unless it's completely private?'

'I should like you to see it. But not immediately—isn't the fleet due back in a day or two?'

'Yes, but I don't see what difference that makes . . .'

I knew exactly what he meant, but wanted him to say it.

He took my hand. 'Look, Aspasia, you're an intelligent woman. We both know there's no logical reason why you shouldn't visit my cave any time you like. But there are several human reasons. In the first place, Pericles doesn't like me—he thinks I'm a corrupting influence and a bad citizen. I probably am. In the second place, he's undoubtedly extremely jealous and would resent your visiting caves even with a friend he trusted. In the third place, you're probably in love with him and don't want to hurt him—as you know you would, however unreasonable it may seem. And fourthly, I'm falling in love with you. It's just as well he's coming back. I shall keep away and you'll forget all about me.'

He was right, yet I still didn't want to accept it.

'Surely you can still come to the house, with Sophocles or Socrates? Pericles is a reasonable man, he can't dislike you all that much . . .'

He was suddenly angry. 'For the gods' sake! Why on earth do you think I've never come before to join in the smart chatter of the "Pericles and Aspasia set"? How many times people have begged me to come, saying "all Athens is there"—and how many times I have promised myself that all Athens could do without me. I've nothing against Pericles personally, he's a great man in his way and probably human in private. But I can't take the false, blind self-righteousness of Athenian society. I let Sophocles bring me the other day because I was curious to meet *you*, and I knew I should be able to talk to you without the Olympian's disapproving eye on us. I almost wish I hadn't now.'

I sighed. 'I'm sorry.'

'So am I.' He was speaking gently again. 'And I doubt if Athens will need to defend her glory by attacking an ally again for a year or two.'

I could hardly bear to lose him. It didn't seem fair that two people so obviously made for each other should have to part like this. I picked up Peri defensively, unsure what to do or say.

'Well . . . goodbye then,' I said awkwardly.

'Goodbye. Be happy.'

He kissed Peri, embraced me quickly and almost ran out of the house. I settled down to play savagely with the baby, who may have wondered why his mother was suddenly so anxious to hurl a ball across the courtyard.

You arrived back two days later, full of love and tenderness. You kept saying how much you'd missed me, how you'd thought about me day and night and had rushed things as much as you could to get back to me. I was overjoyed to see you, too—you made me feel safe. I suppressed my irrational feelings of guilt (after all I'd done nothing wrong) and did my best to show you how much I loved you. Every now and again I found myself comparing you with Euripides—particularly when you were being smug or sententious about the war—and hated myself for it.

I was undecided whether to tell you I had met him. If you didn't know, you would have nothing to worry about—though why should you, in any case? But several people had seen him at the house, and if they told you, you might think it odd that you hadn't heard it from me. It would look as if I had something to hide. I realised I was making an exaggerated problem of it, so on the evening of your third day back took a deep breath and said, perhaps too casually:

'By the way, I met Euripides.'

'Oh yes? Where?'

'Here. Sophocles brought him.'

'I should have thought he'd know better. That Euripides is a useless, lazy, unpatriotic bore.'

'What nonsense!'—the words were out before I could stop myself.

You looked at me sharply. 'Don't tell me you liked him? He's got a diseased mind.'

To my fury I was blushing. 'Yes, I quite liked him. You know I've always admired his plays.'

You scowled. 'They're far too clever. His writing is just a trick to make everyone discontented, and undermine popular faith in democracy, the city and the gods. If I had my way his plays would be banned.'

I couldn't control myself—you were being so totally unreasonable. 'They're the greatest plays ever written,' I burst out. 'You're just prejudiced because he refuses to take any part in the mutual admiration society that governs Athens. He doesn't like hypocrisy and I don't blame him.'

'So . . .' you sneered. 'You seem to care a lot about him. How many times did the *great* Euripides come to our house while I was away?'

'Only once.' The moment I told the lie I regretted it—but it was too late to take it back.

'I see. I suppose you found him irresistibly attractive?'

'No, of course not.' There was an angry silence as I tried to pull myself together. 'Please, darling, don't be silly. He came here once, Sophocles was with us, and I found him rather abrupt and rude. I *do* think he's a great writer, but that doesn't mean I think he's a great person as well.'

You were slightly mollified. 'I admit he's very persuasive with words. What I can't stand is his air of superiority when he's with people who really care about the city.'

I counted to ten and said nothing. Once I could trust myself not to sound choked I asked non-committally if the Samos question had really been settled. You said you thought it had. It had all been bloodless and efficient: you had driven out the aristocrats, installed an Athenian garrison and left a board of Inspectors to set up a new democratic constitution. To make absolutely sure there were no reprisals you had seized a hundred hostages—fifty men and fifty young boys—and taken them to the island of Lemnos, more than a day's sailing away from Samos. I stopped myself protesting at the cruelty of taking innocent young boys away from their families, and suggested we went to bed. At least you hadn't butchered everyone on the island.

You drank quite a lot of wine that evening. And you were angry with yourself for seeming to care about Euripides. So you took it out on me. Once we got to the bedroom you were anything but loving and tender—you pushed me onto the bed, pinned me down and assaulted me with savage fury. I had never known you quite like this, and remember thinking during a brief lull that I ought to make you jealous more often. You were relentless, and apparently inexhaustible; you went on for what seemed like half the night, muttering wild threats to kill any man who ever touched me, to kill me if I ever touched another man. I don't think you knew what you were saying, or even that you were saying anything at all. Yet it all came pouring out in a rush of pent-up jealousy and possessiveness. I did my best not to give the impression I was enjoying it— though I doubt if you would have noticed.

You began to get really rough, shaking me, half strangling me. I was more frightened than excited, and was about to plead with you to stop. But you sensed my fear and relaxed your grip on my neck. 'You won't want a man again for a long, long time,' you muttered. Then you sighed, trembled and let yourself go. I thanked the gods that at last you were going to put an end to it.

There was sudden shouting in the courtyard outside and hammering on the door. I don't know how you did it, but you somehow stopped, swore and listened.

'Pericles, it's urgent'—it was Sophocles' voice.

You rolled off the bed and strode out naked into the courtyard. It must have been something exceptional for Sophocles of all people to disturb you in the middle of the night. But I felt too shattered even to raise my head, let alone go out and investigate.

After what seemed like a long time you appeared in the doorway.

'Could you get up, Aspasia? It's very serious.'

'What's happened?'

'Samos. Some of the men we exiled have gone back with an army of mercenaries and recaptured the island. They've imprisoned the Athenian garrison and handed them over to the Persians. And they've somehow freed the hundred hostages.'

I staggered up, wrapped myself in something and went to join the Council of War, consisting of Sophocles, three other generals whom I knew quite well, and a terrified sailor who had brought the news. There was nothing much I could say as you all paced up and down through the dawn, questioning the sailor again and again. One thing was obvious—you would all have to go back to Samos. For this time Athens' honour really was at stake and she had been made to look extremely foolish. There was no point in saying I Told You So. I noticed you were still naked and went to get you a cloak. It was appalling, shameful and true that my immediate reaction was relief and pleasure—for this meant I could see Euripides again.

The Aspasian War had now become so important that all ten generals were ordered to sail to Samos. You left with sixty ships, only two days after we heard the news. You were so busy I hardly saw you, and when I did just had time to notice how unhappy you looked. We had left much more than an orgasm unfinished that night, yet there was no time to bother with personal affairs. Athens, on this occasion, came first. You were up most of the night before you sailed, making last-moment arrangements with Sophocles and the other generals who were going to follow on as soon as more ships were ready. An hour or so before dawn you came into the bedroom where I was lying wide awake, your armour clanking. You squeezed my hand, then kissed it. I had a lump as big as an apple in my throat.

'I wish I didn't have to go.'

'I know.'

'But not because of anything I said the other night. You do know that, don't you?'

'Yes, darling, of course.'

'Remember I love you, always.'

'So do I.'

You hugged me so tight I thought my bones would break against your breast-plate, then you stood up wearily.

'Look after Peri. And take great care of yourself.'

'You too, darling. Come back soon.'

'I will, I promise.'

You walked out into the dark. And I didn't see you again for nine months.

I never tried to explain to you about Euripides because I knew you wouldn't and couldn't understand. There's little point in trying to explain now. I suppose if I hadn't been left alone for all those months nothing would ever have happened between us. Yet I should always have been fascinated by him, always have been curious to find out exactly what I was missing. As it was, I got to know him and love him. And although you'd never believe it, in a way it made me love you even more. I discovered it was possible to love two people at once—when they were two such completely different people as you and he. But not to love them equally. I loved Euripides because he was so like me, because he thought like me, felt like me, knew far more about me the first time we met than you did after sixteen years of living with me. I have never met a man with such an understanding of women. The one thing we didn't have in common was that I was basically happy while he was tortured. We were both misfits in Athenian society, but whereas I, the companion from Miletos, had come to terms with it, he, the wealthy citizen, hadn't, couldn't and never will. And he was incapable of a satisfactory relationship with a woman because he cared too much, suffered too much and ultimately made the woman feel too much was expected of her. Making love to him was, for me, like making love to another girl—there was the deepest affection, tenderness and understanding, but it was never wholly satisfying. He idealised me as the perfect woman, and made me long for a real, arrogant, thoughtless man. Not that there was anything physically effeminate about him—technically he was a better performer than you. But he lacked any conviction of male superiority, so that for me it was nothing more than a gratifying game between two equals. He knew this, and suffered all the more.

I loved you because you were so different from me. I loved you because you would explode with fury if you read this. I loved you because you wouldn't remotely understand why I spend so much time demanding that women should be treated as human beings, then complain when someone treats me as one. That, my darling, is the way we are. Euripides not only knows how both men and women behave, he also knows why—and this knowledge makes him lonely, unhappy, unpopular. We none of us want to face the truth.

I hate to have to face the truth that I am incapable of living on my own. But it's there. If it hadn't been Euripides during those nine months it would probably have been someone else—though there were few enough men left in Athens. You, Sophocles, Meidias, Socrates, everyone had gone, leaving only the old men, the women and the unpatriotic. I missed Socrates very much; perhaps if he'd been here to look after me Euripides would never have happened. If it had just been sex I missed I could have followed most of the other wives' examples and made do with women (I think half of them preferred it anyway). But I missed conversation, I missed intimacy, I missed the sense of belonging, I missed quarrelling with you, humouring you, listening to you, taking you for granted. Euripides was no substitute for you, but he filled the gap with something new.

Lysicles, my present husband, is no substitute for you either. But once again I couldn't face life on my own. And with Lysicles I knew I couldn't even love. At least most of our friends are still here in Athens, and almost as nostalgic as I am for the days of Pericles.

One afternoon in mid-summer Euripides and I were lying on a rock outside his cave on the island of Salamis. We had been swimming—or rather, he had been teaching me to swim—and were stretched out naked in the sun, enveloped in heat and light and contentment.

'This is what I meant about getting away from civilisation,' he said dreamily.

'Mm.m.m. Let's just hope Pericles doesn't come back tomorrow and demand to know why I'm so sun-burned.'

He patted my brown thigh. 'Don't worry. He won't. They've just sent more ships out to join the blockade. It's going to take a long, long time.' He paused, then said softly, in a different tone: 'I wish it would take for ever.'

'It can't. You know it can't.'

He took no notice. 'We could live here together, just the two of us, and my books. It would always be summer, we would always be in love, we would write great poetry and be worshipped as gods.'

I had to laugh. 'You're the one who's criticised for being too realistic, remember?'

He rolled over and put his arm round me. 'I wish I weren't. I wish I could believe this summer would last for ever. But it's no use deceiving myself. At this very moment you're anxious to get back to the child. And I know you'd never leave Pericles for me. You think you love me, but as soon as he's back you won't need me any more.'

I started to protest, but he put his hand over my mouth. 'No, Aspasia, don't try to be kind. You know it's true. You need company as much as I need solitude—and, sadly, you're the only person I've ever been able to share it with. You need all the worldly things I hate. You need your eminent husband, your demanding child, your house, your pretty clothes, your friends. There is room in your life for everything, from the commonplace to the sublime, and you somehow manage to have everything. I envy you. And since there is room for me, too, I only hope I can go on being a very small part of your life.'

He was right. And I *was* worried about getting back to Peri. We clung together for a moment, then dressed and rowed back to the mainland almost without speaking. How could I help loving a man who understood so much?

We had to be extremely careful about meeting. I felt no guilt about our affair as long as nobody was hurt—and you would have been if you had found out. So I was determined you should never know. Euripides came openly to our house occasionally, but I refused to sleep with him there. The slaves would know and the slaves would talk. Yet we both realised, almost from the beginning, that we were going to make love somewhere, somehow. And the obvious place was his cave on Salamis.

My main problem was finding a convincing excuse for being out of the house half the day—it took some time to get down to the coast and then across to the island. Very few people came to the house (practically everyone was away blockading Samos), yet it just needed one person to spread the word that I was vanishing mysteriously and all Athens would have known about it. We needed an accomplice who was reliable, discreet and understanding.

She walked in one day about a month after you'd left, just as Euripides and I were despairing of ever being really alone together. I can't think why I hadn't thought of her before, but the moment I saw her I knew she would help. In fact we didn't hear her come in, and were making love with our eyes when there was a discreet cough behind us.

'I hope I'm not disturbing anything.' It was Elpinice, looking amused.

'Not exactly.' It was useless to pretend—she had summed the situation up at a glance.

'Well, I'm glad to see you have company. And I won't stay long. I came to ask if you have any spare time now you're on your own, but clearly you're not bored.'

'You have an evil mind. What's your problem?'

'My daughters. I've been doing my best to give them an education, but quite frankly I'm not all that learned myself and I've taught them all I know. I'd just got a tutor for them when he went off to Samos. So I thought it might amuse you to try and make cultured women out of them.'

'I don't see why not. Perhaps Euripides could help, too?'

She roared with laughter. 'The poor girls will become brilliantly unhappy. But it's worth trying. I'll leave you two alone together now—come and talk to me about it.'

It was an ideal arrangement. I did take over the education of Elpinice's daughters and greatly enjoyed it, since they were intelligent girls who were eager to learn. Some days they came to our house, some days I went to theirs. And several times I went to their house as usual, slipped out of the back door wearing a slave's cloak thoughtfully provided by Elpinice, met Euripides just outside the city and spent the day on Salamis with him. I knew we could rely on Elpinice to foil anyone who went to the house asking for me; she was one of the few people in Athens who genuinely liked

Euripides, she was virtually unshockable and, above all, she was completely trustworthy. I knew she wouldn't even tell her husband, close though they were. She had had one or two affairs herself in the past, so rather approved of my doing the same. And I later discovered that she was nursing a personal grudge against you for exiling her brother Cimon years before; it amused her to get her revenge by helping your wife commit adultery.

She asked me one day whether I'd mind if she joined her two teenage daughters at our lessons.

'Of course not! But why?'

'Well, now they're prattling away about Homer and Hesiod I'm beginning to feel inferior. My brother taught me all I know, but getting his lessons second-hand wasn't the real thing.'

With Elpinice there, things became really lively. She had a far more detailed knowledge of Athenian history than I did, so that often the 'lessons' became an exchange of information between the two of us, with her daughters listening respectfully and, I hope, learning.

'You realise we're wasted on each other?' she remarked one evening after a heated philosophical argument. 'There are hundreds of women sitting about with nothing to do except play with each other and their babies. They'd be far better off here, learning something.'

'Just try and get them here.' I sighed. 'You know they wouldn't come.'

'They might if I told them to. Some of the younger wives secretly long for something different.'

'Yes, but you know my reputation. I've never met an Athenian wife in my life except you. They'd be terrified to show their faces in what my sister-in-law calls this "house of shame".'

'Don't be too sure,' she said knowingly. 'I know one or two who have always wanted to meet you but never dared ask. At the worst they can only get a beating from their husbands—who probably come here themselves.'

Three days later she appeared with two women of about my own age who seemed too scared to open their mouths—except to gape. I don't know what sort of den of iniquity they had expected to find; certainly not a perfectly normal home housing a normal mother and baby. They lay gingerly on the veranda looking longingly towards the women's quarters, starting at the sound of footsteps as though they were afraid of being caught on men's sacred ground.

They came back, however, bringing their friends. Within a month there were about twenty altogether, listening wide-eyed to what Elpinice and I had to say, not daring to ask questions. They reminded me of my father's wives.

The trouble was that while it was a wonderful idea in theory, in practice it just didn't work. Ideally, I would have liked to start a sort of women's club where Athenian wives could find new interests beyond their kitchens and their nurseries and at the same time become more interesting to their husbands. There was no logical reason why they shouldn't spend their afternoons discussing the world and trying to put it right, just as their husbands did. But, with one or two exceptions, they were too timid, too frightened of trespassing on what they considered to be men's territory.

The thing I couldn't fight was these high-born Athenian women's complete, unthinkable acceptance of their supposedly inferior status. It had never occurred to them to question it, and although many of them complained about being bored and unhappy, they had no idea what was wrong. If I suggested that perhaps it was because their men ignored and despised them, leaving them to run the house, look after the children and oversee the slaves while they themselves did nothing more than chatter in the market-place or in the baths, they invariably replied: 'But Aspasia, it's *right* that men should be like that. We don't know anything about culture or politics, why should they stay at home with us?'

I had to be very, very patient. Many of them were shy of revealing what they did know, a few were horrifyingly ignorant of anything which went on outside their own houses. Yet they weren't stupid; it was a condition imposed on them from their earliest childhood and which they accepted because they had no choice. By now it was too late to change their deep-rooted conviction that men were a different, superior species and that women were created solely to serve them. No wonder they were baffled and angered by Euripides' plays —in which women defied, dominated and often destroyed their men.

He may have been a women's champion, but he refused to take my 'club' seriously. One day I suggested he should bring his wife, and he shook his head in mock despair.

'It needs a man to explain to you about your own sex. My wife, Melite, is a simple, good-natured woman, constantly worried because she doesn't know how to please me. The more she fusses the more she irritates me. But it's much too late for her to change. Even if you taught her to read and write, to recite Homer and chart the stars, you wouldn't be able to change her mentality—she would be doing it all from obedience and humility and not because she cared.

If you want to change Athenian women you've got to snatch them in their nurseries—it's no use starting at the age of 25, or even 15. The one or two, like Elpinice, who do manage to be individuals, despite their suffocating upbringing, are generally far more unhappy than the others. She was a social outcast before she married Callias, just because she was "different". My wife believes her place is in the home and it would only confuse her to take her out of it.'

'Yes, but . . .' What he said was true, but this didn't mean it had to be right. I felt he was betraying me.

'Surely there's some slow, gradual way of changing things—even if it's only teaching parents that their daughters have a right to use their minds? Women haven't always been treated like this. I don't see *why* they should have to be.'

'I know, my love. And if you didn't lead such a sheltered life among the leisured Athenian aristocracy you'd realise that all women aren't like that, even now. Athens isn't the world, you know: in other cities and countries women are sometimes allowed to fulfil themselves—as women. Even here in Athens there are thousands of female slaves with personality, passion, a love of life. They are a hundred times more interesting than their inanimate, apathetic mistresses, despite the fact that technically they're not free. And it makes no difference that they're not educated—they somehow manage to be people. Of course it's *wrong* that respectable Athenian women should be denied the chance to be whole human beings. It's disgraceful. But that's the way it is. And not even Aspasia of Miletos can change it.'

I sighed. 'I suppose I ought to be thankful. If Athenian women were released from their mental confinement there would be no need for companions. It's so illogical—men want companions because their wives are so dull, yet refuse to let their wives become interesting. And of course they're forbidden to marry companions. They need two women—one to have their children and one to entertain them. It's impossible for one woman to be both. I try, but, although it sounds silly, I do mind not being "respectable"—as much for Pericles' sake as my own.'

He kissed me—we were lying in his cave. 'You know why you're such a womanly woman? Because you spend so much time with men. They admire you, flatter you, adore you for being the exceptional creature you are. You wouldn't really like to exchange them for a group of intelligent women, however brilliant—you'd be jealous, competitive and frustrated. Women don't want to be with each other, they want to be with men. That's why your "women's club" won't work. You're trying to copy men instead of following your instincts as women.'

'My instinct at the moment is to get you ostracised for destroying all my beautiful ideals. You must admit there's no logical reason in *theory* why husbands and wives shouldn't mix together socially.'

'It's a beautiful theory. And you'd hate to lose your position as the only woman in a man's world. Now stop arguing and be a bit womanly.'

I like to think that my afternoon gatherings for women did do a little good—if only to make them see that an ex-companion could be just as 'civilised' as they were. And as they very slowly lost their shyness, two or three of the wives began to take an active interest in what was being said. It was a big drawback that none of them could read and write, and it was far too late to try to teach them (if I had had the patience, which was doubtful). What they seemed most anxious to learn about was the daily life of Athens, the things their husbands did and discussed and decided during the large part of the day they spent out of the house. Elpinice and I painstakingly described the workings of the city government, administration and legislation, explaining how every citizen had a part to play. We tried to explain the international situation, still dominated by veiled hostility between the two big powers of Athens and Sparta. We had to teach them some elementary geography—few of them had ever seen a map. And we kept them up to date on the progress (or non-progress) of the war in Samos.

As soon as you arrived back there you had settled down to blockade the main city on the island. Unfortunately there was a scare about Phoenician ships coming to the rebels' rescue; you sailed off to intercept them, and the people of Samos managed to break the blockade, get in enough supplies and stores to last for months and take a large number of Athenian prisoners. You never found the Phoenicians—they were probably just a calculated rumour.

You then sailed back to Samos in a panic, defeated their army, set up a stronger blockade with a wall right round the city, and settled down to starve them out. The Samians appealed to Corinth and Sparta for help—this could have started a real world war. But luckily both cities decided they couldn't interfere in a dispute between Athens and one of her allies (or perhaps they didn't feel ready to fight at that time). The new Athenian generals elected in mid-summer took another sixty new ships out to you, and by autumn you had 200 ships and 40,000 men surrounding the island capital.

I was proud, pleased and amused about some of the stories messengers brought back. One of your biggest problems, obviously, was boredom—it wasn't easy to keep forty thousand citizen soldiers sitting idly round a city wall for nine months, and it wouldn't have helped to point out that the siege of Troy took ten years. I gathered that everyone was urging you to attack, provoke the enemy, *do* something instead of just sitting there. You hated wasting lives unnecessarily, and realised that the only way to break down Samian resistance was to starve the city out. To keep the troops happy you invented a system of special leave during which they could rest, eat well, organise games, or enjoy whatever other doubtful pleasures Samos had to offer. The army was split into eight divisions, one of which was always on leave. But instead of taking it in turns, they drew lots with beans, and the division which drew a white bean was the one which had a rest the next day. It may not have been fair, but it gave everyone the hope that he might get a holiday tomorrow. Athenians love drawing lots—half the city officials are chosen that way.

You also devised some ingenious siege-engines and battering rams which were totally ineffective in breaching the city walls but kept the troops occupied and optimistic. In the end, of course, the Samians surrendered from hunger. I don't think they had expected you to stay on through the winter, but once they realised you really would sit it out for ten years if necessary, they had no choice but to give in.

You demolished the city walls, seized the fleet, took hostages and imposed the massive fine of 1,276 talents—which was what the campaign had cost Athens. This was more than double the yearly revenue of the Athenian treasury; you had even had to suspend building on the new temples to find the money. The Aspasian War was expensive, unproductive and completely unnecessary. Miletos was undoubtedly pleased to see her old enemy humbled, but this particular Milesian was sickened and ashamed.

As soon as you all got back, after a terrible mid-winter voyage, most of my new women friends deserted me. Some of them were forbidden to come by their horrified husbands, some were frightened of what their husbands would say. It was one thing to come to our house when there were only women there, quite another when it was once more a meeting-place for men. But a few whose husbands were regular visitors begged, pleaded and bullied to be brought along as well. There was really no logical objection the bewildered men could make, with the result that from then on there were generally

169

several 'progressive' young wives among the Pericles-Aspasia set. I loved to observe the surprise and incredulity of our men friends as they discovered that it was possible for one of their own, respectable Athenian women to be sociable, informed and articulate.

I don't think they really approved—they were scared of what it might lead to. And you certainly didn't. You arrived back from Samos utterly worn out, with a hundred problems to solve, nine months work to catch up on, and a secret sense of fury and frustration at the futility of the whole mess. This unpatriotic reaction made you feel guilty, so you tried desperately to convince me, yourself and everyone else that it had been glorious and worthwhile. You were like a stranger for the first few days, detached, preoccupied, ill at ease. I think you were probably shy, too, after being away so long—whatever it was, I found it impossible to communicate with you. I was hurt and disappointed: after an emotional parting from Euripides I had been looking forward with relief and excitement to your coming back. I had wanted to show you how much I loved you, to make up for the sins you would never know I had committed. In my own mind I had built you up into a sort of superhuman father, husband and lover whose mere presence would put everything right. Instead of which you were just a weary, bad-tempered, confused man.

The public funeral for Athenians killed at Samos was held a few days after you got back, and naturally you had to make the funeral speech. When you gave it to me to read the evening before and asked what I thought, I hadn't the heart to say it was just one long pious platitude.

'It's fine. That's what the people want to hear.'

You sighed. 'You mean it's dishonest and hypocritical. Well, that's just too bad. I'm too tired to write golden words like some of your friends. It'll have to do.'

I ignored the reference, but worried about it half the night as you snored beside me.

I found an excuse for not going to the funeral next day—I didn't want to listen to you declaiming about the glory of giving one's life for one's city. But I heard about it from Alcibiades, who came rushing back to announce with glee that you were in a 'murderous mood'.

'Why, what happened?' I sensed disaster.

'Elpinice made him look ridiculous.'

'How? What did she do?' Elpinice was always trying to get her

170

own back on you for exiling her brother Cimon. It was a friendly battle, but sometimes she took it too far.

'Well, he made his dreary old speech which went on and on, and at the end everyone was weeping and wailing and cheering—you know how they do. The women grabbed him as he walked down from the platform, kissing his hand and flinging flowers and wreaths all over him. Anyone would think he was a victorious athlete. He stood there looking pleased and embarrassed until Elpinice pushed her way through and told him he ought to be ashamed of himself.'

I could visualise it all too clearly. 'What did she *say*?'

'She didn't say, she shouted. She yelled in that piercing old voice of hers that he certainly deserved all those flowers and garlands for his "noble" deeds. For he had thrown away hundreds of Athenian lives, not in a war against Persians or Phoenicians like her brother fought, but in destroying a Greek city that is one of our allies.'

My heart sank. She had tried to make you look a fool in front of the whole city. Nothing could have hurt you more.

'What did he do?'

'He looked straight through her, smiled scornfully and quoted some line of poetry about not wasting perfume on women with grey hair. Then he walked away as if nothing had happened. But I could tell, he's in one of his real tempers. If you don't mind, I'll leave you to deal with him.'

He sauntered away, whistling. He was an impossible child, but a useful ally and informant.

You came in much much later, looking grim.

'You know what happened at the funeral?'

I nodded.

'Well, what *is* all this? What's been going on while I've been away, fighting for all of you? How *dare* a woman stand up and speak at a public function? It's unthinkable!'

'You know Elpinice, she does what she likes . . .' I murmured apologetically.

'Yes, I *do* know Elpinice,' you exploded. 'I've known her far longer than you have. And I know she's a loyal Athenian who would never disgrace herself like that in public. Somebody must have put her up to it, and the only person who could have thought of such a thing is you.'

You raged on and on in an illogical, irrelevant tirade in which all the jealousy and frustration of the past nine months was suddenly released and directed against me. The gist of it was that while you had been away bravely and brilliantly defending Athens—it took you only nine months to capture the most powerful city in the East while it had taken Agamemnon ten years to capture Troy—I had been corrupting respectable women, teaching them unpatriotic, subversive ideas, turning them into prostitutes like myself. We had been making love to one another in front of the children, holding horrific orgies; how could I betray you like this when you were all alone in the battlefield, thinking of me day and night, never looking at boys or women? I was yours, I belonged to you, you couldn't bear to think of me even in a woman's arms ...

This reminded you of something else, and you demanded to know if I'd seen Euripides. Half-truths are safer than complete lies, so I admitted he had been to the house once or twice. You immediately forgot all about the women and launched into a new fantasy in which Euripides the traitor had been sleeping in your bed, corrupting your son, stealing your wife, turning all Athens against you and conspiring with the Samians. You went into graphic and completely inaccurate detail about Euripides' technique as a lover, swore you had proof, witnesses, verbatim accounts of our secret meetings, and promised to kill us both in the near future. At long last, having repeated everything about three times, you staggered out of the room ordering me never to come near you again.

By some superhuman effort I had kept my temper. You were so demented there was no point in arguing—it was as though you had a fever which completely upset the balance of your mind. But it was difficult not to be provoked when you challenged me with these preposterous lies. I kept reminding myself that you couldn't *possibly* know about Euripides and me, that I must just pretend not to take you seriously. Vehement denials could have been incriminating. Perhaps if you had been less crazed I would have been tempted to put up some sort of defence. As it was I could only hope that now you had got it off your chest you would come back to your senses.

I waited about an hour, then went into the bedroom. Pericles the Olympian was lying face down on the bed, sobbing: huge, silent choking sobs. I put my arms round you and you gripped my hand tightly. So I knelt on the bed and pulled your head onto my lap, stroking your domed forehead, running my fingers through your wavy, greying hair. The words you were muttering into my thighs were as incoherent as before, but very, very different. I pulled a blanket round us—it was a cold night—and kept watch over you till dawn.

You had a high fever the next day, so I refused to let you leave the house. And you refused to let me leave you. We lay hand-in-hand on the big bed like a couple of young lovers, except that Peri was crawling all over us. You seemed to think he was the most remarkable baby in the world because at the age of nearly two he was beginning to talk. We didn't say much, and when you tried to apologise I stopped you.

'Don't think about it. The important thing is that you've come back, you're here.'

'I didn't think it was ever going to end. It seemed like nine years.'

Everything was right again, after all. And although we had minor repetitions of the same scene whenever you had been away for any length of time, I got used to it and learned to expect it. It was almost worth it for the calm that followed.

A few days later you said casually:

'By the way, I saw Euripides in the market-place this morning and asked him to come and see us. He seems to have improved lately, to have grown up a bit.'

I made a non-committal noise and expected a trap. But then I reasoned this might be your way of saying you were sorry, showing you didn't mean what you had said. You had certainly put yourself out to be charming to any women who visited the house, and had accepted Elpinice's apology with good grace.

I didn't think Euripides would come, yet he did. It was a strain trying to act and talk naturally, but I don't think it showed. We had a few minutes conversation with nobody else around.

'I thought you couldn't bear the social gatherings of civilised society?'

'It's the only way to see you. I can tell you're happy. I'm glad.'

We exchanged a quick smile of secret understanding before he went off to argue with Socrates. As time went by, and he continued to come to the house just like any other friend, I almost forgot we had ever made love in a cave on Salamis—it seemed like something that happened to another woman in another world. And although he probably wouldn't have admitted it, I think he no longer came just to see me, but because he enjoyed the company and conversation. It wasn't as shallow and hypocritical as he had thought. He stopped being a rebel and became a respectable eccentric.

As I write this, my husband Lysicles is away serving as a general in Caria, not far from Samos. And, coincidentally, Euripides has just been to see me with the first draft of a new play, 'Hippolytos'. I am six months pregnant, so wasn't tempted to elope with him to his cave. We talked lovingly and longingly about you, and felt very old.

173

13

THE next three years were probably the happiest of my life. I had everything I had always wanted: an adoring husband, a beautiful son, the company of the greatest artists, writers, thinkers and scientists in the world. Athens was in an exuberant mood—there were no wars, no major problems—and at times I was almost inclined to agree with you that she wasn't far short of being the perfect city. I was in my late twenties and becoming more mature, more sure of myself. I was no longer a girl, but a contented woman. You were nearly sixty and mellowing with age. You, too, had a new confidence which made you more relaxed and understanding. We depended on each other and trusted each other and loved each other. Friends said you looked ten years younger and I looked ten times more beautiful. I certainly felt that way.

I suppose there must have been cold wet days and stifling heat waves, quarrels and misunderstandings, tempers and tantrums—there always were. But I don't remember them in those three years. I remember sunshine and happiness and you playing with Peri on the veranda. He was an attractive, good-natured child, neither precocious nor backward, and we thought he was a young god. I remember plays, concerts, books, the inauguration of the new temples—everyone seemed to be doing something creative. Above all I remember the afternoons spent talking, debating, discussing new ideas, new theories, new philosophies that probed and questioned every established belief about the world and mankind.

Among the plays I particularly remember four by Euripides performed at the Dionysia festival two years after the Aspasian War. I thought they were the finest I had ever seen. The audience hated them, and he came last of the three competing tragedians. For although he kept strictly to the conventional tragic form—not even taking as many liberties as Sophocles sometimes does—his language and presentation were far too modern and realistic for supposedly civilised Athenians to stomach. They particularly objected to the princess's love song in 'Women of Crete', presumably because it sounded like something a lover might actually say in life. (In fact I had heard the song, privately, two years before in the cave on Salamis.) In their opinion a stage character should say 'I worship thee, beloved' when he or she means 'I love you, darling'. And there should never be any suggestion that this love is anything but pure. Euripides was also attacked for dressing the hero of 'Telephos' in rags when he was disguised as a beggar, although it seemed perfectly reasonable to me. Sex, poverty, dirt and other harsh realities of life are for some reason shocking when portrayed on the stage.

The play I remember best is 'Alcestis', because I suspected (rightly) that it was a complicated joke for my personal benefit. On the face of it it's about a young wife who is so dutiful, submissive and unselfish that she agrees to die in her husband's place (this exchange of bodies is made possible by Apollo, playing yet another little joke). The play was intended as light relief after three heavy tragedies, and the audience liked it more than the others, thoroughly approving the wife's self-sacrificing devotion. What they failed to see is that the whole thing is an attack on our society's inhuman attitude to women. To most Athenians it seemed perfectly right and proper that a pretty young wife and mother should die because her middle-aged husband didn't want to—after all, she was only a woman. Her husband's old parents refused to die in his place, nobody else offered, so the obvious person to save him from death was his wife.

Euripides showed up the husband as a hypocritical fool (though I doubt if many spectators appreciated this). He was afraid of dying, allowed his wife to die for him, then started wallowing in self-pity about what he was going to do without her. Once she was dead and he was still alive he could safely moan that he wished *he* were dead, and that she was luckier than he was. His misery, of course, was all her fault. At least his old father was honest enough to admit that he liked life and intended to cling to the little of it he had left; the two men have a furious argument in which each accuses the other of being heartless and selfish. But the one thing neither of them considers is the feelings of the wife. The only character who cares about her at all is her woman servant.

It all has a happy ending when Heracles fights with Death and brings her back. And here Euripides really enjoyed himself—for Heracles is a very thinly disguised Socrates. He talks like Socrates.

he eats and drinks like Socrates, he even plays a Socrates-like trick by introducing the bereft husband to a veiled woman and not letting him know she is his resurrected wife. The whole thing is a delight from beginning to end, and I was surprised to find that Euripides had such a sense of humour.

The Parthenon temple was finished in time for the Great Panathenaea Festival that year. I think it must be the most imposing, majestic building in the world; it certainly surpassed even your wildest dreams. Perhaps the most awe-inspiring thing about it is its perfectly contrived simplicity: every line, every pillar has a flowing grace that seems so natural one can hardly believe it was all man-made, from shapeless blocks of stone. Inside the huge temple there is nothing out of place, nothing cluttered. Its dark, cool, empty space is the perfect setting for Pheidias' gold and ivory statue of Athena which towers over the altar. Although intended to inspire reverence for the gods, and Athena the Virgin in particular, the Parthenon inspires me with reverence for mankind, and in particular for the men working under Pheidias who in less than ten years created this breath-taking monument to the glory of Athens.

I don't think I have ever seen you as happy as the day the temple and statue were dedicated. You had fought for this temple, you had defended it against critics who said it was too big, too vulgar, a waste of the city's money, you had supervised its building month by month, year by year. Now at last it was standing there, dominating the city. And you were able to lead the Panathenaic Procession up on to the Acropolis to sacrifice to the goddess in this beautiful building.

Pheidias' statue of Athena is a work of art in itself. He really achieved his life's ambition: the enormous figure is seven or eight times larger than life-size, a glittering mass of gold with finely sculpted face and hands made of pure white ivory. Yet it would have been better for Pheidias himself if he really had been too frightened to accept the challenge. For through no fault of his, the statue was his downfall.

As a private joke he had included two rather special figures among the fighting warriors on Athena's shield. One was a bald old man hurling a rock with both hands—easily recognisable as Pheidias himself. The other had his face covered by his arm, but was still unmistakably you. Few people realised these portraits were there; those of us who did know thought it was very funny.

But poor Pheidias had a lot of enemies. In the first place, he was a difficult man to get on with and made no attempt to be polite to people he didn't like. In the second place, his triumphs made less talented people jealous. They resented the fact that a mere sculptor should be a close friend of yours with more influence than many wealthier nobly-born men. By attacking him, they hoped to hurt you, too. About a year after the dedication of the statue they succeeded.

First he was accused of stealing gold intended for the statue—an utterly ridiculous charge. Pheidias was scrupulously honest and would have been incapable of stealing even if he was starving. Fortunately he had made the gold plating on the statue detachable in case it was ever needed during a financial crisis; it was taken down and weighed, and of course not a drachma's worth was missing. But during this operation some busybody had noticed the two innocent little portraits on the shield. There was an outraged cry of 'sacrilege!', and the world's greatest sculptor was sent to prison.

Thank the gods you *were* his friend and had enough influence to get him out. He had to leave Athens, however, and went into exile in the Peloponnese. He set up a workshop at Olympia, where he sculpted a gold and ivory statue of Zeus which is even larger than our Athena. People who have seen it tell me it's the most impressive thing he ever did.

So your enemies had managed to exile both Athens' most eminent philosopher, Anaxagoras, and her leading sculptor. It seemed so unfair that these two men should be victims of petty political rivalries, especially since neither of them took the slightest interest in politics. And the banishment of Anaxagoras and Pheidias made no difference at all to your political position. It just deprived Athens of two great talents.

In fact soon after Pheidias left Athens your prestige was increased by a peaceful naval expedition to the Black Sea. Although you didn't want to leave home and I didn't want you to go, we both saw that it was necessary in order to safeguard the city's corn supplies. Athens, with a total population of around two hundred thousand, couldn't possibly exist on the small amount of corn produced from the rocky soil in surrounding Attica, so had always had to import the bulk of the city's basic food. Egypt and Sicily could no longer be relied on as stable sources of supply, and we were trading more and more with Greek colonies and native tribes round the Black Sea.

Your goodwill mission was a great success. There were at least a dozen Greek cities scattered round the great Northern sea, all of them prosperous, but beginning to feel neglected and cut off from civilisation. Their citizens were pleased and impressed that Athens should send an imposing fleet under Pericles himself to help solve their commercial squabbles and offer protection against the inland barbarians. The natives were even more impressed by the size and power of the fleet which sailed wherever it liked, even among lands ruled by the fiercest warrior tribes. You made trade agreements for corn, hides, dried fish, iron and unskilled slaves, and stopped off on the way back to help the people of Sinope overthrow their tyrant. Conservatives at home complained bitterly about the cost of the expedition, which was only a fraction of what was spent on the unnecessary 'Aspasian War'. And the peaceful Black Sea mission did far more good for the city.

You were away for several months altogether but the time passed very quickly. Peri was four years old and exhausting to be with, since he never stopped asking questions. He was growing up among articulate adults instead of gossiping women, and he had become a serious, independent little boy with an absorbing interest in how and why things worked. He asked intelligent questions and expected intelligent answers; I wished he could have started school, but no schoolmaster would take him before he was six. And even then he wouldn't be able to go to one of the good schools for citizens' sons, just because I wasn't Athenian. I gave him a few elementary lessons myself and then Euripides, surprisingly, offered to take over.

'Peri's far more rewarding to talk to than half the best educated men in this city,' he muttered apologetically. 'So far he's got no prejudices.'

So visitors to the house were amazed and amused to see Euripides sitting in a corner deep in conversation with a four-year-old boy. Two or three times a month they went over to Salamis for the day— 'He's got to learn to love books,' said Euripides—and I laughed wryly at the thought that Peri had taken my place as honoured visitor to the cave.

Thank the gods Socrates was still in Athens, too, to help deal with that problem child, Alcibiades. He was brilliant, beautiful, moody and heartless. He bullied the slaves, his mother and the other boys at school. He demanded constant flattery and adulation, trampled on other people's feelings, stole, cheated and lied in order to get his own selfish way. Yet when he set out to be charming it was impossible to resist him. And he knew it.

He must have been about thirteen when you were away in the Black Sea, and half the men in Athens were already in love with him. This, of course, just made him more conceited and more convinced that he was best at absolutely everything. In fact he was very good at most academic subjects and most sports, and a very bad loser on the rare occasions when things didn't go entirely his way. Wrestling was a sport at which he didn't always win—naturally enough, since his slim, graceful body didn't have the weight and power to stand up to some of the heftier boys in his class. As a result, he 'hated' wrestling and played truant from the wrestling school whenever he could. If he was forced to go there, he cheated: we had a report from his wrestling teacher Sibyrtios complaining that Alcibiades had bitten a chunk out of another boy's arm when he was losing a bout. His opponent screamed with pain, let go his hold and accused our young Alcmaeonid of biting like a woman. 'Oh no,' retorted the little god, 'like a lion!'

If you had been at home you would undoubtedly have given him the beating he deserved for this piece of silliness—he was old enough to know better. As it was, I tried to lecture him and failed miserably. I am not the best person to preach about fair play and upholding the family name, and Alcibiades was all too aware of this. He apologised sweetly, promised never to do such a thing again, then gave such a funny description of the other boy's face that in spite of myself I burst out laughing.

His next escapade was anything but funny. It happened at the wrestling school again, where one of the attendants collapsed and died after being beaten on the head—presumably with a club. Nobody saw it happen, nobody could explain it. But Alcibiades had been at wrestling school that afternoon, had lost badly in at least three bouts, and was in a furious temper. Of course he swore he knew nothing about it and assumed an air of offended innocence at the idea that anyone should suggest he might. Yet the fact remained that he couldn't account for where he *was* at the time and I strongly suspected that he was responsible. He was always unbearably arrogant towards slaves, servants and anyone he considered his social inferior. He very probably took it upon himself to 'teach the man a lesson' for some imagined insult, then managed to deliver the fatal blow before his victim realised what was happening.

'What on earth am I going to do with him?' I asked Socrates. 'As long as Pericles is away he seems to think he can literally get away with murder. And he's only *thirteen*—imagine what he'll be like in ten years time.'

Socrates shrugged. 'I doubt if there's much you *can* do. He takes after one or two of the more notorious Alcmaeonids, who were so brilliant they were almost insane. This obsessive need to be first in everything eventually caused their downfall—hence the legend about the Alcmaeonid curse.'

'Don't be so defeatist.' I was extremely worried, since in spite of everything I was very fond of Alcibiades. 'He needs a man he can admire and look up to. But he's got no father, he's never been close to Pericles, and he has no respect at all for his mother. There's no point in sending him to Ariphron—it would probably make him behave even worse. Anyway, he knows I haven't the authority to do it.'

'It's useless to try to change him.' Socrates sounded very serious. 'The only way to deal with Alcibiades is to ignore his bad qualities and encourage his good ones. He does have them, you know: he can be generous, affectionate, sensitive even. You must have noticed that he behaves reasonably well with me, for the simple reason that ever since he was a small boy I've treated him as an equal. I don't try to order him about or make him submit to senseless rules. Alcibiades will do anything reasonable if you *ask* him. But he won't be disciplined.'

It was true that Socrates did seem to have a magic effect on Alcibiades. I willingly agreed to let the boy spend as much time with him as he liked, and the two became almost inseparable. The beautiful aristocratic boy and the shabby gross-featured stone-mason made an extraordinary couple and were talked about all over town. Neither seemed to mind.

Your own son Paralos came back from his military service about this time, much more grown-up after a year in a garrison fort. Yet he was still a very dull, ordinary character, without a trace of the Alcmaeonid brilliance that Alcibiades had inherited. We saw very little of him, since he had his own friends and was out most of the day. When he was at home he was always quiet and unassuming, apparently overawed by the celebrated people who were generally there thinking out loud. He listened respectfully and seldom asked questions. I liked him—there was nothing to dislike—and found it difficult to communicate with him since he appeared to have no strong thoughts or feelings about anything. You were equally baffled, for he was so terrified of you he would hardly open his mouth in your presence.

His elder brother Xanthippos made up for it. Fortunately he had moved into a house of his own several years before, so never bothered me directly. But whenever he saw you in the market-place or at the baths he asked you for money. He was notorious for his wild parties at which his uncle Ariphron was usually present. And between them they succeeded in stirring up public opinion against us in a way that nearly ruined our lives for ever.

The whispering campaign started soon after you got back from the Black Sea. We took no notice at first, thinking it would die down as others had in the past. But this time your enemies were in earnest. They had got rid of Anaxagoras, Damon and Pheidias without weakening your position at all. They knew there was no point in attacking you openly. So they launched an offensive where they knew it would hurt you most—against me.

The man behind it all was Hermippos, a talented but vindictive comic poet who bore a grudge against anyone who was luckier or more successful than he. He particularly hated you because of a decree you had introduced imposing a mild form of censorship on slanderous comedy (it was only in force for three years). Your political enemies and disgruntled relatives made use of his talents to poison public opinion. Hermippos was undoubtedly the author of most of the anonymous letters and pamphlets that began circulating in the Assembly and market-place, but there was no way of proving it. And even if there had been, there was no law against it.

Athenians love scandal. They especially loved scandal about you. So for two years they eagerly devoured every piece of sensational fiction Hermippos served up to them.

They learned that I was a Persian spy, sent to seduce you and force you to deliver Athens into the hands of the barbarians. They heard that I was an atheist and blasphemer. I lured respectable Athenian women to our house so that you could make love to them (you, poor darling, were represented as an insatiable womaniser, at the age of nearly sixty; nothing could have been further from the truth). I had turned your house into a brothel where I corrupted free-born wives and their young daughters. I had cost the city thousands of talents by starting the 'Aspasian' war. And so on and so forth.

It was miserable and humiliating and there was nothing we could do about it. It didn't matter so much to me—nobody whose opinion I valued took the slightest notice, and I wasn't concerned about what the rest of Athens thought. But for you it was different: every day you had to mix and work with people who might believe this scandal about your wife; you had to stand up and address the Assembly knowing that half your fellow citizens were sniggering at the thought of what went on in your home.

When Peri finally started school, I began to suffer too. Not being a future citizen, he couldn't go to any of the smart schools in the centre of town; we had to send him to a school outside the city walls reserved especially for foreigners, illegitimate sons and any other child fated to be a social outcast. It hurt you terribly that your son should have to go there, but we had no choice. He needed the company of other boys and couldn't go on for ever learning only from Euripides—he would have become even more of a misfit. So he trotted off with his 'own' attendant slave, and seemed perfectly happy for the first few days.

Then one afternoon he burst into tears as soon as he got home. I was horrified—he was a child who hardly ever cried.

'What is the matter, darling?'

'School,' he sobbed. 'I don't want to go to school any more. Don't make me.'

'Why ever not? I thought you liked it.'

'It's the other boys. I *hate* them! I'll kill them!'

He was so upset he was almost incoherent. But at last, after patient questioning, I discovered that some of the older boys had been taunting him about me. He didn't understand what they meant when they called him 'the prostitute's son', but he knew it was something hateful.

I was furious. I was wild with anger. I didn't want him ever to go back there again. It took the combined eloquence of you, Socrates and Euripides to persuade me that he couldn't be protected from this sort of thing all his life so had better get used to it now. Euripides had a long talk with him about the failings of human nature, which he appeared to understand. But why should one *expect* a six-year-old to be so brutally exposed to them? His attendant reported that people pointed and jeered at him in the street, too. I hated them.

When Hermippos was satisfied that all his criminal fantasies had taken root, and blossomed into generally-accepted truth, he delivered his final blow.

You came home one day white-faced and trembling.

'They can't do it,' you raged. 'It's unthinkable, it's preposterous. I'll find a way to stop them ...'

'Stop what?' I was alarmed—you looked ready to murder the entire population of Athens.

'Stop them destroying me, destroying everyone round me ... I thought they'd done their worst already, but this is the end!'

'But who are "they", and what have they done now?'

'I can't tell you. I won't tell you. You mustn't be used in this way ... It can't possibly happen in Athens, the city I love ...'

'Please, darling.' I put my arms round you but you hardly noticed.

'Pull yourself together and tell me what it's all about. It can't be as bad as all that.'

There was a long silence before you looked me in the eyes and sighed.

'It's worse than anything you could possibly imagine. They're going to prosecute you. You, Aspasia, my wife . . . They will ask for the death sentence . . .'

I didn't know what to say. There wasn't really anything to say. At that moment I was convicted, sentenced and dead already.

'I see. What are they charging me with — as if it matters?'

'Everything and anything. Impiety, sacrilege, atheism, immorality, spying . . . I can't bear to think about it.'

'No.' It seemed remote, unreal, a nightmare involving someone else. I couldn't believe, suddenly, on a normal summer afternoon, that I was going to die. My strongest emotion was indignation that Athens should do this to *you*.

'I suppose Hermippos is behind it?'

'Of course. He's prosecuting personally. He served the summons on me in the market place today.'

'When will it be?'

'The first hearing is before the magistrate tomorrow. The trial proper will be in a few days' time.'

'Am I allowed to defend myself?'

'No. Neither foreigners nor women can speak at their own trials. You're both.'

'That's true.'

We sat there silently, stunned. I felt completely helpless — there was absolutely nothing I could do. I had no rights at all, and any action I tried to take would only make things worse. I might as well have drunk the hemlock poison there and then.

'Of course I shall defend you,' you said suddenly.

'Pericles, darling, you mustn't. You could ruin yourself as well.'

'That's just what they want.'

'Well, don't do it. Don't you see it's a trap? If they find me guilty, as they undoubtedly will, Athens and the world will see that you haven't even the influence to save your own wife. You will never be respected again. It's bad enough as it is, without you being publicly humiliated. I won't let you.'

'But I've got to.'

'Of course you haven't. We can easily find someone else — Meidias perhaps. Not that there's much point to any defence — after all the gossip of the past two years the jurors will be convinced the charges are true. I suppose I could always leave Athens here and now and take Peri with me. Then there wouldn't be any trial.'

'Yes, there would. And they'd never let you come back.'

You walked up and down the veranda, frowning. The veins were standing out on your head and your fists were clenched. Then you wheeled round, looking determined.

'Aspasia, I love you. Nobody is ever going to take you from me. They are not going to drive you out of the city. They are not going to make me watch in despair as someone else half-heartedly speaks up for you. It isn't you they're putting on trial, it's me. So I am going to defend myself, to plead for my own life. If you die, I die too. If you are exiled, I go too. I can't live without you. So I intend to fight for both our lives. Don't argue . . .'

Your arms closed round me and we stood there clinging to each other.

I tried to argue. I tried to get our friends to reason with you, to convince you that this was suicide. You replied stiffly that you knew what you were doing. You hardly ate or slept for three days and I worried that you might collapse.

You didn't tell me much about the preliminary hearing at which a clerk took down the 'evidence' for use at the trial. I know your son Xanthippos testified that he had often heard me say the gods didn't exist—something I had always taken great care not to say in his presence. A political enemy of yours came up with a ludicrous story about his daughter, claiming you had seduced her in our house at my instigation. Neither of us had the slightest idea the girl existed. About ten slaves you had never seen or heard of produced detailed descriptions of orgies, intrigues and secret assignments. Someone must have coached them well and given them enormous bribes. For in this progressive, civilized city slaves' evidence can only be taken down under torture, on the assumption that they are incapable of telling the truth.

Our steward Evangelos begged me to let him and some of the household slaves give evidence for me but I wouldn't hear of it. I would have felt as though I was torturing them myself. And in any case it would have been assumed that we had bribed or threatened them to speak in my favour. The whole case against me was vague, so undefined that it was impossible to answer specific charges. It was a question of convincing the jury that the whole thing was a deliberately-constructed web of malicious lies—or being convicted as a blasphemer, procuress and spy.

On the day before the trial I pleaded with Socrates: 'Can't you try to make Pericles see sense? Convince him that Athens needs him, tell him he's destroying his beloved city if he does this for me. You know he listens to you, so just tell him anything as long as it sounds logical.'

Socrates shrugged. 'At this moment I have the impression that he *wants* to destroy Athens. And I don't blame him. Also, for once in his life he's quite deaf to logic. He is sincere when he says he can't live without you. So he's doing the obvious thing by trying to save you.'

'You don't think I should just take Peri and go?'

'Certainly not. It would make you both look like cowards and give the impression that you must be guilty of these ridiculous charges. Pericles would be a wreck without you, and very soon they'd find some excuse for prosecuting him as well—successfully.'

'I'm bound to be found guilty. They might as well not hold a trial.'

He sighed. 'In this great democracy of ours everyone must have what is laughingly described as a fair trial. I'm as upset about it as you are. We all are. The thing is, my dear, the only chance you have of being acquitted is for Pericles himself to defend you. If Euripides or I were to do it, for example, you would certainly be convicted because of our personal unpopularity. Pericles is loved and respected by most citizens. Remember it was he who introduced payment for jury service. The people listen to him, they are impressed by him. He is also a great orator. And he will be speaking about something he cares about deeply. He may be able to save you; nobody else could.'

You and I both lay awake all night, holding hands, saying nothing. We knew it might be our last night together. You may have prayed and I wished I believed in a god to pray to. Just before dawn you got up, put on your tunic and cloak, then stood beside the bed for a moment, looking down at me.

'Aren't you going to wear your helmet?'

'No, not today.'

You picked me up in your arms and kissed me. 'Don't worry darling. They're not going to have you. Try to sleep.'

You went quickly out of the room as I settled down to wait.

But I found I couldn't face that morning on my own. Deino-mache was no help, although sympathetic—she was already weeping and wailing as if my conviction were a foregone conclusion (which it more or less was). I sent a note to Chrysis, who came round straight away and made a noble attempt to stay cheerful. I had kept Peri back from school, so we half-heartedly told him some of Aesop's fables for about the twentieth time—so badly that he kept on correcting us. Elpinice arrived, uninvited but welcome, and the three of us chattered determinedly about her girlhood, my arrival in Athens, my first banquet, and so on. We had heard it all before and weren't listening now—we were all three thinking about what was going on in the law courts on the other side of the city.

The hours dragged by. The slaves were hovering anxiously round the courtyard, wanting to help but not knowing what to do. Evangelos and Amycla kept bringing offerings—a jar of the best wine, a bowl of cakes, a plate piled high with exotic fruit. I couldn't eat, but drank several cups of wine. It gave me a detached feeling, as though I were someone else watching four women and a little boy sitting on a veranda waiting for guards to come and take the youngest woman away to die.

Your son Paralos walked through, hesitated, then came over and kissed me. I was touched, and wanted to cry for the first time. He went out without a word, but we knew he was on his way to the trial.

I didn't know what the procedure was, and hadn't wanted to find out. Would they bring the hemlock to the house, at once? Would they take me away? I had never heard of a case where a woman was sentenced to death. Men were sometimes kept in prison for a few days before being given the cup of poison. I hoped that with me it would be immediate. I had heard that death by hemlock was painless, at least: you became slowly paralysed, then died.

'When they come, take Peri into the other part of the house,' I told Deinomache. She nodded mutely, tears streaming down her cheeks.

'And for the gods' sake try to keep him happy. Always.'

I found I could hardly speak myself. 'Elpinice, please stay with me. We'll hear them coming because there's bound to be a crowd following the guards in the hope of seeing something . . . interesting . . .'

But we didn't hear you coming. You walked through the front door alone, your shoulders drooping, your legs dragging as though you had been sapped of all your energy. Yet one glance at the look of grim satisfaction on your face told us everything.

'Darling!' I rushed towards you as you staggered forward. You took me in your arms and held me for a long, long time, standing in the middle of the courtyard. Then you announced to the world at large, over my head: 'They'll never try that again. Aspasia was acquitted by 437 votes to 64. Hermippos will have to pay a thousand drachma fine.'

Cheering broke out from the other end of the courtyard where all the slaves had assembled silently. You looked at me for a moment, your face haggard, your eyes already half-closed.

'I'm tired. I'm going to bed.' You lurched towards the bedroom and must have fallen asleep almost before you got there. For when I looked at you later you were lying unconscious across the bed, still with your cloak and sandals on.

As soon as you went I had collapsed on the nearest couch. I laughed, I cried, I screamed, I howled and finally came to my senses to find Elpinice slapping my face and Peri looking extremely alarmed.

'That's enough,' I gasped. 'I'm all right now. Peri thinks you're trying to kill me.'

The horribly bad joke I'd unintentionally made brought on another fit of hysteria. But eventually I recovered enough to explain to Peri it was just a game. He seemed relieved, as he was by the general gaiety that then replaced the morning's tension. I suppose I should have sent him away somewhere while it was all going on. But where? We only had each other.

It was Sophocles who gave me a full description of the trial, after dozens of people had come to offer congratulations and sing your praises. You slept through all the noise and excitement and were still asleep when Sophocles and I strolled to a corner of the veranda and lay down in the twilight.

'Do you want to hear all about it?'

I nodded.

'He was magnificent. He was superb. I've known him for fifty years, ever since we were at school together. I must have heard him make hundreds, even thousands of speeches. But I've never seen him like he was today.'

Sophocles stroked his beard thoughtfully, and went on in his grave, deep voice: 'His performance in court today would have won the prize at any drama festival. Because it was real, it was sincere, it was deeply moving. It was better than any speech I've ever written in a play. But I know I can't write like that because I'm not capable of the sort of love he feels for you. The beauty of it was that it *wasn't* written—he spoke spontaneously, straight from

187

the heart. And the jurors and spectators who are used to hearing the Olympian speak from his head were astounded by this new, human Pericles pleading in public for the woman he loves.

'There was a special jury of 501—the usual collection of old men who scrape a living by sitting in court and judging their fellow citizens. They hardly fitted on the benches. The magistrate was Stymodoros—I think you know him. A nice enough man who looked very uncomfortable at having to preside over such a sensational trial. And half Athens was there for the free entertainment. I have never seen a court so crowded.

'I won't bother to tell you what Hermippos said—I doubt if I could bear to repeat it. All the spurious evidence had been read out, all the lying witnesses had confirmed their outrageous statements. Pericles' son Xanthippos was smirking, unable to conceal his glee. Then Hermippos got up on the speakers' platform and would still be there now if Stymodoros hadn't told him four times that the water-clock had already run out. He almost had to be carried down as the foolish old jurymen stamped and shouted their approval of his speech. (The trouble is they are mostly poor, ignorant and enthralled by scandal. I know they're supposed to be elected from the whole list of citizens, but it's only these old dunces who have the time to do it, need the money, and therefore volunteer.)

'Hermippos was very clever: he hinted at every sort of debauchery and depravity without making any specific allegations —the jurors' fertile imaginations could supply the details. He brought in a mass of irrelevant detail about Miletos, your friends when you first came here, even your friendship with Socrates. Unfortunately, as you know, speakers at Athenian trials are not obliged to keep to the point. They can say whatever they like as long as they don't over-run their time. He invoked patriotism, love of the family, respect for ancestors, reverence for the gods. He painted a picture of a monster woman who single-handed is capable of turning the city over to the Persians, making all respectable wives into whores, corrupting the children and, worst of all, provoking some dire punishment from the gods on the whole city because of her sacrilege. He was cunning enough to portray Pericles as the innocent victim of this scheming Medusa, ensnared and infatuated but in no way to blame. Needless to say everyone was staring at him to see how he was taking it. He stood there expressionless, without moving a muscle.'

Sophocles sighed. 'I must confess, my dear, that by the time Hermippos was forced to stop talking the case against you looked very black indeed. The tragedy was that none of the jurors, or very few, had ever met you. They had heard plenty about you, all supporting Hermippos' case. They had to choose between what they mostly believed to be common knowledge (and therefore true), and what one man with an extremely personal interest in the matter was going to tell them.

'The atmosphere was tense as Pericles climbed up on to the platform. Everyone there had heard him speak dozens of times in the Assembly and knew him to be a great statesman and general. But this was different. This time the Olympian was spokesman for himself, not for his policies. He was alone. And he was bare-headed. He looked smaller, more vulnerable without that ever-present helmet.

'He began mildly, almost conversationally, by saying how lucky we are to live in a city which honours freedom and justice. We are free, he said, to live as we like, to form and express our own opinions. It is this freedom which attracts eminent thinkers, artists and scientists from all over the world to Athens. And Athenian justice is rightly famous all over the world for its fairness and common sense. It is well known that Athenian juries listen equally to both sides of a case, that they throw out prosecutions based on spite, political revenge or groundless gossip.

'The jurymen were looking pleased with themselves—they love to hear this sort of flattery. "And that is why," said Pericles, still talking very calmly and quietly, "I have no misgivings about appearing before an Athenian jury today to contest these vile, malicious accusations against my wife and myself. You will say I am infatuated. If I am infatuated so are the four hundred citizens whose names are in the clerk's box, all of whom are prepared to come forward and swear there is not one word of truth in this conspiracy of falsehood and slander. They include generals, magistrates, councillors—the men you have elected and trusted to be your leaders. They are all willing to give evidence. But I knew this was unnecessary. I knew I could rely on the wisdom of Athenian jurymen to give me a fair hearing. You are free men, intelligent men, not easily taken in by tricks and clever talk. Neither you nor I nor any of my loyal friends believe in sorcery and witchcraft. We know, reasonably, that no human being can be under the spell of another, man or woman. We are free to accept what we find to be right and reject what is wrong."

'He paused, and his tone changed. "Yet I admit to you, fellow citizens, that I have chosen to be ensnared and infatuated by my wife Aspasia—if those words describe the love I feel for this remarkable woman. I knew what I was doing. I know what I am doing today. And I have no regrets. She is not like our women of Athens, for she was born in a foreign city. She was raised among different customs and different standards, which would be strange and unnatural for our own wives and daughters. You find *her* strange and unnatural; you distrust her because she is different, because she is not like the women you know and respect. But in free Athens it is no crime to be different. It is no sin not to conform. It is a crime to be mean and dishonest and cruel, like the people who brought this prosecution. But Aspasia is none of these things . . ."

'His voice was trembling now,' said Sophocles, 'and there was hushed silence in court as he went on: "I swear to you that at heart Aspasia, for all her foreign ways, is a woman like any other and better than many. She has been a faithful and loyal wife to me for nine years—during which time you have elected me your leader time and again. Would you have done this if you had believed one word of this despicable scandal? She has been a loving mother, both to our own son Pericles and to my young wards. She has been mistress of my slaves and hostess at my banquets. She has been . . . and is . . . my life."

'At this point he broke down and wept. Pericles, the Olympian, wept in front of half the city.' Sophocles sounded as if he still couldn't believe it. 'He sobbed for a few moments, then raised his head and told the jury that even though you are a woman and a foreigner you are still a human being—as are all women and foreigners. You are also a very patriotic, loyal human being who trusts Athenian justice. He said that if they convicted you he would be so ashamed of his city, his own Athens, that he would leave and never come back. He believes in you and loves you. So in judging you they were also judging him. He was making no attempt to defend you, or himself, from the wicked charges brought against you, because no reasonable man could take them seriously. So he stood alone before the jury—his friends and fellow citizens—imploring them to apply the justice for which Athens is so rightly famous.

'There was a long, long silence as he walked slowly down from the speakers' platform. Then the court broke into an uproar. The jurymen shouted and stamped and cheered—I have never heard anything quite like it. There was really no need for them to cast their votes, as the pebbles rained into the *No* jar and there was only an occasional, secretive clink for the *Yes* side. Hermippos will be fined for bringing a prosecution which received less than a fifth of the votes.'

Sophocles stood up to go. 'It really was the most dramatic scene I've ever seen—in or out of the theatre. I think the jury were expecting a flood of involved legal argument. Instead, he kept it short, simple and sincere. And by taking them into his confidence, by admitting he loves you—an unheard of thing for a statesman to do in public—he completely won them over. They were being allowed to share his intimate private life and thus to see that even Pericles the Olympian is as human as they are.'

I kissed Sophocles. 'Thank you. Now I feel as if I had really been there.'

I went to look at you, still sound asleep, then wandered round the house in a semi-daze, letting it all sink in. It was difficult to believe the nightmare was really over.

You stirred and muttered when I got into bed, and your hand groped for mine. The next morning we both woke up smiling.

Writing this, and remembering, makes me overflow with love for you. Most of the pain has gone now, leaving memories and emotions that will be with me for ever. I am absurdly happy, still, that you could have risked so much for me. Only I knew quite what it meant for Pericles to break down in court and plead for a woman's life. I hope I made it worthwhile for you afterwards.

The happiness doesn't go with my present state of official mourning, due to my husband Lysicles' death in Caria. Sad, I suppose, that having achieved his lifelong ambition to be a general he should be killed on his first campaign. But I can't honestly pretend to be anything but pleased. I married him because at the time I couldn't face being alone. Now I am stronger; and I have learned that solitude is better than the company of brutes and boors. I have Peri. I shall have the new baby. I have all my friends, and shall now move into a house of my own. The marriage was necessary at the time, but a mistake I won't make again.

I must at least try to look sorrowful, for the sake of Lysicles' relatives. Though all I want to do at the moment is go out and find someone—preferably Sophocles—who will talk for hours about you.

14

T HE last years went so quickly it's hard to sort out what happened when. They were clouded by war and fear and sickness and bewilderment; the bubble of Athens' greatness was slowly deflating, giving way to shock, resentment, bitterness. Strangely, the more recent events are, the less well I remember them—it's almost as if I didn't want to accept them and imprint them on my memory. I can remember every detail, every word of unimportant incidents and conversations fifteen years ago. But the last five or six years are one big blur spotted with haphazard memories.

The continuous, ever-present thread running through them was, of course, the war. Because it was in a sense *your* war, and because you felt personally responsible for bringing Athens into it, it came to dominate our lives, day and night.

It all began quite soon after the sensation surrounding my acquittal had died down. For more than ten years the balance of power sanctioned by the Thirty Years Peace had stayed more or less unchanged, and the big powers—Athens on the one hand, Sparta and Corinth on the other—had been very careful not to meddle in each other's business. But it was an extremely uneasy coexistence. And both sides were becoming increasingly aware of a third power rising in the West—the Greek colonies in Italy and Sicily, led by Syracuse. If there were a war, the West would become very important indeed. And it wouldn't be on our side.

You were worried. You had admitted during one of your speeches to the Assembly: 'I see as it were a cloud of war rising from the Peloponnese'—that is, from Sparta—and you knew there was no way of averting the storm. You began quietly to prepare for war by reorganising the treasury and cutting down public expenditure. Building on the Acropolis gateway was stopped and has never been resumed since.

Suddenly, you were an old man. Your hair and beard went grey almost overnight and the skin on your face began to sag. Mentally you were still in your prime, but the effort and responsibility of being in the public eye all day, making speeches and decisions, defending your policies against the pacifists on the right and a growing group of noisy, extremist war-mongers on the left took more and more out of you. You kept up a public image of strength but collapsed in private, with me.

I remember your saying wearily one evening: 'There's no way of avoiding war with Sparta and Corinth—in the end. They're too afraid that Athenian power and Athenian ideals might come to dominate the whole Mediterranean. If only they could. And *I'm* afraid, myself, of what could happen when I'm gone. The Assembly is full of young men who know nothing about war but long to achieve military glory. They're quite capable of plunging Athens into a bloodbath, destroying everything we've created in the past ten years. I personally have had more than enough military glory—all I want now is peace, quiet, and you. Yet I'm not being conceited when I say that if there's going to be a war it's got to be soon, while I'm still here to control it. If we must fight we shall fight *my* way, without throwing away Athenian lives. I'm sixty-one now and shan't live much longer. We have to declare war within the next five years or not at all.'

I think it was the same evening that our love-making began to go wrong. You were excited, you wanted me, I was eager for you. But try as you might, you couldn't do anything about it. The reason was obvious and we both knew it: you were old, you were tired, you were worn out. And we both knew there was no cure. Yet, understandably, you refused to accept this final fact. You went on trying, desperately, and the more you tried and the more you worried the worse it became. You were obsessed with helpless rage, guilt, jealousy, alternating between abject apologies for being so useless to me and groundless fears that now you were impotent I, still in my early thirties, must surely have found a younger lover. There was little comfort or reassurance I could give you except to tell you truthfully that I loved you and it didn't matter. We found various inadequate solutions, but they always made you feel guilty.

It was only towards the end when we had given up even trying to make love in the normal way that you made a sudden, unexpected recovery. Perhaps it was because you had at last stopped worrying and facing each night as an ordeal. Whatever the reason, for the last year or two, although not exactly a giant in bed, you did feel you were a man again. It made a big difference at a time when practically everything else was going wrong.

Alcibiades, on the other hand, had just discovered the joys of being a man and seemed determined to prove he was as good at this as he was at everything else. He was already patronising the brothels, and spent more time at my old house with Manto and the other girls than he did at home. Half the men in town were also hopelessly in love with him; he graciously granted them the honour of sleeping with him in return for lavish gifts. I think he actually preferred women, but didn't really mind what he did as long as it gave him a thrill. He asked me, very politely, if I would sleep with him 'to teach me your skill', and called me old-fashioned when I declined the privilege. (I never told you about this; you would not have found it funny.)

He was unutterably conceited and stunningly beautiful. But he made a big mistake when he tried to seduce Socrates. He simply couldn't understand why Socrates, who was known to take a normal, healthy interest in boys, wasn't crawling at his feet like the rest of his suitors. He knew Socrates liked him, he was convinced he was irresistible, so what was wrong?

Socrates, much amused by Alcibiades' attempts to conquer him, gave me a day by day report. The young god had come to the conclusion that Socrates must be nurturing a secret passion for him but was too shy to say so. *Socrates Shy?* So he set out to make himself available. He devised elaborate arrangements for the two of them to be alone together; Socrates simply talked. He invited Socrates to wrestle with him; Socrates just wrestled. He invited him to dinner; Socrates left early. Finally he thought he had trapped his victim (who by this time seemed the most desirable man in Athens). He 'tricked' Socrates into drinking at least ten cups of unwatered wine, then suggested that since it was so late he should stay on the spare couch in his bedroom. Socrates—who can drink a hundred cups of wine and still stay semi-sober—agreed, and didn't protest when Alcibiades lay down on the couch beside him. But although the boy smothered him with enough embraces to make any normal man crazy with desire, Socrates simply lay there like one of his own stone statues (he told me afterwards it was one of the most difficult things he'd ever done; but since he genuinely loved and cared about Alcibiades he felt it was time he was taught a lesson).

Alcibiades had never been so insulted. It was such a blow to his pride that the next day he vanished. At first we weren't particularly worried, but when he'd been gone about three days we started making enquiries. Manto hadn't seen him, he hadn't turned up in the market-place or gymnasium or any of the drinking-clubs. We even checked all the State brothels, but he wasn't nursing his injured conceit there either. Your brother Ariphron heard about his disappearance (presumably through the slaves) and told you fussily that you ought to have it proclaimed by the town-crier. After all, he was only seventeen, and boys do foolish things . . . You told him there was no point in panicking: if Alcibiades was dead, we wouldn't gain anything by finding out a day or two sooner; if, as was likely, he was alive, it would be humiliating for both him and the family to have his escapade announced all over the city. Besides which, Alcibiades was no ordinary seventeen-year-old and far too fond of himself to do anything silly.

You were absolutely right. The next day our steward Evangelos told me he'd heard from a slave who had heard from a friend that Alcibiades was sulking in the house of a young man named Democrates who had been courting him for months. He was drinking, gambling and inflicting his bad temper on everyone there. A couple of days later he turned up at Manto's. And eventually he slunk home, looking sheepish.

Once he'd recovered from the initial shock he was intelligent enough to realise what a fool he had made of himself. Some time afterwards, talking about Socrates, he told me: 'You know, Aspasia, he's the only person in the world who really makes me feel ashamed of myself.' An extraordinary admission, coming from Alcibiades. In fact Socrates did have a magical effect on him, transforming him into a model of thoughtfulness, consideration and respect. I don't think they ever did become lovers—yet they were far closer to each other than many established couples.

By this time Socrates had become a sort of itinerant lecturer: wherever he went he was surrounded by a group of adoring students all trying unsuccessfully to copy his very individual 'philosophy'. He often used to come and hide in our women's quarters, just to get away from them. And not long after the drama of his non-seduction, both he and Alcibiades went off to war, much to your relief. Alcibiades was becoming too much of a nuisance round the house, so you were thankful when his eighteenth birthday came and he was called up for military service. I don't know whether Socrates went just to be with him; despite his eccentricity he was a conscientious soldier who was always among the first to pick up his shield and go when there was a call to arms.

They shared a tent during a long campaign against a town called Potidaea right up at the very North of the Aegean. Encouraged by Corinth, it had defected from the Athenian alliance. And it was just one more step towards total war when Corinth sent troops to help it hold out against the Athenian army. There was a pitched battle between Athenian and Corinthian soldiers outside the town, in which Alcibiades' glorious career nearly came to an abrupt end. He was badly wounded and would undoubtedly have been killed or taken prisoner if Socrates hadn't come to the rescue. With incredible courage he stood over Alcibiades' body, fighting single-handed against several groups of Corinthians looking for plunder. Then, not content with saving Alcibiades' life, he refused to accept the prize for bravery which he fully deserved, insisting that Alcibiades should have it instead. The generals thought (wrongly) that you would be pleased if an Alcamaeonid got the prize, and gave it to him. So Alcibiades came home to be acclaimed a hero—simply because Socrates had saved his life.

Socrates himself stayed on with the troops besieging the town right through the bitterly cold Northern winter. He became known as a sort of hero himself, because of the way he endured the cold. There was one particularly freezing spell, with snow and ice. The soldiers all huddled in their tents, wrapped up in furs and fleeces. But not Socrates. He went out *barefoot* as usual on the slippery ice, wearing nothing but his tattered old cloak.

He became even more of a celebrity during the spring when he had a Thought. (You and I were used to Socrates' Thoughts, which went on for days and could not be interrupted for anything.) His Thought struck him at dawn, in the open air in the middle of the camp. He stood still and began to consider it. At midday he was still standing there, Thinking. At sunset a platoon of fascinated soldiers settled down for the night round him, to see how long he was going to stand there. And it wasn't till dawn the next day that he finally shook his head, blinked, muttered something they thought was a prayer to Apollo (he told me that what he really said was: 'By Apollo, I'm hungry') and shuffled off in the direction of the kitchen.

The siege of Potidaea went on for nearly three years altogether, but Socrates came back to Athens that summer after being in the North about twelve months. I think he missed Alcibiades—although he never admitted it openly, he really was very much in love with your precocious ward.

He must have admitted it to himself however, and perhaps come to the conclusion that it was becoming too important to him. At least I can't think of any other reason why he should have taken the extraordinary step of getting married. We were all astounded, particularly since his bride Xanthippe, was about the ugliest, most bad-tempered woman in Athens.

Socrates explained, infuriatingly: 'My ambition in life is to study mankind. This marriage is a test: if I can endure Xanthippe, I know I shall have no trouble in putting up with anyone else.'

To tell the truth, he didn't sacrifice himself too much. He still stayed out all day and most nights; he refused to wash or alter his appearance, despite her constant nagging; he still had as many boy friends as before; and he never gave her any money because he never had any.

For unlike other philosophers, Socrates refused to accept fees for his improvised lectures. He argued that since he knew nothing and was simply searching for knowledge when he embarked on a half-day discussion, he wasn't entitled to charge his audience for listening to his display of ignorance.

The siege of Potidaea was still dragging on and Sparta was flooded with envoys asking for help against us. The ruling council had agreed in principle; but their king Archidamos (a personal friend of yours, and unusually far-sighted for a Spartan) wanted to play for time. He realised they weren't yet ready for what could be a disastrous world war. You knew we were as ready as we ever could be, and still believed the war could be over quickly as long as you were there to control it. So you precipitated things with the 'Megarian decree'.

Megara is a city halfway between here and Corinth which makes a living from exporting textiles. It is a Corinthian colony, hated by Athens for massacring an Athenian garrison the year before peace was signed. It seemed a good place to pick a quarrel over. So a decree was passed forbidding all our allies to trade with Megara—which meant economic disaster for the Megarians. The *official* reason was that they had ploughed up some sacred land (it was always necessary to find a religious excuse for an act of aggression).

It seems they always had to find a way of blaming me personally for wars, too. Someone (undoubtedly Hermippos again) cooked up a story that would have been laughable if it hadn't been so malicious. He spread the word that a group of young Athenians, including Alcibiades, had made a drunken expedition to Megara to kidnap the city's most illustrious companion. In retaliation the men of Megara stole 'two of Aspasia's choicest girls'. Then to get *my* revenge I persuaded you to impose economic sanctions. It was perfectly true that two of the girls living in my old house had gone home to Corinth when war began to seem likely — at my suggestion. And Alcibiades may well have carried off a female prize after a wild party. But you knew nothing about any of it. You supported the Megarian decree because it seemed a wise political move at the time.

The Spartans voted for war on the grounds that we had broken the peace treaty by attacking Megara. And they began to make slow preparations for invading the countryside round Athens in the spring. During the winter, just to show they were really 'peaceful' at heart, they sent ambassadors to say they were prepared to cancel the invasion if we revoked the Megarian decree, called off the siege of Potidaea and expelled 'the Accursed of the goddess' — that is to say you. They had suddenly and conveniently remembered the Alcmaeonid curse.

I remember Meidias asking indignantly: 'Do they take us for fools? They can't seriously think we'd let Pericles go at a time like this, when we need him most. You can rake up a curse in anyone's family history if you try hard enough. It's just an excuse to get rid of the general they're really afraid of!'

In fact it probably did you more good than harm. Public opinion agreed with Meidias and your personal prestige shot up.

I didn't and don't like war. I don't know why it has to happen. But it seems that men and cities will always be greedy for power and property, never content with what they've got. And that winter I had to agree with you, reluctantly, that war was necessary. I also agreed whole-heartedly that it must be as quick and bloodless as possible. You thought it wouldn't take more than a year or two to show Sparta, finally, that Athens could not be crushed. We just had to stand firm and defend the city. On no account must we start reckless invasions ourselves.

You were due to speak in the Assembly in answer to the Spartan ambassadors' demands. We wrote your speech together, trying to present your case as honestly as possible. Alcibiades thought the final result was luke-warm and conciliatory. But Alcibiades would.

We pointed out that it was madness to give in to Spartan demands backed with the threat of war. Once we had agreed to these proposals they would come back with new ones. The more Athens conceded the more Sparta would want. It would be never-ending blackmail. The Megarian decree might appear to be just an unimportant issue not worth bothering about, but the principle at stake was a big one: if we revoked the decree for fear of Sparta, we would be at her mercy for ever.

We said Athens was prepared for war. She had a vast fleet and plenty of reserve funds. But we made it clear that all country property would have to be sacrificed. Country people would have to come into the city and let the Spartans plunder their land. It would not be easy, but land can be planted again whereas lives can't. We could not possibly hope to defeat the vastly bigger Spartan army. But we could hold out for ever inside the city and the walled road down to the sea. We were prepared to revoke the Megarian decree on our own conditions—first and foremost that the Spartans should allow their allies self-government. We were ready to submit to arbitration. But if we were attacked, we would defend ourselves.

Fortunately the invaders still hadn't arrived by the time of the Dionysia drama festival. It had an air of forced gaiety about it that year, as if despite all your reassurances nobody was quite certain it would take place the next year, or ever again. In fact that was the last month of peace. Now, four years later, the war still shows no sign of ending.

Both Sophocles and Euripides had entered plays. Both were beaten by Euphorion, son of the great Aeschylos. He was a mediocre poet, and I think the judges voted more for his father's memory than his own merit.

Not that Euripides could possibly have won even if the judging had been strictly fair (he came last, as usual). For the powerful, passionate, tragic heroine of one of his plays was everything an Athenian audience most detests.

They were shocked and disconcerted by 'Medea' (exactly as Euripides intended them to be). They were frightened and fascinated by this uncompromising portrayal of naked jealousy, love, fear, revenge, madness. They would have liked to shut their eyes to the message that instinct and emotion can triumph over moderation and self-control. But once they started watching they couldn't look away.

Medea is generally regarded as a wicked monster. She was so upset when her husband Jason divorced her to marry a younger, prettier, wealthier woman that she took rather drastic revenge— killing both the bride-to-be and her own two children by Jason. As all good Athenian women know, you should just submit obediently if your husband wishes to divorce you. And it makes no difference if, as in Medea's case, you happen to have saved his life and helped him win the Golden Fleece.

Euripides' Medea is not a monster. She is a profoundly passionate, highly articulate, deeply wronged woman. Jason, if anyone, is the brute, for his complete indifference to her suffering. He simply doesn't want to know about it. So that eventually, crazed by love, blinded by jealousy, she *forces* him to take notice of her—if only with horror and hatred.

The play sums up everything Euripides and I have ever said about women. It contains no jokes, unlike 'Alcestis'. It is a tragic, impassioned plea for woman's right to be treated as a human being. Even the generally timid chorus insist that women too have intelligence, and that 'a time will come when the female sex is honoured'.

It was appropriate that 'Medea' should be produced in the last month of peace, at the end of a decade dominated by reason and moderation. It was a warning that so-called 'civilised' values as represented by Jason count for nothing when confronted with savage animal instincts. And the longer this war lasts, the more civilisation is crumbling before cruelty and violence.

If you could have foreseen the tragic consequences, I think you might have agreed to revoke the wretched Megarian decree. But there were so many things we couldn't possibly have predicted. Therefore, as soon as the Dionysia festival was over, we began to prepare for the Spartan invasion.

At least ten thousand people had to be evacuated from the country and villages to the city. Many were peasants who lived from the land, some were wealthy families who lived on country estates. They had to bring *everything* possible with them—the less they left behind the less there would be for the Spartans to plunder and destroy.

Grumbling, resentful, muttering about their crops and harvests, they began to stream into Athens. It was very hard for them—no enemy had been on Athenian territory since the Persian Wars fifty years before, and now we were simply going to let the Spartans overrun their homes without putting up a fight. Their livestock was ferried across to the islands of Euboea and Salamis (Euripides was terrified his priceless book collection in the cave would be eaten by goats). And the refugees themselves, with wives, children, mattresses, pots and pans, even the woodwork from their houses, settled down to camp where they could. Not many had relatives they could stay with in the city. So the streets were suddenly filled with makeshift shacks—cramped and uncomfortable, but at least they gave shelter from the sun. There were refugees living on the walls, under the trees, in all the shrines and temples that hadn't been safely locked up. Everywhere there was complaining and discontent. As always in a crisis, the soothsayers and oracle-mongers did a roaring trade. And as always, everything that went wrong was blamed on you.

The Spartans finally arrived—a massive army of 60,000 men systematically sacking and burning houses, crops, vines, everything they could lay hands on. Our army, at full strength, would hardly have been half the size. And Athenians, unlike Spartans, are not trained to be soldiers from the day of their birth. It wasn't much comfort to know we were supreme by sea; our navy could do nothing against this sprawling mob of fighting men. You were worried that your old friend King Archidamos might spare your own country estate—either out of courtesy or as a clever move to suggest you had made a bargain with the enemy. You diplomatically offered to give your land to the city if this happened.

They got as far as a big village within sight of Athens itself, and settled down to raze it to the ground. Archidamos obviously hoped this would provoke you to come out and fight, which was just what half Athens was urging you to do. It was cruel for the villagers to have to sit doing nothing while their homes and vines were destroyed in front of their eyes. It was almost unbearable for the young men to hang about the hot, crowded, stinking streets, knowing there was an invading army half an hour's ride away. They wanted action, refusing to see this would cost thousands of lives. There is nothing glorious, you commented bitterly, about senseless suicide.

There were groups of people in every street holding their own War Councils, consulting oracles, believing any soothsayer who promised victory if they went out to fight. They demanded that you should be deposed for 'cowardice'. They tried to summon a special meeting of the Assembly. But you refused to let them, realising that in the mood the people were in they would vote for any reckless plan. (It was a question of sense before democracy. I tried to make you feel less guity by pointing out that in wartime there had to be one man in charge. The people had voted to fight the war your way and couldn't change their minds after one month.)

You appeased them a bit by sending out cavalry to harass the Spartan patrols. And you hurried up preparations for a big sea raid on the Spartan peninsula, the Peloponnese. A hundred ships sailed right down the enemy coast, attacking villages, disrupting communications and generally intimidating Spartan allies.

At long last King Archidamos realised he was not going to tempt you out to fight. Provisions for his vast army were also getting dangerously low. So after about twenty days within sight of Athens the Spartans marched away, burning and looting as they went.

To work off the city's anger you immediately led ten thousand men against Megara, cause of all the trouble. It relieved their feelings to do to the Megarians exactly what the Spartans had done to us. Then you came home to prepare wearily for the whole thing to be repeated the next year. The first campaign had ended, as you hoped, with very little loss of life. But it wasn't really much consolation.

You were very conscious of this when you had to write the funeral speech for the few men who did die fighting. You were discouraged, you had lost faith in Athenian democracy and justice, you had almost lost sight of what we were fighting for. You had discovered, too late, that your ideals of freedom, justice, beauty, courage, could never really be attained. At the age of 63 you had become a realist; just when Athens badly needed a dose of sincere idealism.

You flung the paper away in disgust, rubbing your sore eyes. It was late, and you had been working on the speech all day.

'It's no good, darling. I can't do it. I don't believe in it any more. How can I write in praise of a city where justice doesn't prevail, where democracy doesn't work, where the rule of law has become the rule of spite and intrigue?'

'Let me look.'

You handed me the pages you had written. It was true—they read like a lament for the living instead of a eulogy of the dead.

'I see what you mean. I wish I could help. But you know I've always hated patriotic funeral speeches. At least this is honest.'

'But it won't do. Just because I'm dejected, the rest of the city doesn't have to be as well. I wish they'd chosen someone else to make the speech.'

You were very, very depressed. I put my arms round you and tried to comfort you. It was unbearably sad to see you like this, disillusioned with the city you had believed in and trusted and loved. I remembered how many times we had argued and how many times I had secretly laughed at your unswerving faith in Athens. I could remember everything you'd said, could practically hear you saying it . . .

'Pericles!'

'Mmm?'

'Pretend you're a scribe and write this down. Don't interrupt . . .'

I dictated to you for about an hour, as your expression changed from weary resignation to incredulity to delight.

'There you are,' I concluded. 'There's your funeral speech.'

'Aspasia. Darling. I don't know what to say. It's absolutely right. But you've told me a hundred times you don't *believe* any of this . . .'

'No, but *you* used to. I still think personally that three quarters of it is basically dishonest, that its values are all out of proportion, that it glorifies the wrong virtues. But it's just a synthesis of the many, many lectures you've given me on the subject. I have a good memory. And even I admit that it's what the people need to hear.'

You looked at me as if I was the goddess Athena, then kissed me in a way that would have been blasphemous with any goddess.

And that is why I always deny I wrote the funeral speech. You wrote it yourself, over the fifteen years before I repeated it back to you.

I took Peri with me to the funeral because he wanted to hear you speak. We stood hand-in-hand on the edge of the vast crowd outside the city wall, as I did my best to answer his questions about what was going on. A young man standing near us overheard and asked politely if he could help me out: he explained that the bodies had been cremated on the battlefield, and the bones had then been laid out in a tent for two days before the funeral so that relatives could take their offerings. Now the coffins would be brought on wagons to be buried in the city sepulchre. After the burial the most impor- tant man in Athens would make a speech — on this occasion it would be the great Pericles himself. The young man said his name was Thucydides and he would be making notes on Pericles' speech because he was planning to write a history of the war. I thanked him for being so kind and didn't tell him I could have recited the speech to him then and there. (I met Thucydides again a few months ago and reminded him of our encounter at the funeral. He apologised profusely for not recognising me under my veil and promised to show me the history when it is finished.)

It was a chilly day in late autumn, perfect for the occasion. For it was also the autumn of the Athens you had loved, the Athens whose praises you were now going to sing.

You looked godlike and remote standing on the high platform, your helmet glinting in the watery sunlight. You spoke slowly, gravely. And although I had heard it all before and disagreed with most of it, I was deeply moved. More because of you, perhaps, than what you were actually saying. For you were no longer a tired old man proclaiming a string of platitudes. You were an immortal delivering an inspired message to mankind. I felt that for that moment at least you had regained your own faith in honour and justice and freedom. I hoped for your sake you wouldn't lose it.

I must admit I'd done a fairly good job of expounding your views without slipping in any of my own. You began by praising Athenian democracy, justice and social equality. Athenians, you said proudly are tolerant, unprejudiced and law-abiding. Their lives are fuller in every respect than those of people in other cities. They have more recreation, more beautiful possessions, a better standard of living. They live in peace and have no fear of war: unlike some peoples they make no secret of their military strength but invite the world to come and look.

Wealth and poverty have no importance: all citizens are equal and all citizens take an equal share in governing their city (those who don't are called useless). Athens as a whole is an education to Greece, and individual Athenians an example to all other Greeks. This is why Athens has achieved such greatness. And this is the city for which soldiers have nobly given their lives.

There were good, strong words about the honour of dying for one's country (it sounded convincing at the time) and a few words of faint comfort for parents and relatives of the fallen. I had restricted myself to just one line about the women of Athens, saying their greatest glory is to be as inconspicuous as possible. Pure hypocrisy, coming from me or you. Yet the people desperately needed to be reassured about traditional values and virtues; it was not the moment for revolution and reform.

The speech was hailed as a masterpiece. I wish any of its sentiments had been true.

15

THE next year we were more prepared for the Spartans. The country people had come into the city again during the spring, still grumbling. But at least they knew what they had to face—or so they thought. And they had little left for the invading army to destroy. That year you also hit back far harder at Sparta—though still without giving the king the satisfaction of a major battle. You yourself led a fleet of two hundred ships to attack one of Sparta's most important ally-cities, nearly captured it, devastated the country round it and made successful punitive raids on enemy towns and villages along the coast. Prospects were looking better.

But we in Athens didn't care about your naval triumphs, or even about the hostile army camped half a day's march away. Spartans, Corinthians, Persians—anything would have been better than the horror raging in the city itself. It was an enemy we couldn't possibly have expected or foreseen. It killed more citizens than a hundred Spartan armies could ever have done. It shattered the morale of the survivors. It destroyed all hope of our winning the war quickly and efficiently. If I were religious I would say it was a mighty punishment from the gods on a city that had grown too proud. Not even Apollo could have found it funny.

There had been stories that people down at the port were suffering from a strange epidemic and that some of them had actually died from it. We thought perhaps the Spartans had poisoned their fresh water reservoir, and didn't worry; in Athens itself we get our water from wells. Then one stifling summer day I heard of eleven different cases of slaves in the city suffering from what sounded like a most unpleasant disease. I ordered our own servants and slaves not to go near the port or the brothels. The day after, several citizens were reported to have gone down with it. I kept Peri home from school and asked Paralos and Alcibiades not to go out unless they had to. Two days later hundreds of men, women and children had caught the epidemic, including a boy friend of Socrates' who had been at our house the day before. I tried to find out what, if anything, to do to prevent it but nobody seemed to know. And then I had a blinding headache . . .

I was one of the first to get the plague, and one of the very few to survive it without horrible physical deformities. I was feeling perfectly healthy, when there was a sudden, searing pain through my head. I hoped it was sunstroke, summer fever, anything but the ominous, unknown disease that was sweeping the town. But next morning my eyes and mouth were red and inflamed. By evening I was sneezing and hoarse. And my stomach was full of knives.

For the next eight nightmare days I coughed and retched and gasped for water, which had no effect at all on the red-hot burning inside me. It was like being on fire and all I craved for was to drown myself in a pool of cold, cold water. I couldn't bear anything to touch my skin and paced naked up and down the room where I had locked myself in, unable to sleep, unable to keep still, wishing I could die and get it over with.

A doctor had been once, but had no idea what to do. Then he caught it too—as did practically every doctor in Athens. The only person I saw after that was the slave who brought me jug after jug of water. There was little point in isolating myself, since the whole city was exposed to it by now. But I should have hated anyone to see me in that repulsive state and thanked the gods you weren't there.

The plague was like a gnawing rat that starts at the head and eats its way slowly down the body. By the seventh night it was touch-and-go whether I could resist the heat of the fever. There was a furnace inside me. But the next morning the burning had gone; instead I was sick in the stomach and beyond. It was more unpleasant still, and left me too weak to raise my head.

But I recovered. And I realised later that despite the agony I'd been through I had really only had a mild attack. Many people died from being literally burned up by the fever on the seventh or eighth day. Others died from exhaustion after the second phase. Sometimes the plague travelled down to hands, feet, genitals: survivors were left crippled or impotent or blind or, worse still, completely out of their minds.

When I finally emerged into the world again, after about twenty days altogether, I found it in the grip of panic and terror. Tens of thousands of people had the plague by now, including most of the

206

refugees from the country who were camping in the streets. Your beautiful Athens was an appalling, horrific sight: the bodies of the dead and dying were heaped in the temples and the streets; half dead, naked bodies were staggering blindly through the city searching for water; the fountains and wells were crowded with demented semi-humans trying to get relief. All the elaborate funeral rites were completely forgotten—people abandoned their dead relatives, or left corpses on other people's funeral pyres or threw them on pyres that were already burning. It was sacrilege, but nobody cared.

Whole families died because there was nobody to nurse them. Their friends, understandably, refused to go near them for fear of catching it themselves. Not that nursing did much good—the rich and the poor, citizens and slaves all died the same way. There was an infectious attitude of complete despair: once people realised they'd caught it they simply gave up hopelessly, losing all their powers of resistance.

This at least was something I could help to fight. When Sophocles' wife came down with it I insisted on going to see her every day to convince her it was possible to survive. She did. It seemed unlikely that I could have it a second time, so I did what little I could for our friends. For the first time ever I could come and go freely in Athenian citizens' houses. Nobody cared if I was a companion or foreigner or witch—they were simply grateful for help, particularly husbands who were trying to look after their wives, children or slaves.

Meidias' wife had died. Then I heard that he was sick, too. I went to his house (a thing I would never have dared do before) and found the now familiar sight. There were no slaves—they had either died or deserted. He managed a painful grin:

'I never thought you'd have to nurse me.'

'I wish I didn't.'

'I'd like to kiss you goodbye. But I can't . . . like this . . .'

I swallowed hard. By this time I could tell at a glance how serious a case was. His really was hopeless.

I stayed there all night and he died early in the morning. His last, choked words were: 'I wish I'd bid more for you at the banquet . . .'

The Spartans spent forty days ravaging the country then left for fear of the plague, which was doing more damage to Athens than they could hope to do. It was too late, then, for people to escape the epidemic by going back to their ruined country homes. The refugees in their cramped shacks had been dying like flies. And for me the worst ordeal of all was walking through the streets to other people's houses. I am not particularly squeamish, but every time I went out I was sick.

I was also scared. Law and order had disintegrated: empty houses were being looted, corpses stripped of whatever belongings they had, dying men beaten up in broad daylight. The general feeling seemed to be that law-breakers probably wouldn't live long enough to be brought to trial or juries survive to try them. Anyone who had money was determined to spend it while he could, on pleasure — after all, tomorrow he might be dead. Lavish parties and wild orgies contrasted horribly with the smell of death.

At least a quarter of the population of Athens died in the plague, which dragged on for about eighteen months, flaring up again the following summer. Our house seemed extraordinarily lucky that first year : after me, only two slaves got it and they both survived. I took in several children who had been orphaned, and organised a make-shift school in which they were taught by anyone who was healthy and available. I was terrified for Peri, but what could I do to protect him?

You were appalled and shattered when you finally got back from your naval expedition. You had only been away a few months, yet Athens was unrecognisable. I think you secretly believed it *must* be the vengeance of the gods — otherwise how could fate be so cruel? The people, however, wanted a human scapegoat. And needless to say, they turned on you.

They couldn't actually blame you for the plague itself, which as far as we knew had been brought by sailors from Egypt. But they blamed you for the fact that it spread so quickly and disastrously. It might not have been half so bad, they said, if all those country refugees hadn't been crammed into the city, living in squalor in the streets. And it was your policy which brought them there.

Without your knowledge, ambassadors were sent to Sparta to ask for peace. The Spartans made impossible terms and the ambassadors came back empty-handed. That, too, was considered to be your fault. Obviously you had to do something to defend yourself and try to whip up a little optimism (which you didn't feel). So you summoned a special meeting of the Assembly and gloomily, despondently, we wrote another speech.

We said it was understandable that the people should be angry and upset. But couldn't they try to be logical? After all, the plague was something you could never have predicted. They had supported and trusted you for years, and you were still the same man. If they believed in you for so long when things went right, it was unreasonable to turn against you when things went wrong through no fault of yours.

We explained that Athens was supreme on the sea. She had an empire and had got to keep it whether she liked it or not—for the protection of her allies as well as herself. Modern Athenians must not let down the memories of their noble forefathers or the reputation of their glorious city. And if by any chance we were beaten in this war, our city must be remembered as the greatest in the world.

We both realised it wasn't very encouraging to admit that Athens *could* be beaten. But in the present situation it seemed unrealistic even to suggest that she might, eventually, win.

The speech won you a grudging vote of confidence from the Assembly, which agreed to carry on the war. Yet no amount of patriotic feeling could make the people forget their private grievances: the mass of them, relatively poor to start with, had lost practically everything they owned. The rich had lost their country estates and complained they were destitute. There was no incentive to work hard at building up a new income or business, for the war was still going on and the Spartans would inevitably come again the next year. The Athenians were bored, frustrated, depressed. It was human, though unreasonable, for them to vent all their bitterness on you.

Hermippos, unfortunately, had so far survived the plague. He and a loud-mouthed orator called Cleon harangued the Assembly, sent their agents out into the streets, resurrected all the old rumours about you, me, the Alcmaeonid curse and so on. They accused us of living in luxury while the rest of Athens was starving, and circulated the whisper that the plague was divine punishment for our impiety and immorality (not that anyone in Athens had much faith in the gods any more. No amount of sacrificing or omen-taking had stopped the plague. What was the point of going on?)

The people were in a mood to believe anything they were told, particularly the remaining peasants from the country. In our 'perfect' democracy they had as much right to a vote in the Assembly as everyone else, although they had seldom used it in the past and understood little about politics. We weren't at all surprised when the Athenians voted to depose you from your office of general.

Your face was grey and dead, like wet clay. You walked with a stoop and your eyes were dull and listless. You had no energy to fight back. I was desperately worried you might get the plague, for you would have had no resistance to it. Not that it seemed to claim old people or sick people more than anyone else. In fact it had just spread to the army camp besieging Potidaea, where over a thousand tough soldiers had died.

Suspension from office meant your accounts had to be examined. It was quite unreasonable to expect anyone to have kept their books up to date that year—when you had to organise emergency rations and subsidies for the starving and homeless you paid them first and sorted out the accounts later. Nobody believed for a moment that you had been embezzling state funds. Yet the books were, undeniably, in a mess.

Your enemies wanted a spectacular trial on the Acropolis itself— with the idea of making it look like some sort of heinous religious crime. It would have been theatrical and impressive and very bad for you. You appeared not to care, but I nagged and bullied every friend and acquaintance I could find to get the procedure amended. It would have been too, too tragic for Pericles the Olympian to end his career by being convicted as a criminal in his own beloved Parthenon. You were already a broken man; this would have killed you.

They managed to get it changed, so you were tried in the law courts, before a special jury of 1,501. They couldn't make sense of the books. You hadn't been given the chance to look at the extremely complicated accounts while preparing your defence. The jury therefore accepted the Prosecutor's word that five talents were missing, and fined you fifteen. It was better than we expected.

All that winter you sat at home brooding, hardly noticing what went on around you. I suppose the rest did you good. But all your life you had been an active man, at the centre of everything going on in the city. Friends who came to see you went away shocked by this shadow of your former self. The politicians were mostly embarrassed to come. And the few who did were struck by your complete lack of interest in the intrigues and manoeuvres that had been your life.

I tried to keep the children away, thinking they would annoy you. But one day I came in to find you with a group of eleven- and twelve-year-olds sitting on the floor round your couch. And you were actually smiling. It seems they had been arguing about the details of some battle in the Persian War, and Peri suggested they ask you. From then on you spent a lot of time with them, describing (and often defending) important decisions, crises and victories in your own long career. They found it a hundred times more interesting coming from you than from a dull old school-master. And you began to look better.

'They're not corrupted yet,' you explained, half-apologetically. 'They have open minds and they ask intelligent questions. As a matter of fact they're rather nice people. I'm sure we weren't like that in my day.'

I kissed the top of your white head and wished there was more I could do for you.

You seldom went out, except to funerals. Your sister Anactoria died of the plague in the autumn. We weren't exactly overcome with grief. A month later your eldest son Xanthippos died too. We couldn't even pretend to be sad. Particularly since it meant that Paralos was now your heir and would succeed you as head of the house. He was never going to be a brilliant man, but at least he was no discredit to you. He was nearly thirty by this time, more sure of himself—and less frightened of you now you were no longer the omnipotent Olympian. For a short time the two of you were closer than ever before.

Then, when the plague broke out again at the beginning of summer, Paralos came down with it. The house was in a state of agonised suspense for ten days, as we tried every known form of treatment and remedy. But I knew there was no hope, and on the tenth day he died. You were left without legitimate heirs—a dreadful blow to an Alcmaeonid. Worse still, it meant that Ariphon or his son Hippocrates would become head of the family and inherit what was left of your money.

You were heart-broken, particularly since you had recently become so fond of your son. As you laid a wreath on his coffin at the funeral, you broke down and wept. I could hardly bear it.

It was no help at all to know that you adored Peri. He was bright, handsome, intelligent—everything an Alcmaeonid should be and your legitimate sons weren't. Because I was his mother, he couldn't succeed you and couldn't become an Athenian citizen. He would be excluded from government office, have no vote in the Assembly, no part in city life. He would always be inferior, socially, and about the only things he could do would be to pay his taxes and fight for the wretched city. I felt responsible and almost wished we *had* exposed him after all.

The day after the funeral Alcibiades came to see me (he had recently moved into his own father's house, where he was reputed to hold wild parties. Probably true, but he was twenty-one years

old and it was none of my business). After a few gallant pre-
liminaries he came to the point:

'I was shocked to see how Pericles looked yesterday. Do you think
he'll get over it?'

I sighed. 'I don't know. I hope so. He took it very badly.'

'It's very important that he should. You see, we want him to
stand for general again.'

'What? You must be mad. In the first place the people wouldn't
have him. In the second place he wouldn't agree to do it.'

'Calm down, calm down'—he loved being patronising. 'You don't
know the people like I do. They've discovered they're no better off
without him, worse in fact, so after their little flirtation with the
pacifists and radicals they want to go back to their own true love.'

'But you've seen what he's like. He's disillusioned, he's lost
interest. He's an old man and I don't think he could take another
betrayal . . .'

'Honestly, Aspasia, we've got to have him back'. He was very
serious now. 'He's the only man who can command authority and
respect. The other generals are all fighting each other, nobody has
any idea what to do next, they are all beginning to realise that
Pericles' policy was the only sensible one, but hate to lose face by
admitting it. It'll end in civil war, let alone war against the Spartans.'

'But can't you see it's not fair to him? He's taken too much
already. It could kill him.'

'Look, dearest, be sensible. It will kill him anyway to sit here at
home brooding about Paralos and watching the city go to pieces.
As general, at least he will have something to do to take his mind
off it. It could even save him, if things go well.'

'Well . . . I suppose you *could* be right . . .'

He saw I was weakening and leaned forward eagerly. 'The thing is,
you see, that I know he won't agree unless *you're* on our side. You
can persuade him to do anything. Be a good girl and help us.
Please!'

He flashed one of his radiant smiles. I felt my heart sinking and
reflected moodily that even when he was five years old I had never
been able to resist him.

'All right. I'll try. Come and talk to him tomorrow. But for the
gods' sake try and make sure they're *kind* to him.'

You were violently opposed to the idea at first, saying you had
already tried and failed and that now it was time for someone else
to be in charge. I pointed out that there wasn't anyone else capable.

For the sake of the city you had once cared about so much, you had to go back. If you didn't, you yourself really would be responsible for the disastrous mistakes that other people were bound to make.

It was cruel, but it worked. When Alcibiades came back the next day with an impressive delegation of your friends and ex-colleagues, you listened to what they had to say and admitted simply that it seemed you had no choice. Therefore you accepted. You were standing up straighter and looked more determined than I had seen you for months. I think the rest really *had* done you good.

You were duly elected that summer and immediately engrossed in state affairs again. The Spartans, as it happened, didn't invade the Athenian countryside that year but concentrated on attacking some of our weaker allies. It was considered a good sign, and the war wasn't felt so much at home. Despite the plague, our house was once more an extension of your office.

Alcibiades kept his word about making sure they were kind to you (although only twenty-one, he already had far too much influence in politics). You strode up to me one day dragging a bewildered Peri by the hand, looking as excited as if the Spartan army had just surrendered.

'Meet Pericles, son of Pericles!'

I blinked. 'Haven't I already had that pleasure?'

'No, no. From now on you must treat my son with respect—as befits a future citizen!'

I could hardly believe it. 'But how on earth . . . ?'

Your deep chuckle sounded almost like your old self. 'I knew nothing about it. I saw Alcibiades in the barber's and thought he was looking conspiratorial. Several people gave me odd glances as I took my place in the Assembly. We got through the day's business and to my surprise nobody left, even though there was an exceptional attendance. Then Hagnon, the general, presented a motion—that due to my recent bereavement and in order that my illustrious house might not be left without heirs, the people of Athens should pass a special law conferring citizenship, when he comes of age, on my surviving son Pericles, now aged twelve. He said this act should be seen as a mark of the esteem and regard in which I am held by the Athenian people.'

Your surviving son Pericles looked totally confused by this unexpected honour as I flung my arms round him.

'Go on, what happened then?'

'That was the reason there were so many people there—they need at least six thousand for an act of citizenship. The gods know how they found them with all the troubles there have been. Anyway, there was a roar of applause when the motion was carried. And everyone was ordered to attend the next Assembly, without fail, for a vote of ratification.'

That evening our young future citizen dined with us for the first time, a garland perched on his curly head. Euripides, who was there, said caustically that Peri was much better off as he was. But you were so happy not even he could spoil your pleasure. Later, in bed, we did our best to conceive another citizen.

The act was ratified and you both had to go up to the Parthenon to make some sort of formal vow to the goddess Athena. I had a lump in my throat as I watched you standing side by side in the vast, dark temple, a white-haired old man and a handsome wide-eyed boy, promising to serve the goddess and the city as your family had for generations. From then on you always called our son by his full name, Pericles. But to me he could never be anything but Peri.

It made a difference to me, too. For as the mother of a future citizen I was very nearly respectable. Admittedly a lot of the social barriers had already broken down due to the war and the plague, but they could easily be built up again. You were probably more pleased than I was—I remember you grinning with satisfaction and saying: 'Nobody can insult you now. You're an Athenian by adoption. And you'll have a citizen to protect you when I'm gone.'

You were full of life and energy then, convinced you would live at least another ten years. After all, you were only sixty-five. But just when everything seemed to be going right again the plague claimed you, too. Although it was only a very mild attack it left you weak and worn out; you simply hadn't the physical strength to go back to work. For two months Athenian policy was decided at your bedside, or from a couch on the veranda if it was fine. Your brain was as good as ever and at least you weren't in pain. But as autumn came and it got cooler we realised you were dying.

We were rarely alone together, for all Athens came reverently to pay its respects. It was as if you were the oracle and I the high priestess acting as mediator between you and the world. Death, in Athens, is a very public occasion: like birth, or marriage, it must be witnessed by as many people as possible to leave no doubt that it really occurred.

In the evenings when they had finally gone we said very little. There was nothing to say. You slept peacefully, for you were profoundly tired. I prayed for a miracle and refused to think of what would happen afterwards. Friends said I was brave; in fact I was being a coward, shutting my eyes to the inevitable pain, putting it off while I still could. There would be plenty of time for weeping and wailing when the mourners came. As it was, I wanted you to see me smiling. I never could bear saying goodbye.

You were very calm, very peaceful. Some of the women had hung a lucky charm round your neck and you showed it to Sophocles, laughing. 'Look what I've come to, allowing this super-stition. I must be very far gone indeed . . .' Sophocles had tears in his eyes as he turned away.

For three days you were semi-conscious, lying there motionless, occasionally opening your eyes as if to check who was there. The room was full of people, day and night: generals, ex-generals, writers, poets, scientists, artists—all the men who helped you make Athens great. Sophocles, Socrates, Euripides, Alcibiades and dozens more came and went and came back again. On the fourth day they were whispering among themselves about your achievements and victories, almost as if you were already a corpse who couldn't hear. Suddenly there was a feeble sound from the bed. Everyone turned round in amazement as your lips started to move.

'Thank you, dear friends, for all you say . . .'

Your bony hand was clutching mine and I could feel the effort you were making.

'But you only mention things that have happened to many generals . . . as much by luck as by skill . . .'

All eyes were on your sunken face as you went on shakily:

'You must speak of my greatest triumph . . . that no Athenian ever wore mourning . . . because of me.'

You looked at me as if appealing for help. Then your eyes shut again. There was a hushed silence that seemed to last for ever. Moments, or perhaps it was hours afterwards someone put a coin in your mouth for the ferry to Hades. You were dead.

It is one year and three months since you died: in that time I have been married, widowed and had a baby. I hardly noticed. I have been too busy re-living the sixteen years with you. When I started writing, back in that bleak winter, I couldn't admit to myself that you were dead, that it wasn't all a bad dream. I couldn't face life without you, and it was only the long hours spent writing that prevented me from taking my own life as well.

Now I have gone through your death again, I can finally accept it.

I am sad, but not desperate. I am an older, wiser, more sorrowful Aspasia, but I am Aspasia again—not the spineless shadow who sat weeping and alone.

I seem to have written away the misery by remembering and describing the happiness. You are almost more a part of me than you were when you were living. And you will be with me for ever. So now I can stop living through the past and look at the future. Appropriately, it is spring. Peri is playing the flute and wants me to buy him a helmet. I have the new baby, born ten days ago (I have called him Axiochos, after my father). I wish he were your child. But in a way I'm happy that he is altogether mine.

I shall now shut this book, which I dedicate to you with all my love. My baby and I are going to start learning how to live.

Epilogue

THAT was just under thirty years ago. I'd forgotten all about this book, but came across it yesterday when looking for the text of the funeral speech I dictated to Pericles. A friend asked me to help him with a speech so I thought I might as well show him the 'masterpiece'. I seem to have become an authority on funeral speeches—though quite honestly it's time I was writing my own.

In case my descendants ever read this and are curious to know what happened to the central characters, here are some brief obituaries. I seem to have survived them all.

Athens, first of all. The war dragged on for twenty-six years and she finally surrendered to Sparta six years ago. The whole saga of disaster is in Thucydides' excellent history, published last year.

Euripides went on writing and being unpopular, spending more and more time in his cave. Then years ago he finally decided he'd had enough of Athens, so went into voluntary exile in Macedonia where he died the next year, aged 76. He had written ninety-two plays but only won first prize four times.

Sophocles lived till the ripe old age of 91. He was loved and respected till the day of his death, seven years ago.

Socrates. Dear, funny, ugly, brilliant Socrates. Last year he was tried and sentenced to death for 'not believing in the gods and corrupting the young' (he had been trying to teach them to think). He had no Pericles to plead for him. Typically, he joked till the last moment, then drank the hemlock like a hero. He was 71.

Alcibiades became the personification of Alcmaeonid brilliance—and insanity. He was involved in innumerable scandals, became a reckless general when he was far too young, was exiled, recalled in a blaze of glory and exiled again. Seven years ago the Spartans set fire to a country cottage where he was sleeping with a prostitute. He dashed out bravely through the flames but was killed by an arrow; the girl had the decency to bury him. He was only 45, but did more harm to Athens in his short career than the Persians and Spartans put together.

Peri was different. Peri was one of the good Alcmaeonids. He became a good general and competent politician—his father would have been proud of him. When he was just 35—eight years ago now—he and five other generals won a great naval battle off Mytilene. But political rivals accused them of failing to pick up survivors, and the six were sentenced to death by the Assembly without even a proper trial. Socrates was on the presiding committee and did his best to block the sentence. But Peri was killed by the city he loved. He was about to get married and perhaps produce more accursed Alcmaeonids.

So now, finally, I am really alone. Except for my son Axiochos whom I love more than any man I know. He looks like his father but his mind is mine. And he, at least, is not tainted with the Alcmaeonid curse. He is 29 now: very soon we must choose him a wife. There are dozens of eligible young girls whose fathers want them to become Aspasia's daughter-in-law. It will amuse me to go and inspect them—for even in modern, post-war Athens marriages are still arranged.

I have had a good life. Sixty-seven whole years of it. I am old and withered now, but they say I look serene. I have held court on my own for the last half of my life, a queen receiving her respectful subjects. I have slept with many men, but loved none since Pericles. For as I wrote thirty years ago, and it is still true, he is a part of me, probably the greatest part. As soon as Axiochos is married, I shall have had enough.

I leave this to my son's children and their children after them—as proof that Pericles and Aspasia were human beings.